American Insurgent

Phil Rabalais

Dedication

Firstly to my wife and daughter, who tolerated long hours and late nights while I pursued one of the only other passions I have other than my family. Also to them and several close friends for providing the blueprint for characters too rich and genuine for me to have ever made up all by myself.

Secondly to my cohost Andrew and the patrons of the Matter of Facts podcast with whom I shared this book throughout its production, for their encouragement and critique.

I also owe a debt that I cannot repay to a few authors who both inspired me and guided me down this path: to Franklin Horton (author of the Borrowed World series) for his encouragement and for showing me this goal was achievable, to Doug Hogan (author of the Tyrant series) for his unrestrained and helpful advice and technical assistance, and lastly to John Ross (author of Unintended Consequences) for unknowingly inspiring another writer to tell a cautionary tale from his own perspective.

Many thanks are also in order for all of the people, and they are numerous, who have discussed the subject matter presented in this fictitious book with me to offer their own perspectives, their thoughts, and their knowledge. Without all of them, though they may not be named, this book would have fallen very short of its intent to provoke thought and question in the minds of the readers while trying to entertain them.

Table of Contents

Foreword: History Repeats

Much rhetoric is thrown around regarding the civilian ownership of firearms in the context of the United States of America and its people. A modern guarantee of the autonomy and supremacy of the citizenry, or merely a leftover from a bygone era? The savior of peaceful people that enables them to protect themselves, or the source of violence that destroys countless lives every year? These are debates for which I do not ever anticipate a universal resolution, but the one idea that always stood out to me was the idea that an attempt to completely curtail the common man's ability to own and carry firearms would lead to a civil war. In moments like this, where bold claims are made, I always look back to history to see when (not if) it will repeat itself again. Within our own history, in 1775, just such an attempt was made by the agents of King George III of Great Britain. These soldiers sought to capture the magazines that supplied the local militias with powder for their muskets, rifles, and cannon. The intent of this endeavor was obvious, to subdue the colonial militias through their disallowance of use of their arms. Let the irony of the American Revolution being kicked off by the first gun grab in this country's history rest in your mind as you read forward.

The rest of the details surrounding the Battle of Lexington and Concord are well noted in history. A group of men known as the Minutemen sought to warn the colonists and their militia forces of the impending antagonistic actions of the crown's troops, such that a counter may be organized. I have always surmised, referencing our own history, for example, that were our own government or indeed any force to broadly remove arms from the people's hands that a similar response may be brought forth.

When I have had occasion to discuss this topic with natives of other countries, they are often very confused by America, with its odd customs and unique history. We are not a nation granted its freedom by a monarchy grown weary with its upkeep, nor are we a country ruled by mob or founded under an authoritarian state. America is uniquely a nation in which the power to govern the country and the individual is closely guarded by the people, a representative democracy used to bind the government's action to the will of the people through their ability to replace their representatives, and which guards incredible personal freedoms from infringement or abridgement by the state. It is also a nation that paid a great cost in sweat and blood to wrest its very soul from the hands of a tyrannical monarchy.

And woe to the man or men who forget the longing for freedom and the spirit of revolution lives on today in every American.
— Phil Rabalais

"Every normal man must be tempted, at times, to spit on his hands, hoist the black flag, and begin slitting throats."
— H. L. Mencken, *Prejudices: First Series*

"What country can preserve its liberties if their rulers are not warned from time to time that their people preserve the spirit of resistance. Let them take arms."
— Thomas Jefferson, letter to James Madison, December 20, 1787

Quiet Broken

A ringing cell phone broke the quiet calm of John Arceneaux's suburban home just north of New Orleans, Louisiana. His wife looked at him with the same worried, questioning eyes he had seen dozens of times in recent history, as she gazed at him from across the room with their daughter. He regarded the phone with curiosity, trying to decide if it was friend or foe. He lifted it, accepted the call, and greeted the unknown caller with his characteristic gruff, all-business tone.

"John speaking, may I ask who's callin'."

He spoke with ever so slight of a Southern drawl, and the blue-collar mannerisms he was raised with, polite, but no pushover. The caller's voice was one he was unfamiliar with, yet John knew who he was...or more accurately who he represented. Ever since the laws changed, when the searches started and confiscations began taking place, a small yet vigorous group of men and women known as the Minutemen had drawn a line in the sand. Their mission was simple: to resist the confiscation of the small arms of law-abiding citizens by government agencies through any means possible. Part and parcel of this mission were phone calls like this one, sometimes hundreds per day nationwide, warning people of impending searches and raids in their area. The first of these calls were met with skepticism and dial tones, to the peril of the homeowners who found themselves subject to a search of their premises with or without their consent. Confiscation was a foregone conclusion. Jail sentences for gross offenders, owners in violation of the "Arsenal Laws," which limited the number of firearms and ammunition anyone may possess, were doled out for those who had flagrantly violated the previous laws for the past four years before that most egregious violation of civil liberties was enacted—the full repeal of the Second Amendment to the US Constitution.

John's face betrayed no alarm, for he felt none. He was not a member of this group, but being a gun owner and Second Amendment advocate prior to the repeal, he had followed their activities. He had expected this day to come eventually, and he had reflected upon his decision carefully. He knew instinctively that his life would change forever if he followed through on the course he had set for himself and his family. He had prayed on it and had come to the inescapable conclusion that the country he had enlisted to defend was no longer his own, and the men who approached his door lacked the authority to confiscate his lawfully owned property. Contrary to what they believed, just because you can convince 51% of voters to show up on election day does not grant you the righteous authority to strip from citizens those rights they had BEFORE they were written down on a piece of parchment in the eighteenth century. The government did not grant these rights, and they had no authority to rescind them.

John listened to the warning, the warning he had heard rumors of throughout the former gun community, and set his mind about the task at hand. The intelligence offered was far more than a random crank caller, he was getting details about the size of the force, their equipment, their backup, a road map to disrupt their operation. Then he heard something he had not expected.

"If you slip out the back door and head northeast from your present location through the wood line, we can have someone pick you and your family up."

The thought had never occurred to him to abandon his home and leave his property to be torn apart and taken from him, nor to turn tail and run like a coward.

"No, sir," John replied. "I believe I'll deal with these uninvited guests personally, though if I'm still around after this, I'd sure like to meet you and your group."

Silence hung in the air, the caller obviously faced with a situation he had foreseen yet scarcely believed. On the other end of this phone, through a repeater service to prevent the call from being traced back to him yet barely a hundred miles away, was a man about to escalate this cold war into a full-blown shooting match. He had always known it would only be a matter of time until the wrong person was pushed too far by the confiscations and door-to-door searches, and then their quiet little resistance would have a decision to make. Fortunately, it was a decision made months ago by unanimous vote. The Minutemen would assist in any way possible, through civil disobedience as long as possible, and through direct action when hostilities boiled over. They had cast their lot and guarded themselves against reprisal from the state for all this time, and finally things were about to get deadly serious.

"I understand your intent. Is your background military?" the voice asked.

"Yes, sir, was in the sandbox back in 2004, then New Orleans in 2005," John answered.

"Roger. Exfil after things cool down; ensure you aren't followed. We'll be watching for a man with a woman and child. Don't trust anyone; verify your pickup. And don't leave your ordnance behind."

The line went dead. John pulled the phone back and regarded it curiously. He had expected to abandon his home with his wife and child after this fight and make a run for it. Now the invitation for help escaping emboldened him. No, after all they had survived, this would not be what broke them. What lay on the other side of the next ten minutes might be a mystery, but what lay before John was not. He went to his safe in the closet.

Years ago, he had built a false wall into a closet and hidden a gun safe, then rebuilt the drywall over it. Without tearing apart the closet, you'd never know the veritable arsenal of firearms this quiet suburban home held, nor the quantity of ammunition and tactical gear. Prepper, survivalist, gun guy—whatever you called John, he was a man who believed in the Second Amendment as a preacher believes in his Bible. The right to keep and bear arms was enshrined for the sole purpose of ensuring the citizenry of the United States were free from government harassment or infringement in their pursuit of owning and carrying arms for the defense of themselves and their communities. In the seventeenth and eighteenth centuries, that meant muskets. Muskets gave way to centerfire rifles, then self-loading rifles, and the centuries of firearm development granted more and more firepower to a single man than the previous generation ever imagined possible. Some were absolutely appalled at this development, believing only nation-states and their agents were to be trusted with such power. Thomas Jefferson and his fellows would have seen things quite differently, perhaps even fondly.

John took precious little time to tear down the drywall, as it intentionally hadn't been secured terribly well. The combination lock spun with a practiced hand, and the door opened.

"We're really doing this, aren't we?" John's wife, Rachel, asked.

"Yes, honey, either that or we stand by and let those men destroy our home and haul us off to prison like common criminals. If you and Kay want to run out the back door, I'll deal with this by myself," John replied, deadpan and without reproach.

Rachel knew John well; they had been married more than ten years. He had his imperfections, but she had found the longer they were together, the less she questioned his judgment. He was not prone to rash decisions, nor selfishness. Quite the opposite, he was one of the most selfless people she had ever met, and he saw his place as a husband and father as one of tremendous responsibility rather than one of convenience. If he had set himself upon this course of action, then she had but two options: join him and fight by his side, or abandon him. She reached for a rifle.

Rachel had grown up in a far more rural community than her husband had, one in which deer rifles and shotguns often accompanied students to schools so that once they had finished their studies, they could quickly find themselves in the woods, hunting game. Guns were commonplace, though not the guns her husband had collected. Next to her wood-stocked .30-06 hunting rifle stood her husband's AR-15, arguably the scapegoat that started all of this mess. Both her Remington 74 and John's AR were magazine-fed, semiautomatic rifles, yet a concerted effort by the media, politicians, and their useful idiots had convinced enough registered voters these firearms were the root of all evil and must be taken from people's hands. Of course, back then, house-to-house searches were out of the question. Tip-offs led to confiscations, but people tolerated this indignity by telling themselves "they should have followed the law; no one needs an AR-15 to hunt." Yet her hunting rifle was still legal at that time, until further indignities demanded the removal of telescopic sights (the so-called "Sniper Rifle" laws), then the required conversion of magazine-fed rifles to single shot, then the licensing requirements for all centerfire firearms. And now, men with the exact same rifles as her husband were coming to ransack her home and take him from her. She reached up on the shelf and helped herself to a box of .30-06.

John quietly accepted the unspoken intent his wife was displaying; she was in this fight if he was. He said a prayer, not the first nor last, that his decision to fight this out would not cost him his family's lives. He hoisted his plate carrier with Level 3 plates out of the bottom of the safe and threw it over his neck. With it came the IFAK, individual first aid kit, and spare magazines for his AR-15. This rifle, groused about by generations of soldiers for being underpowered—it wasn't, but privates will be privates—had been so thoroughly demonized by politicians that the average civilian thought quite literally the rifle would cause the death of all Western civilization were it left in the hands of common people like John. He lifted his wife's armor, which she accepted with a grimace. She had commented on more than one occasion that men had obviously designed these "medieval torture devices," made all the more evident by the fact that no one had ever considered a woman's figure when the plates were molded or bent. In this situation, safety trumped comfort, and she tolerated their weight and lack of accommodation for the female form.

"Kay honey, come in here," John called to his young daughter. As John's daughter approached, quite brave for a six-year-old but obviously very worried about why her two parents looked ready to walk through Mogadishu, he placed a gentle hand on her shoulder.

"Honey, there are some people coming here now. I think they want to hurt me and Mom and take us away from you. We aren't going to let that happen, but I need you to be safe and sit in this closet until this is over. Can you do that for me, honey?"

Kay quietly nodded, then impulsively hugged her father so hard he could feel her compressing his ribs in spite of the hardened steel plates guarding his body. The closet, John knew well, had its walls reinforced with cinder blocks and sandbags behind the drywall, part of a very unconventional home improvement plan he had undertaken years ago to turn a walk-in closet into a combination gun safe and panic room. Topped off with a steel security door, it wasn't impervious, but it would give his daughter the best chance of not being hit by a stray round of ammunition piercing the drywall of their home. He looked at his wife as if to ask if she should stay in the panic room too, but she only responded by hugging her daughter, then shutting the door.

Husband and wife took up their positions, using the plan they had determined and rehearsed years prior as a response to home intruders. At that time, they had anticipated gang members or perhaps looters, not trained and heavily armed agents of the state, but the principles remained the same. Overlapping fields of fire would maximize their firepower, while pre-rehearsed shooting lanes kept them from flagging each other. John had a hundred and twenty extra rounds of ammunition, plus an extra sack of magazines he hoped not to need. If this surprise attack worked, they would catch their assailants in a crossfire that would surprise and confuse them. No one before today had resisted, not beyond some terse words and scuffles. No one had struck back. No one had stood their ground and said NO.

Today, someone said enough was enough.

The Exfil

John, with Rachel and Kay in tow, loaded their car as quickly as they were able. He had hurriedly thrown their family bug-out bags in the back of the hatch, along with a few extra cans of ammunition for the arms they carried. John was not only a gun guy, but also an ardent prepper and was not one to stock the bare minimum of anything, yet all of his years of stockpiling were about to be shed to the essentials as they rushed from their once happy and peaceful home. No neighbors came outside to bear witness to the aftermath of the violent chaos that had happened in their quiet community.

Rachel took care to shield her daughter's eyes from the evidence of the firefight she had hoped and prayed would never come, staying relegated to ominous warnings from her husband of what might one day come to pass. With the task at hand done, they left never expecting to see their home again. Though the message had alluded they should exfil on foot, John preferred the mobility and load-carrying ability a vehicle provided, though he wondered where their mysterious backup would link up with them. If he failed to find them, he had every intent of taking the back roads to leave the area, and they would figure out where to go from there.

John need not have worried though, as they had barely left their neighborhood when the familiar ringing of his cellular phone broke the heavy silence in the car.

"Still with us, friend?"

"Yes, we are," John replied.

"What is your situation?"

John paused for a moment, knowing a cellular phone was easily tracked and listened to. "No casualties, minor injuries, we are exfilling on wheels."

"Roger that. Leave in the direction you drive to work, over the bridge, continue northbound. We'll pick you up there. Ditch your phone so you can't be tracked." The line went dead.

The phones were immediately erased (thanks to Apple for building that handy feature into them) then discarded out open windows. John continued to drive with his sidearm in his lap and the other firearms well clear of the windows to prevent alarming people who might opt to call their local tip line and report their sighting. The thoughts passing through his mind were multiple. How had this mysterious voice known his location or the path he drove to work? How had they come by their specific intel regarding the raid? And into whose hands was he delivering his family now by blind faith alone? John was placing his trust in his own judgment, as he often did. He could find no motivation for the force that urged them forward now if not to assist them in their escape.

As he crested the overpass heading north, he saw a pickup truck on the side of the road. Apparently broken down, its owner was under the hood, checking the engine. John would not have stopped with his family during normal times, and he certainly did not now. What did pique his curiosity was the radio clipped to the man's belt. Not a CB, not a ham he was familiar with. It almost had the look of military gear, which sent his alarm bells ringing. Was this a trap? He saw the man look up and reach for the radio as he passed. If he was driving into a trap, he was committed now.

Two miles up the road, a vehicle approached him from behind. The small SUV gained on him, but not in a threatening manner or with any speed differential that insinuated an intent to ram him. He pulled up alongside John's car, and as John looked over, he could see the driver giving him a thumbs-up. He completed his pass, his hazard lights flashed a few times, then he had the lead of this two-vehicle convoy. The pickup truck, suddenly cured of its ailment, then joined them from behind. Rachel and Kay took in these events in silence, as Rachel held her daughter's hand in one of her own, and her Smith and Wesson 9 mm in the other.

Their journey continued along the back highways to a larger property than most. As John followed faithfully behind the other vehicle, he noticed the lookout. A young man was hidden away in the wood line that bordered the home. He would have a nearly unobstructed view down the highway in the direction they had come, and John surmised there was probably a similar lookout at the other end of the property. These two men could provide good early warning for the residents of any vehicles entering the area. John's journey ended at the end of a long driveway that wrapped around behind a large home. The driver of the SUV exited, and John tightened his grip on his CZ while rolling down his window.

"I'm glad to see you made it safely to us, but I figured if you made it through Iraq and New Orleans, you would make your way." The mysterious voice had a face.

"Thanks for the warning, I doubt we'd have had time to act otherwise. Not to sound rude, but who are you, and who are these men behind me, and who are the two men in the wood line?" John inquired.

Now it was Mark's turn to be surprised. He hadn't figured John would notice the lookout, and a quick glance at the wood line confirmed they were hidden as they always were. *This guy doesn't miss much, does he?* Mark asked himself rhetorically. "Let's get you and your family inside, and get this car in the shed out back so it's out of sight. We'll make some introductions then decide how to handle the trouble you've found yourself in," Mark replied casually.

With that, John and his family unloaded from their vehicle, holstering firearms as they stepped out. Mark was quick to notice the old Army surplus web belt on John's waist married to modern MOLLE mag pouches and a Kydex duty holster, while Rachel tucked her shield in a simple IWB holster. Kay clung to her mother's hand, unsure of her surroundings. One of Mark's men took the open door as invitation and hopped in the car to move it under cover while Mark led the weary family into the home.

Within minutes, both lookouts checked in, reporting no unauthorized vehicles, nor any sightings of drones or aircraft. The TOC, Army jargon for tactical operations center, likewise checked in, reporting no unusual radio traffic, nor evidence their encrypted comms had been penetrated. Kevin sat at his station and faithfully listened to the largely unsecured comms of the local agency personnel who had discovered the scene at John's home, much to their dismay. Kevin's hand flew across his notepad while the computerized system transcribed the raw conversation, and he jotted down what he felt were the more pertinent details for Mark, who preferred the human touch over raw volume of information.

Four casualties, all with multiple gunshots, one apparently executed by a single shot to the head at close range. Inspection of the home indicated very few if any shots fired by the downed agents, with the overwhelming majority of fire being directed at the front doorway from within the home. One agent, one who apparently paid attention to his weapons training, noticed a disparity in the brass cases that littered the living area and the size of the holes in the drywall, concluding that at least two shooters with different caliber firearms had participated in the "attack." A further search of the house revealed the gun safe they had been ordered to search for, which had been largely emptied of firearms. The only things left were children's BB guns, also heavily restricted to the point of near total illegality, but not the cache of assault weapons and sniper rifles they had been told to expect.

Their information had come courtesy of another three-letter agency, one that had embarrassingly graced the media several times in past decades with allegations of spying on the American people. It was they, after the laws were passed requiring all civilian-owned firearms be surrendered, who found a way to pry the needles from the haystack. Decades prior, a program was initiated that caused the NICS (the National Instant Criminal Background Check System) to catalog all 4473 forms that were checked against it. While this was in clear violation of federal law, the end was believed to justify the means should an extremely high-profile case merit such measures. Once this was unearthed, it provided an impressive assistance to the search and seizure operation that was taking place all around the country. The

10

government finally had what it had always wanted: a complete record of any and all firearms sold through federally licensed dealers going back decades. While some would inevitably slip through the cracks, the seizures would energize the political base that supported the disarmament initiative and lead to more tip-offs and people turning in neighbors.

The empty safe and grizzly scene on the front lawn only meant one thing to the assembled agents: the subjects, John and Rachel Arceneaux, were armed and extremely dangerous. They would report up the chain and move on to the next target on their list.

Mark was sitting in the living room, his unofficial command post and the center of their cell, when Kevin entered and passed him the notes from the radio transcript. He stood by Mark's chair and quietly regarded their new guests and marveled at how absolutely ordinary they looked. Rachel and Kay could have been any mother and daughter from any suburban neighborhood, but beneath her curly brown hair lay a hard set of eyes. John had the posture and mannerisms of a military veteran, with two dark brown eyes framed by close-cut hair and a short beard. He sat opposite Mark, not relaxing like a man who had just escaped a horrific scene but like a coiled snake. Despite a bit of middle-age spread and years out of uniform, Kevin surmised John was every bit as dangerous as the agent's accounts over the radio indicated.

Mark broke the silence. "I imagine you have a lot of questions, not the least of which is who we are. We are members of the Minutemen, one of many cells that are spread around the country. We have undertaken the task of spying on the agency assets who are involved in these gun confiscations, and attempting to warn their targets. In the past, we have provided assistance in smuggling the families out of the area, resettling them when we can or changing their identities. Often our...subjects do not reach us and are taken by the agents. To date, you are the first subject who actually fought back against them, and from this radio transcript Kevin intercepted, it sounds as if you won convincingly. Do you want to discuss that?"

John's eyes darted to his daughter, who sat right next to his wife, holding her arm. Her mannerisms were guarded and anxious, but she could be easily forgiven for that after the morning she had lived through.

Mark understood; they would discuss what happened without her present. "Some other time. Right now, we need to discuss how to handle the situation we all find ourselves in. To date, we have been running an intelligence-gathering operation, occasionally aiding and abetting felonious gun owners out of the area so they could resume their lives elsewhere. Our intent was to fight a cold war against our enemy, though that has heated up considerably in the last few hours. The entire weight of the agency is currently tearing apart the state looking for you, so while I am not opposed to helping you relocate, I'm not sure that you wouldn't be found at a later date."

Mark paused for a breath, and John spoke. "I didn't...do what I did back there to run and hide. I'm tired of hiding. Years ago, I started to hide my political views. I hid the fact that I owned guns. I stopped going to gun ranges even before they shut them all down. I have done literally everything to keep these people off my family's doorstep so they would leave us in peace, and they came anyway. I struck first because I couldn't run from this fight, and I don't think I can run now. If you see the situation differently, please tell me; otherwise my question is what do we do now?"

Mark considered John's question carefully, as it did not sound rhetorical. Here was a man backed into a corner who had fallen back on his instincts and now was contemplating his next move. And Mark had to admit he wasn't in favor of John and his family running either.

"The Minutemen have conducted this operation as we have up to now, waiting for someone to strike back. We believe this may have the effect of emboldening others to act if we market it correctly. To put it bluntly, we want to have you stay here and join us and tell your story if you are willing. If not, you are free to leave now or at any time."

John hung his head. He could almost feel tears of frustration welling up behind his eyes. He wasn't a fighter, though he would if provoked. What he felt most was guilt that his family had been dragged into this mess. Why hadn't he just surrendered all his guns years ago? Why hadn't he just given up like his neighbors did? Now he was a fugitive, his wife and daughter were on the run, and he had destroyed any chance at his family having a normal life. All for what? Not for some chunks of plastic and steel, for his pride maybe?

"I'll give it some thought. We will take you up on your invitation to stay here for at least the time being and get our bearings. I would like to talk with you more about this proposal, and then with my wife. Either we agree to your terms together, or we both walk."

Mark nodded his head, understanding the family dynamic as he got to know this man. John could be decisive and painfully direct when the situation called for it, but looked for and trusted his wife's judgment when time and thought could be afforded to a complex decision.

Mark regarded John and Rachel's daughter. "Hi, honey, what's your name?"

"Kay," said a small voice, wary but not frightened.

"Kay, I have a son about your age. He's probably out in the backyard with his mother, tending the garden, if you and your mom would like to go meet them." Mark's eyes flitted up to Rachel's, silently communicating that he wanted to speak to John alone.

Rachel picked up on the cue. "C'mon, honey, let's go make some friends in case we're here for a little while."

Mark noted a very different accent from her husband's. As the ladies filed out of the room, Mark stood and motioned for John to follow him.

They stepped out into the foyer, and Mark offered a cigar from his humidor. At the sight of a cigar, John visibly uncoiled, and Mark recognized that he had finally broken the ice a little between him and this enigma who had walked into his home. A quiet suburban husband and father, yet a vicious fighter when provoked, a man who wanted peace but had outfitted his home and family for the fight of a lifetime. And now, here he stood with Mark, toasting the foot of his cigar while regarding him with those dark and intense eyes. It was not a threatening look, but one that almost seemed to cast aside your face and peer into your soul. Mark could imagine those eyes peering down a set of rifle sights at the front door of a home. And Mark asked John what happened...

Memories

"When I got the phone call, I had been expecting it. I'd heard of raids around town, just rumors. There's a lot of overlap between the prepper, gun, and veteran communities in this area, and we were all worried. Hell, a LOT of us had kept our guns and told the state to cram it. We never really believed they would actually start putting bootheels on doors and dragging people out. And when the rumors started, that's all we thought they were. But I had this sinking feeling in my gut I just couldn't shake that this was on the level. Years prior, when those stupid bans started, I hid a gun safe in the wall of my closet because I wasn't handing those guns over no matter what. But I didn't raise a fuss; I stopped attending the protests. I kinda feel ashamed for all of that since I was such a big 2A supporter in this area before that, but I felt like I had a bull's-eye painted on my back, and I didn't want to bring that home.

"I talked to Rachel about what I had heard, and she thought it was BS too, but we kept hearing it. Then people started turning up missing. Then people started getting cell phone video of these raids and passing it around until their phones mysteriously stopped working. Cell companies said their phones had been hacked and they needed to be fixed, but when they got their phones back, these videos they had shot were gone. People would upload them to social media and they'd get deleted or blocked. It was like a George Orwell novel, and I wasn't just reading it, I was watching it around me. I got scared, like no BS scared. I talked to my wife about pulling up stakes and leaving town, but she insisted this was our home. I only had one response: if they came for us, I would fight. She just nodded her head. She knew her husband.

"Then the day comes I get this random phone call telling me the storm troopers are coming, ready or not. I'm not mincing words, I jumped them. I didn't want a fair fight against lopsided odds when the other guys are wearing plates and carrying machine guns. I jumped them; as soon as the first one came through the door, we lit them up. The first three fell over each other trying to back out of that doorway and just kept taking shots. I emptied the whole thirty-round magazine before I saw them fall backwards. Rachel had been shooting too through the walls towards the front door, and that .30-06 just sings going through drywall, doubt it ever even slowed down. When I reloaded and went to check, I find one of these guys still alive, but he's all sorts of messed up. He's not pleading for his life or upset his buddies are dead, he's telling me to lay down my arms and not to resist like he's arresting me. I put him out of his misery and looked back towards the doorway to see my wife. She looked at me in a way I had never seen before, and I can't decide if I like it yet or not. She's seen me take people's lives, some would say in cold blood while others would say self-defense, and that is something she will never forget about her husband. I wish these men had just left me and mine in peace, but here we are now. And I don't have the first idea what to do.

"I know what I heard about the Minutemen. Government calls them a terrorist organization, an American insurgency. They've been accused of running guns, human trafficking, drugs—you name it, some three-letter agency wants their heads for it. But I don't get my news from the media, and the alternative media says these guys are like the Robin Hood of the gun community. They've been warning people what was coming way before the laws and restrictions, before the confiscations. After their warnings were ignored, they still kept fighting any way they know how to. And all this time I stayed in my quiet little home and minded my business, you guys were risking your asses trying to do the right thing. As if that isn't bad enough, you're almost proud of me for abandoning the fight then getting my wife into this crap in the end.

"You think telling this story will get other people to step up to the plate and fight back, maybe change things. Maybe

16

you're right, but how many people are going to come out on the wrong end of those firefights? How many wives and daughters are going to get hurt because someone decided to be Billy Badass and try to stick it to the man? And how long is this going to go on before the government gets fed up and stuffs a JDAM right through the front door? Don't you realize who these people are? They throw around million-dollar bombs at toolsheds in the Middle East because they got nothing better to do. And you want a dozen or so guys to become public enemy number one?!" John's speech wound down, like the last puff of air blown out of a balloon.

Mark struggled mightily to wrap his head around everything John had just set at his feet.

"Mark," John asked, "what the hell do you have in mind? I'm not arguing this can't continue, but a lot of good people are going to get hurt if they go off trying to follow the example I just set. I have four lives on my conscience, and I'm trying to get to heaven without any stains I can't wash off."

Mark launched into a diatribe. "John, you came out on top. Maybe luck, maybe skill, maybe our intelligence or all of it together, but if YOU came out on top, others can too. You know, I heard your podcast years ago; I was a quiet little fan of yours."

It was John's turn to be surprised. He had run a podcast years before, mainly preaching Libertarian values, small government, pro–Second Amendment, and preparedness. It had grown a modest audience and had made him some lifelong friends, but when the political winds shifted and social media and tech companies began to blatantly purge any and all content creators they viewed as dangerous, his show was abruptly but quietly shut down. No one would host his bandwidth, and his social media accounts were all deleted. To hear Mark recall all of this sent John's mind racing. Who was his host, and how deep did this previously unknown connection go?

"You always said this would happen. Hell, you predicted the Arsenal and Sniper Rifle Laws years before they were proposed. You were yelling at Fudds telling them their bolt guns would be next, like you were Nostradamus and nobody believed you…but I did. I was linked in with most of these guys already. And the more things turned, the more apparent it was we needed to take action. Minutemen isn't a single organization; we're modeled after a network of terrorist cells. Every cell is independent, with its own leadership and resources. We know precious little outside of comm frequencies and call signs of the other cells, so if one is infiltrated, they cannot penetrate the entire network. No one person is in overall command. We all pursue a common goal in our own ways, to disrupt the government's attempt to strip our arms from us. When our intelligence revealed you as the next target, and you made it clear you wanted to fight them, we made the decision to assist you afterwards. I see no reason your actions wouldn't energize others, either to join our cause or even to operate on their own.

"John, you were the one who said if a hundred million gun owners stood up and said NO, the state would have to back down. Well, if this continues, we're going to get weaker every day until our numbers won't be enough to stop them. If we get those gun owners on their feet, all of them, this will stop. Those four guys thought they were kicking the door on a single family. If they'd rounded the corner and come face-to-face with a couple of dozen armed people, you think they'd push the issue or go home? Your story, your voice, YOU can make these people see that surrender isn't the only option and unite them. You could help us do that. It's your decision. I know you don't want anyone else's blood on your hands, but how many more people are going to rot in prison if we stand by and don't do something?"

That last bit stung John, which Mark did not intend. He did feel like he'd abandoned the fight. He had cowered rather than fought, and the fight came to his door anyway. He had taken men's lives in self-defense, but now he was being asked to openly advocate insurgency against his own country. He understood innately that an asymmetrical and unconventional war was the only one with any chance of success against a technologically superior foe. They had the home-field advantage, as these agents were inevitably being massed from surrounding locations and couldn't be familiar with each and every neighborhood they were searching.

Mostly, they had the advantage of blending in with noncombatants, a lesson the US military had learned from fighting insurgencies in foreign lands. It is inherently difficult to separate combatants from noncombatants when they all speak the same language and look the same, and the penalty for accosting noncombatants is the delegitimizing of your force and the mission.

He had indeed uttered those words years prior, that if all the people united, the state had no option but to capitulate to their will. Even the "useful idiots" who voted for an ever more progressive agenda lacked the numbers and the spine to stand up to a majority population of angry citizens intent on having their rights respected. He saw Mark's point and his vision, and he did not question his motives nor his logic. The feeling nagging at John was actually something more personal to him; he questioned if he was the man to be leading this…insurgency. He questioned if this was what he wanted his life's legacy to be, the man who tore his own country apart. He had enlisted young because he loved his birthplace and loved what it stood for. And now, his country had followed in the footsteps of every Marxist dictatorship the world had ever seen, jettisoned the natural rights of its citizens, and was currently wiping its bloody boots on every word in the US Constitution and the Bill of Rights. Sure, some part of him wanted to watch that country burn, but it pained him terribly to come to that realization. He didn't want to see his country torn apart, but perhaps slapped until it was brought back to its senses.

"Okay, Mark, I'm in pending a discussion with my wife. Let's sit down and figure out exactly what you have in mind and how we're both going to keep from getting our heads shot off in the process."

Mark smiled. He had hoped for that reaction, though he could visibly see the conflict that boiled inside John. "Any hesitation?" Mark asked.

"I just hope we don't go down in history as the two who set a match to what's left of the United States of America, Mark. I didn't serve my country to be the one who burned it down." John sighed.

Mark gave John a knowing look and nodded as they walked back inside.

Conflict and Resolution

"What do you think, honey?" John asked his wife. He had always sought and greatly valued his wife's counsel in moments like this. John was, by his nature, a very decisive person. He always found the shortest distance between two points, the most direct path to his objective, and then he pounced on it. He was nearly unable to weigh the consequences of the options before him. Once he had decided on a course of action, he would not shy away from any hardship IF he believed the end justified the means. This strength, he would admit, was sometimes his greatest weakness.

Rachel was very different. No less committed to following through on a decision she had made, she debated the merits of different plans and considered not only the objective but the cost of her potential actions. John making a decision was using a sledgehammer; Rachel used a scalpel. If her only fault was occasional indecisiveness, her strength was the ability to digest extremely complex situations and, given appropriate time, come up with a solution that mutually satisfied all parties involved. She could win a fight without actually fighting, a born negotiator. It was this strength John looked to now.

"I don't know, honey. I understand Mark's point about trying to force a change before it's too late, and I don't fault you for the decisions you made that brought us here, but I would be lying if I said I didn't have some reservations about continuing down this path." Rachel reached down and gently took her husband's hand, that same rough and calloused hand that had worked so hard to build a life for her and their daughter. The same hand that had gently and tenderly held her through moments of joy and sadness. The same hand that promised endless tenderness to those he loved, promised incredible violence to those who threatened his family. She had seen very clearly earlier that day the duality that was the man she loved: the husband and father, and the soldier. She had met him two decades earlier while he was in uniform...

"I'm going to marry this man," a younger Rachel told her friends and family. He was nothing but a picture she held, hundreds of emails and Yahoo Messenger chats, a soldier pouring his heart out to a woman he was falling for thousands of miles away back home while he was in Iraq.

John had joined the Army National Guard young, with all the idealism of a young man who wanted to serve and protect his home. When he had made his commitment, the Twin Towers had not been struck, Iraq and Afghanistan were just countries on a map, and the War on Terror was not yet a phrase coined to describe a decade of fighting half a world away. Yet when his orders came, he went.

Months later, a friend of his from high school moved into an unassuming apartment complex near a local state college and struck up a friendship with another young woman recently moved down from a more rural town. A picture on her refrigerator, depicting a young man heavily tanned from the desert environment, lean and muscled from his deployment, caught Rachel's eye immediately. The day he came home and was released from duty, his first stop was home to grab his car. His second stop was to her.

After the first few years Rachel watched the Army side of her husband fade but never disappear. He had softened, grown more patient, turned into a wonderful husband and a great father, yet she always knew that behind that lopsided grin, beneath those dark eyes, he was still capable of incredible viciousness and violence were he to be cornered or threatened. On an occasion or two, if his family were in some small way threatened, she could see and hear the old him resurface.

This morning, she had seen it come out, all the way out. She had watched this gentle man morph into a soldier again and ruthlessly kill four men without pause, and then just as quickly turn back into the husband and father trying to shield his family from the ugliness of what he had done. He was not ashamed, for he felt justified; he was just trying to protect his family. Always trying to protect.

"Rachel, I meant what I said. If you think we should cut bait and take our chances, then let's cut bait and go. We have our bug-out gear, that'll cover us for several days. We have plenty of ordnance to protect ourselves, med gear if that becomes necessary, our emergency shelter, and enough fuel to put some miles between our home and ourselves. If you think that's the smart decision for this family, I need to hear it."

Rachel knew John was not saying this to abdicate his responsibility, only that he was deeply conflicted and saw no clear answer to the decisions he faced. It was moments like this, without clear direction, he was at his most vulnerable. He was afraid to make a decision that would later turn out to be ill advised, and hence sought the counsel of the only person in his life he trusted to give him direction.

"John, I don't think running is the answer. I think Mark is right, either we fight this fight today while we are strong, or we wait until we are too weak to fight it. People should have been going nuts years ago when you were out campaigning and protesting about these laws, but they all shrugged their shoulders. And they still are, waiting for their turn to get marched off to the next camp for the politically inconvenient. I'm just worried about my family. I'm worried about my husband and my daughter. The rest of the world can figure their own problems out if they would just leave my family alone."

And John nodded his head, for similar thoughts had crossed his mind on multiple occasions. It was why he stopped his advocacy, didn't fight when his podcast and blog were shut down, stopped going to the state capital, stopped writing congressmen. He was not a quitter, but he had hoped that if he stopped proudly wearing his bull's-eye on his back, the people who came to his door that morning would never come. This was America, after all; things like this weren't supposed to happen.

"Well, honey, I'm pretty worried too. The problem is I know history. Every time an insurgency, and that is what we are proposing here, arises, the state will spare no effort or expense attempting to crush it. The insurgents' only possible way to survive is to call more people to their cause, which spreads out the government's resources and disrupts their control. If we don't fight this fight, they will find us and destroy us. If we do fight, we may be destroyed anyway. I see our only path forward is to jump in with both feet and do what Mark is suggesting. He wants to start by using our story like a lighthouse to guide other ships in the storm. We were the first ones to stand up and say NO MORE. If others follow suit, the state may have to reconsider its policies or risk their legitimacy completely crumbling. The more heavy-handed their methods, the more people realize the time to shit or get off the pot is right NOW. If we can keep our butts out of the immediate line of sight, we may pull this off, and the Minutemen have the resources to shield us for the time being. But I can't do this without you."

Rachel gave a long blink and nodded her head. John was such a dichotomy, both hard and soft at the same time. On the outside, he was nearly six feet and two hundred forty pounds of tanned skin, tattoos, and calluses with just a bit of "dad bod" thrown in, but underneath he was an incredibly emotional person. He depended on his wife to calm the storms in his mind and his heart, to help him make sense of the emotional currents that ran through him. It did not take an incredibly perceptive person to look at those deep-set dark eyes to see he was worried about many of the same things that worried her, only he didn't seem to be able to find the words to make sense of all of them. He just felt worry, and unable to find a course of action that suited him, the worry chewed on him.

"If you think this will make a difference, let's do it. I know you won't do anything to intentionally jeopardize our family. What's Mark's plan?" Rachel inquired.

"Initially, pirate the AM/FM radio frequencies and broadcast. The government has the internet pretty locked down, but he and I think we know some avenues that will be much more difficult for them to control. And once we get the information into the hands of the Minutemen's other cells, the agency will have its hands full trying to block multiple coordinated attacks. I'm sure they're already hard at work trying to cover up what happened, wish we had taken pictures and collected some evidence to corroborate our story, but that wasn't high on the priority list. But their commo guy Kevin caught the whole radio transmission from the scene 'cause the stupid bastards weren't running secured comms, and that'll be hard to ignore. It's going to be an information/disinformation campaign for now, not direct action."

"By direct action you mean…"

"I mean neutralizing enemy forces," John finished.

Rachel shuddered, maybe internally, but maybe it showed. She had taken no pleasure in shooting at the men who had come to her home that morning, even though she felt fairly justified defending her husband and her family. What her husband wasn't saying, and did not have to say, was that "for now" meant it was an option not off the table. If an occasion arose where John felt justified in launching a preemptive strike, or if their location was discovered and they were attacked, then John would cut a bloody path through anyone who got in his way. He didn't have to say it, it was just a part of who he was. He had promised her years before that he would never let her or their daughter be harmed, and she had seen firsthand the training he subjected himself to for years to carry through on that promise. Firearms training, range days, the expense of ammunition and firearms—John never compromised on taking care of his family's financial needs, but he saw this as another aspect of taking care of them, and he committed to it fully.

"What can I do to help?" Rachel asked.

"You already have, honey," John replied, squeezing his wife's hand. Then he hugged her, turned on his heel, and walked back toward the house to find Mark. His demeanor had changed in that instant. Gone was the quiet, brooding, unsure man who looked longingly for his path and his task. In his place was the soldier, a man who believed in the righteousness of what he was about to undertake. A soldier who had been assigned an important mission that he could not fail.

Mostly, he was a man with the full support of his wife, his other half. He was a man who knew he couldn't be beaten by anyone.

"Mark, let's get started," John stated matter-of-factly while leading Mark back into the house.

"You're sure, John? You two came to a decision that quick?" Mark replied questioningly.

John nodded his head. "The longer we wait, the colder the trail gets. Let's hit them right now and get this going. I wish we had some evidence of what happened to corroborate that radio transmission your guy Kevin grabbed, but I guess we'll have to roll with what we have—"

"Actually, we do have evidence," Mark replied casually, turning around to the console behind him. Seconds later, John was looking at a bird's-eye view of his home, and nothing looked out of place. Then an SUV pulled up, blocking their driveway; four men in tactical gear and carrying rifles at low ready approached his front door. One carried a battering ram, which John realized was how they had knocked his door in so quickly. He had hardened that door years prior, using three-inch deck screws to secure the striker plates and hinges, and the door was an old solid wood job that was fairly heavy. One swing with the ram, and the men were stacked up, running in…then falling backwards as fast as they had walked forward. With their black uniforms and the height the video was shot from (a drone most likely) their wounds were not obvious, but the one surviving member of the failed raid was obviously in pain. Then John watched himself walk out the front door, rifle at low ready. He viciously stomped on the man's hand that still held a rifle, reached down with a knife to slice the sling, then kicked it away. A quick glance at the other three showed no movement. John slung his rifle, drew his sidearm, and shot the man once in the head. He then proceeded back into his home, and the video ended.

"I'm sure at some point it occurred to you we knew far too much about your home and your routines to be casual observers. We knew about the raid days in advance. We have a man on the inside, but that is all I can say. We did not know the time, only a window during which it was supposed to happen, so we quickly moved one of our drones into position to observe you and figure out what their response time would be. Once our other drone saw them depart their HQ this morning, we knew how long you had before they showed, and were able to give you details about their raid. We could not have anticipated your...response. So, to answer your concern, we have every bit of evidence. Our only issue is IF we proceed ahead with this, we are handing that same evidence to the state. If they catch you, they have ironclad evidence of what you did."

John took it all in. He had been keeping an eye out for suspicious vehicles, but had not even considered a drone and silently kicked himself for that oversight. "Are we sure they don't have active drones too? One could have spotted my departure and tracked me here."

"We saw no evidence of drones. Satellite reconnaissance is something we have far less control over. It's a risk we have to take," Mark said.

"So what you're saying is," John started, "the only way to pull this bad tooth is to stick our head in the lion's mouth and hope he isn't hungry today."

Mark smiled ruefully. "I think that's a fair way to put it. But if you want to commit and want to start right now, let's sit down and figure this out."

With Me, or Against Me

"Do you think they'll go for it, Mark?" John asked. It was impossible for that normally stoic voice not to betray a note of worry.

The two of them had argued endlessly throughout the evening on how to handle the information. Mark argued for condensing and editing everything, and John wanted full disclosure. In the end a compromise was reached. Now to disseminate it, they surveyed their options. Mark had enough radio equipment, made more frequency flexible than was legal under normal circumstances, to pirate several bandwidths in the AM and FM bands. The transmissions came with a danger that they could always be tracked back to the source, but short transmissions would narrow the window for the local agencies to accomplish such a feat.

It was a foregone conclusion that they would blast their content through social media using all available platforms, and an equally foregone conclusion that this content would be relentlessly scrubbed as it went viral. It was a necessary expenditure of energy to attempt, if only to get it into the hands of the public and get the rumor mills stirred up. Also, the risk was minimal due to Mark and Kevin's reliance on VPNs, so-called virtual private networks, which shielded their IP address from those who would attempt to discover their whereabouts. No security measure was perfect, but this one proved fairly robust.

John had also recommended utilizing P2P, or peer-to-peer data transmission using torrent files. These would not depend on any server or singular storage to maintain their viability. Once released into the wild of the internet, and once it found its way into enough hard drives, it would be nearly impossible for the federal agencies to remove. Best of all, any attempt to remove these files from private hard drives would send the operators and the media itself into histrionics at the obvious infringement on the right to free speech. The federal government probably still remembered the stinging rebuke they received in the court of public opinion for their attempts to regulate and banish 3-D printable guns and the other intellectual property of Defense Distributed years earlier. The Streisand effect was obvious then, as the more agencies and states attempted to crack down on the transmission of these files, the more they traded hands. John believed they could leverage a similar effect now, which Mark and Kevin agreed was likely.

The real question mark was the Minutemen themselves. Each cell operated independently, without cohesive overall leadership. This made it incredibly difficult to root out the entire organization, as you had to destroy each cell individually, but also made cooperation among different cells voluntary. John was the first one to point out that, just as he had fought against those who claimed to support the Second Amendment yet gave ground on every issue, a similar battle might be on the horizon among the various cells of the Minutemen. Certainly, it was likely that at least some, and possibly many, of these cells might not be enthusiastic about extending their mission statement beyond simple passive resistance to aiding and abetting a fugitive and advocating outright insurrection against a nation-state.

"John, I have to believe these people will see what we are doing here and join us. If I'm wrong, then we are all in a lot deeper trouble than I originally thought." Mark sighed.

"I hear you, Mark. I'm just saying be prepared for that pushback. These are your people, not mine. None of them wanted to reenact Lexington and Concord on my front lawn before I did it; none of them stood in front of these agents while they hauled people off to prison and tore their homes apart. They didn't want to get their hands bloody or their boots muddy, and now you are about to tell them to ruck up and get ready for a war. I would be amazed if at least some of them didn't balk. The real question is, do any of them know your full name or location? Can they turn on us to save their own skins? Because once you and I let this missile out of the silo, there is no calling it back, and the state is going to put incredible pressure on everyone and anyone they have to in order to bring us to heel," John said emphatically.

Mark glanced at him and nodded. They had bought themselves into this table, and win lose or draw, they were going to play the game.

"Kevin," Mark said, "send this to our other cells. Eyes only, not for immediate retransmission. Indicate we intend a full release eight hours after this is transmitted, and we ask them each to match our release simultaneously. Even I'm not positive how many cells are out there today, but we were well over a hundred two years ago, and growth was always part of the mission statement. Let the government try to shut us all down and see how far they get. Once our statement is out in the public eye, we'll figure out our next move. Step one is just to get this out before the agency starts feeding the media its version of the events."

"And what then?" John asked.

"And then we wait," Mark answered. "It is impossible to predict what the exact response of these agencies is going to be, much less our cells or the populace. If I had to levy a guess, I would assume the immediate response will be an attempt to silence our transmissions followed by some fairly draconian curtailment of freedoms, at least in this immediate area. That will not be viewed favorably by the populace, and it may be something we can use to sway public sentiment to us. The battle is going to be fought for public opinion, not with bullets just yet. The state has tried their very best to do to us what they did with the Weaver family and Mount Carmel, to smear our reputations and mischaracterize us. And just as then, many people bought their lies rather than investigate the claims for themselves."

John had made these same references years ago. It didn't take a rocket scientist to figure out Randy Weaver and his family were assaulted by the government, not because they were mass murderers and violent felons, but because they were accused of possessing a shotgun shorter than the legal length without having paid the ATF the requisite two-hundred-dollar tax stamp. Mount Carmel and David Koresh were demonized quite thoroughly, called religious cooks and Koresh accused of child molestation, but no one bothered to wonder WHY THE ATF was the agency that discharged that initial search warrant and conducted the raid. If the charge was statutory rape and child abuse, why weren't the local or state police tasked with snatching Koresh right out of his chair at the local coffee shop and bringing him in for questioning? Why was this department involved in shooting and burning these people out of their building? And why were the allegations of child abuse only brought up AFTER the disastrously mishandled raid to justify such heavy-handed tactics.

The Minutemen were about to fight a similar war against disinformation. The state had similarly demonized them thus far, and their newly found affiliation with a family accused of murdering four government agents in cold blood was going to make the entire organization the focus of an intense public smear campaign, to say nothing of the countryside being torn apart looking for their cells. John only hoped these men were prepared for the long row that needed to be hoed, because he suspected none of them would make it out of this without getting a little dirty.

Out back by the garden, Kay made friends with Mark's son, George, while the mothers stood quietly off to the side. Rachel regarded Mark's wife, Vicky. They had introduced themselves, but said little since Rachel had spoken with her husband. The silence was deafening as she waited for news of what was being discussed inside, and just as she was preparing to break the silence, Vicky did just that.

"Your daughter is beautiful. George doesn't have many friends since we live so far out of town. I haven't seen him come this far out of his shell in a long time," Vicky said, as if oblivious to what Rachel and her family had been through that morning.

The absolute normality of this polite chitchat astounded Rachel. "I don't want my family to be a bother in your home, but I believe my husband intends to take Mark up on his invitation to stay on for a while."

Vicky smiled and shook her head. "Rachel, you and your family are no bother. I have supported my husband's work for years. I knew who you were and what was about to happen to you before you did. I was in the room when I heard your husband announce his intention to fight back, and saw the question in my husband's eyes. I nodded immediately; how could we not lend you our help? If the roles were reversed, I would hope someone would come to my family's rescue."

And suddenly Rachel had a new perspective of her quiet host. Vicky well knew the perilous situation around her family, but had the mental fortitude not to let it rule her daily life. Instead, she focused on her husband and her son, just as Rachel had for years even as she knew the great danger that could come to their door at any moment.

"I appreciate that, Vicky. Still, I want to earn our keep around here, so any help you need around the house or property, please let us know. My Sicilian grandmother would be ashamed if you didn't at least let me help out with a meal here and there. And John is a fair hand at carpentry and mechanics work."

Vicky nodded politely. "I accept. Just know that you aren't a burden to us. You are either a guest or you are a member of this household, depending on whether you intend to stay on temporarily or permanently. Either way, your company and help are welcome."

And so the ladies sat and watched their children play and get to know each other, and Rachel felt a sense of warmth and belonging. No longer was her family hiding from their neighbors; no longer were she and her husband disguising themselves. They were among kindred spirits, men and women who saw their mission as a righteous one to restore the country they loved to its true path. Rachel felt at home, yet felt unease. While this might be a place they belonged, she felt the impending hostility that was sure to come their way looming on the horizon. She felt just like she had that morning, holding her rifle, watching her husband's face harden and his eyes darken, waiting for the sound that would tell her it was time to fight or die…

I hate this damned armor, Rachel thought for not the first time. At the expense of sounding crass, it chafed nipples like it was made of sandpaper, and did its best to crush her feminine figure into a decidedly flatter profile. It dug into her shoulders, into her armpits, and if she did not stand absolutely straight up, it would pinch on her belly and waist. It was, aptly described by her, a medieval torture device. It was also the only thing that might be standing between her life and death, so she tolerated it. She looked down the hallway and into the kitchen at her husband.

John looked in his element, if you overlooked a bit of beer belly poking out from beneath his armor. John had worn somewhat similar armor when he was deployed to Iraq for Operation Iraqi Freedom and was a firm believer in using this potentially life-saving tool when you expected trouble, like the kind of trouble coming their way. Spare magazines draped across his chest, with more in a bag next to him on the floor with his medkit. His hands tightly gripped his AR-15, with its buttstock firmly in his shoulder and his eye lined up with the rifle's red dot sight. He had set his wife up in a shooting lane where she would be far from the immediate line of fire, and of course put himself right in the path of potential danger. That was her husband; if someone was going to get shot, he was going to demand he be the one in front rather than someone else. This home-defense plan relied on him being the center of the assailing force's attention while he attempted to push them back with suppressive fire. Rachel's .30-06 had more than enough power to drive through most armor their attackers would be wearing, and shooting from the side as she was set up, she would be able to cut them down quickly IF they managed to make it past the foyer. With John in front of them, that was a big if. She knew he intended to cut these men to pieces before they had any opportunity to hurt her family.

The bang on the front door startled her, and she accidentally tightened up on the trigger. Her husband's endless drilling of weapons handling kicked in, and she let her finger back off, stared down her shooting lane parallel to the hallway, and waited. The eruption of fire from her husband's rifle made her wince, as did the guttural yell that came from the man she loved. He wasn't just shooting, he was hurling his very anger and outrage at these men who had just knocked his front door off its hinges. She watched with mingled horror and wonder as the cords in his neck and arms stood out, that usually happy face changed to one of rage, and her husband stood and began to advance. She could not see around the corner of the hallway, but she fired at the doorway through the walls to try to help her husband. She need not have worried, John was advancing because these men expected to find a family cowering in the corner, not a monster in body armor waiting to exact revenge for their disturbing the peace of his home.

She worked to reload her rifle quickly, then stood and advanced slowly to find her husband. She came to the corner of the hallway and turned left to look out the open doorway just as her husband's foot came down with all his weight on a man's hand. The sound of shattering bones was hard to miss, as was the cry of pain. John took the man's rifle from him and surveyed the other three bodies for movement. She watched as her husband slung his rifle, extracted his handgun from its holster, and shot the man in the face. Her own feelings were in turmoil. This man was no threat, lying on his back with several shots in his chest and unarmed, but seconds ago he had tried to hurt her husband. She wrestled with these emotions as her husband looked up at her. His eyes softened; his face changed; whatever he had called forth to take these men's lives was gone in an instant. "Rachel, go get Kay and get our bug-out bags. We have to get out of here. Right now," John said.

Rachel nodded and went to go get their daughter. When the door to the panic room opened, she saw Kay sitting on the floor, knees to her chest with her arms wrapped around them and her head down. She slowly looked up, worry giving way to relief. She jumped up and hugged her mother. "Where's Daddy?" she asked.

"Daddy is coming. We're all okay," Rachel answered. "Honey, we have to go right now. Can you help us get our camping bags (Rachel's euphemism for the family bug-out bags)?"

"Sure, Mom." It would only be moments later Rachel would curse herself for not thinking that Kay would walk right past the front door, where four dead men lay, in her pursuit of the camping gear. And it would be nearly an hour of holding her daughter's hand while they drove for their lives before Kay would speak again.

Rachel reflected on this, the longest and most frightening day of her life since the car accident that almost ended it decades before, and she felt a tear slide down her cheek. She knew their daughter's life, and hers, had been irreparably altered by the events of that morning, and wondered how she would try to provide a normal childhood for a young woman hiding from her government with two felons for parents. For ever so brief a moment, she questioned the decision she and her husband had made, and then abandoned the thought. She no more wanted to go back to their quiet suburban home without her husband than she liked the situation she was in, but at least here her family was together and their new hosts were welcoming. They would do as they had always done; they would survive until the time came they could thrive again. But they would survive.

Idle Hands

"Where did your guy drop off our gear?" John asked.

Mark replied, "We set you up in one of our spare rooms. Figured the three of you would want to be together, so there's a king bed and a full in that room, plus closet space. Everything from your car is in there, and your car is out back in our barn under a tarp. We'll have to check it daily, maybe move it somewhere more permanent to keep the critters from chewing on the wires, but for now it'll do."

"I've always made a religious habit of cleaning my guns after use. Do you have some space I can tend to that and not ruin your furniture or bedding?" John inquired.

Mark nodded knowingly. "Yeah, I'll give you a hand bringing everything to our attached garage. We set it up as a workshop years ago when we built the unattached garage. I have a workbench and should have everything we need. Want some company?"

"Only if you don't mind me smoking a cigar out there. We left in a hurry, but I had the good foresight to snatch my travel humidor. Can't leave home without the essentials," John said ruefully, painfully aware he might never see his home again.

Mark led John to his new room and helped him grab up the very firearms he had used to extinguish four human lives that morning. Mark knew guns and immediately recognized John's AR. He was less familiar with John's sidearm and was surprised to see a Remington hunting rifle among the guns not in bags or cases. "That's an odd choice for a defensive weapon," Mark remarked.

"Rachel didn't grow up shooting scary black rifles in her rural hometown; she grew up sitting in deer stands with her father. That rifle was the first firearm more potent than a BB gun she was given as a teenager, and she's attached to it. I'm not a huge fan, tends to jam if I don't religiously scrub out the chamber after use, but .30-06 makes an impression, and she is surgical with it," John replied as he followed Mark to the workshop. Once there, he found a bench not unlike the one he left at home (another pang of pain), constructed solidly of four-by-four legs, two-by-fours, and decked in plywood. It was sturdy, all business, and showed the stains of gun oil and carbon from use. "Do you guys get a chance to do any shooting? I mean, you're way out in the sticks, but, hell, someone would have to be deaf not to hear the sounds of gunfire," John asked.

"We don't have many neighbors this far out, and the few we do have plenty of guns and no love for the government. They would no sooner turn me in than themselves. The only reason you got hit today is because you live in the suburbs. They haven't made their way this far out in the country yet," Mark said easily. "Talk me through what you have here. A Remington 74 Auto in .30-06, I don't recognize your sidearm, and that AR has to be homebuilt."

"This is a CZ P-09. Double action/single action, 9 mm, polymer frame. It's a service gun, four-and-a-half-inch barrel with nineteen-round magazines; then I added the Surefire X300 tactical light to it and plus-two base pads to the magazines. Twenty-one rounds plus one in the chamber makes for one hell of a potent bedside gun. I built this AR a while back, rifle-length gas system and buffer, fixed stock, eighteen-inch barrel. I stuck a light on the front, red dot sight and a magnifier. I figured I wanted something that would be a modernized M16A2 like what I was issued when I enlisted, so I opted for something that would work from point-blank range out to about three hundred yards. I could've put a magnified optic on it, but that makes short-range shooting a little trickier. If I need something with more range, I have a bolt gun that'll put three rounds on top of each other at a hundred yards," John explained as he started breaking down and stripping the guns with a practiced hand. "I never did care much for Glocks or other striker-fired handguns. Got my start with a 1911 and always like the way a good trigger on a hammer-fired gun felt. Once I fell into CZs, I was hooked."

Mark listened as he pulled out some cleaning supplies. John had his own preferences, but beggars can't be choosers, and he accepted Mark's offer of supplies and help. The two lit their cigars and enjoyed a moment of silence while they let their hands and the task at hand occupy their minds.

Neither man needed to tell the other they were using this chore as an excuse to keep busy and keep their minds off the uncertainty they felt about what would transpire in the next eight hours while the messages fanned out to the other cells. They had no choice but to impatiently wait to see if the other cell leaders would accept their decision and agree to assist, or if they would leave them to fight this newest battle alone. Mark urged optimism. John was not an optimist. He was a hard worker, but he was also a man who prepared himself emotionally for the worst-case scenario at all times, and his mind worked feverishly to consider his next course of action should this one sour suddenly.

"I won't ask why you're doing this, helping us. I figure you're either completely insane or an ardent ideologue. I do feel compelled to ask how far you are prepared to go to see this through. This fight could get awful bloody, and if you aren't ready to march that road, I need to know now," John said suddenly.

Mark regarded his guest, almost let his outrage get the best of him, and realized another piece of John's puzzle. He and his family were already neck-deep in a bad situation, and he was counting the pros and cons of staying with Mark and his group. He was also giving Mark an out if he didn't want to put his family in harm's way. John needed his help terribly, but not at the expense of their lives unless Mark was committed. John wasn't doubting Mark's commitment, he was expressing clear concern for Mark's well-being and, more importantly, for his family's.

"I don't doubt you, Mark. I just know it would hollow me out if anything happened to my wife and daughter. I don't want anything to happen to yours either. And after what I did this morning, I might as well be a pound of plutonium. Anyone who takes my family in is in danger. You have to know that, and what could happen," John explained.

Mark reflected on John's candor and found little to argue with. He had accepted the loss of his freedom and his estate when he decided to help John's family. He expected to have to spend an inordinate amount of his inheritance and wealth to keep his family out of prison. He had not considered that the price to pay might be their own lives. His mind tried to wrap around this thought, he and found it difficult to believe the situation was even that dire. "Are you suggesting that if we were discovered, we would not be taken into custody but simply executed?" Mark asked, careful not to inject the disbelief he felt into his words.

"I think," John answered, "their next move will broadcast their intentions loud and clear. They didn't come to my door with a clipboard to conduct a compliance check; they knocked my door off its hinges and came in with M4s at low ready. That isn't how you deescalate a situation. Neither do you raid a compound with a hundred guys with MP5s, or shoot a man's wife with a sniper rifle. Those are the sorts of operational postures meant to beat your opponent into submission, not give them the opportunity to come quietly."

"And what would you have done if they had politely knocked on the front door?" Mark asked.

"I would have left the door locked and let the little pecker necks figure out their next move. Like refusing to speak to a police officer without your lawyer. If they forced entry, they were mine. If they had not, they would still be on their merry little way to stomp the next citizen's rights and have a beer after work. What happened is simply a reaction. They attacked; I hit them back when they weren't ready for it. My worry is they may respond by driving that door down with guns blazing on the next guy."

And that was another thought Mark had not considered, that the reaction to John's attack and Mark's attempt to shield him from the agency's eyes would result in their posture becoming MORE aggressive rather than less. If the agency reacted by doubling down instead of backing down, then John was right; everyone would end up dirty when this was over.

As if on cue, Kevin walked into the workshop. John's mind, as it tended to, seemed to freely analyze and file away details...like the fact that no one he had seen on this compound carried a firearm. He intended to carry his sidearm at a minimum and hoped that wouldn't be a point of contention. It would be something he would have to bring up delicately to his new hosts. Kevin began, "We've gotten some preliminary responses from the other cells. A lot are quiet, which means they either haven't checked their encrypted email yet, or they are considering the information. Some of these cells operate via strict democracy, and those will take some time to come to a conclusion. More cells than I had hoped for gave the green light, mostly the ones farther out in the country in their respective areas. But we may have a problem..."

"The cells in the urban city centers," Mark finished. "They feel the pressure the most because they are closest to the detention centers, closest to the center of the search webs."

"And they're the ones who probably shrugged their shoulders at every infringement up to the last one," John snarled. His anger was evident; it spread out across the room like a fogbank, clinging to every surface. "It was always the but'ers: 'I support the Second but...' They would beat the drum for the Second Amendment one day, then say 'we have to be reasonable' the next. Fair-weather friends sold us out every time we needed them to hold the line on gun rights. Then when the Second Amendment got totally repealed, gone, most gun owners looked around and shrugged their shoulders like it never mattered in the first place!" John's fist came thundering down on the workbench.

"Kevin, do we have enough support to move forward without those cells?" Mark inquired.

"I don't know, Mark. The urban-center cells have access to a huge population of potential holdouts, and they are right in the areas we need for AM/FM broadcast and pirate cable channels to try to warn people right where the searches are taking place right now. If we don't get them, we might end up pushing a rope," Kevin replied.

"So what will it take to get them up off their asses?" John snarled. "Those weren't the Girl Scouts who showed up on my doorstep this morning, and you can't even try to convince me mine was the first house they pulled this act on. They aren't conducting searches and compliance checks, they are wholesale breaking into people's homes with guns drawn! When will enough be enough?!"

"Listen, John—" Marked started and was curtly cut off.

"No, you two answer me one question. What has happened to the other gun owners on the naughty list? The ones who do come quietly and don't smoke check their attackers? They get a slap on the wrist? A finger wagging? Pay some fines? You had a drone above my house BEFORE you knew I intended to fight, that means you've been watching them too. Tell me what happened to everyone else!"

Mark hesitated just long enough for John to read his eyes, and he read John's. John suspected he knew the answer to the question, and Mark was about to confirm John's worst fears. "Most of the time the entire family is hauled off to a detention camp; kids go with a CPS worker. We've tried to get close enough to see what's happening in the camps, but our drones got knocked out several times. The agency's control over those sites, even their immediate airspace, is total. We know where they are, but nothing of the living conditions. Some citizens were beaten before being taken, a few severely."

"Go on," John said coldly.

"Some were killed, even when they didn't fire a shot." Mark sighed.

"And you knew, and you sat here and did nothing. And these other cells knew and have likewise sat on their asses. These jackbooted thugs are imprisoning and murdering people for exercising the rights promised to them by their country, and no one seemed to get upset enough to raise a finger. And now," John said levelly, "you two are surprised they don't want to get their hands dirty when an honest-to-God war is about to break out?!"

Mark and Kevin could not meet John's gaze. The cold fury, indignation, and raw anger in his eyes was the most incredible thing they had ever seen. He looked like a wild animal finally out of his cage and ready to hunt.

The Caged Tiger

Rachel found her husband finishing his cigar on the back porch. She thought she heard him yell and started walking back towards the house to find him there. His body was tight, shoulders hunched forward, the knuckles of one hand near white while the others fought mightily not to crush the cigar it held. She did not have to ask if something was bothering him, or what. She only had to sit next to him and lay a hand gently across his shoulders for him to let it out.

"It's worse than I thought. They aren't just arresting people for trial, they're rounding up entire families and hauling them off to detention camps. Like this is Communist Russia, for God's sake! How in the hell do people stand for this? When were their neighbors or friends going to stand up and demand justice for these people? It's like the country I knew is gone, and all the people with the balls to do the right thing are already gone," John said, his tone halfway between a cry of despair and a sigh of resignation. She could feel how alone he felt.

"What is happening?" Rachel asked.

"The other cells are in disagreement about whether or not to proceed," John replied. "The ones out here in the country, like Mark's, are ready to go; the assholes in the cities don't want to get their hands dirty. Isn't that how it was a decade ago when we were still fighting for gun rights? It was always these clowns in urban areas, the but'ers and 'law-abiding gun owners,' who kept demanding we hard-core gundamentalists stop making them look bad. Sit down, stop making people scared, obey the law, and look where that got us. Second Amendment repealed, and now anyone who didn't kiss the government's ass and pass over the guns willingly is being sent off to the gulag, and STILL they don't seem to care enough to stand up and fight!"

"What about Mark?" Rachel asked.

"What about him? He knew all of this was going on. Was he in that house with us to help when the rubber hit the road? Was he out marching the streets with a rifle? Did he go assault these camps?"

"Is that what you want to do?" Rachel gasped.

John sighed. "Yes and no. I don't know what to do. I want to go back in there and tear Mark's and Kevin's heads off and stuff them into each other's hind ends for sitting here in the safety of their little compound while people are hauled off to camps, but I can't blame them. I said for years, one man shooting is a nutcase, a hundred is an insurrection, ten thousand is a revolution. They would have been cut to pieces if they were the only guys doing it. Still, I'm angry, and that's why I came out here, to think and get ahold of myself."

Rachel chuckled under her breath. "You threw something, didn't you?" She knew her husband and his proclivity for explosive anger. He wasn't by nature a violent person, preferring to take his frustration out on inanimate objects rather than people. He had practically turned throwing tools into an Olympic sport over the years, or offending parts if they were light enough for him to shoulder.

"Yeah, I don't think Mark will make a habit of leaving hammers lying around on his bench after having me for a houseguest. What do I do, honey? I have to figure out some way to get these guys off the bench and in the game, or we're just spinning our wheels. If they don't join us and bombard the citizens with the truth, the agency is apt to release their own statement and use what we did against the Minutemen. That will justify an even more heavy-handed tactic than what they are already using. What I did will get more people hurt unless I can convince these people the time to fight is right the hell now."

Rachel reflected. This was not a battle to be won through yelling, but through negotiation. What they needed to do was to court the other cells, not shame them...though a little shame might not hurt. They were all idealists at heart; otherwise they would not have undertaken this endeavor.

Perhaps if an appeal to the safety of the people would not rally them, a slight wound to their pride might.

"Does Mark have some system to communicate simultaneously to all of the cells?" Rachel asked.

"He would almost have to," John replied.

"Then why not talk to them? I don't want to watch my husband march off to get shot any more than the next person, and you almost have me convinced that's what needs to be done. Maybe you can get them to join us, with a little persuasion and coaching."

"Use honey before vinegar, huh, honey?" John smiled.

"Of course, love, that's how I get you to see things my way most of the time." Rachel smiled. She kissed her husband and hugged him, as much to reconnect as to reassure him. She could always calm the storm that was her husband; it was one of the reasons he married her. And in those times she could not calm that storm, she could at least redirect it, just as she was doing now. His frustration was only due to a lack of direction, and setting him on a path to victory was all that was needed to change his entire personality.

And so John, now with a purpose, stood and turned to face the house and was looking right into the faces of Kevin and Mark. "Listen, guys, I need to apologize—"

"You don't owe us an apology. We're all frustrated. We just don't all react by hurling tools through drywall," Mark said without a trace of anger. He was grinning.

"Well, I behaved like an ass and took it out on you guys. My wife is right; we need to garner the Minutemen's full support to this new cause. Do you have some method of simultaneous secure comms with them? Something other than encrypted email?" John inquired.

Mark glanced to Kevin. "We do have a system, but it's been used very sparingly. As secure as it is, a continuous signal is easier to trace and find, no matter how many other networks we bounce it through. If someone is looking for it, they'll find it eventually," Kevin explained. "The question is, is it worth the risk? What do you have in mind?"

"I'm going to do exactly what I spent years doing before I went silent. I'm going to do my best to rally your people… our people. They have to see that the present course is not yielding the desired result. Some won't support us no matter what, but if I can convince the majority our course of action is the proper one and the naysayers aren't yielding any outcome, we have a chance," John replied. "And if I'm not the one to convince them, I'll yield to you, Mark, but someone has to try. We're sitting ducks here without their support."

Mark nodded. "No, I think you are the one to speak to them, and this system was set up years ago for just such an eventuality."

Now, John thought, *what button do I have to push to get these guys in this game?*

In, or Out

John started into the microphone. "Ladies and gentlemen of the Minutemen, my name is John Arceneaux. This morning I received a call on my phone, like thousands you people have made to try to warn those gun owners who have not yet turned over their arms of the danger that was approaching their door. In many cases, you have assisted these people in escaping to parts of the country where the raids have not reached, or integrated them into your organization. Mark issued me just such a call this morning, only I did not run. I had heard rumors of the confiscations and the incarcerations and the abuses heaped upon people by these agents, and I had decided years ago I had had enough of it. Three years ago, I decided not to comply with their laws, their registration, their bans, and I hid my gun safe behind a false wall in my closet. I won't go into details, but suffice to say I had enough firearms and ammo in that safe to ensure I would never again see daylight were I caught and tried. I cast my lot that day, and when the day came to stand and fight or bow, I fought.

"My wife stood by my side, my daughter hid in our panic room, and—I will not mince my words—I shot and killed four agents. They did not come to my door with clipboards and smiles, wanting to inspect my home. They did not ask to check my serial numbers or see if my guns were in compliance. They used a battering ram to knock my door off its hinges and entered my home without warning, each holding a full-auto M4 carbine that NONE OF US could legally own any longer even if we paid our extortion money to the ATF. I considered this breach of my home an act of war against a citizen of this country, and I reacted accordingly and unapologetically. I killed them and placed my family in a very precarious situation in the process.

Mark and his group aided my escape, and we are preparing to release ALL of the information, drone footage, and radio recordings of the attack and post attack on every social media platform, every AM/FM radio frequency, every avenue we have available to us. The resources of a nation-state are limitless, and if we alone undertake this, we will be stopped, our message will stop, and we will be hunted down. That is inevitable.

"If you join with us, release the information we have provided simultaneously, the agency will be so overwhelmed they will not be able to stop our message. The time has come to decide if you are in this fight or out. If you stand on the sidelines, know that you are abandoning not only us, but tens of thousands of people to the same fate that awaited me. Maybe hundreds of thousands. You can ease your guilt with phone calls and warnings, but you know, as I do, many of these people do not have the preparations and training to mount an appropriate defense of themselves. If we do not act, they will be rounded up and carted off just as many have already. I do not mince my words, based on my attack this morning, the agency may opt for an even more aggressive stance. The next house they hit, they may not use a battering ram, they may just shoot on sight. Save money on prison housing costs, 5.56 is cheaper than feeding and clothing prisoners. And if that happens, we have stood by and watched people who have never committed a crime be executed because their government decided only it should be able to use force to protect its interests.

"In 1775, the original Minutemen faced a similar choice as you do today. They could have issued their warning, moved the powder stores as they did, and not confronted the British troops. They could have stayed home and not stood in front of the world's greatest army and refused to be disarmed. But those men stood there and said NO, no more. They told the British they would not be disarmed, they would not scatter, they would not yield. They took casualties, and the further casualties of the American Revolution cut a bloody swath through the people of this fledgling country.

But no price was too great to pay for their freedom; no matter how many sons or brothers they sent to the lines never to be heard from again, the price was worth paying. The price is worth paying today. Stand with us, and if this turns into a shooting match, then let's fight it out knowing the cost is worth paying." John released his microphone button, and the transmission ceased. He leaned back in his chair and released the tension he felt. He had done his best to energize them; he only hoped it worked. What he did not expect was a response.

"I don't think engaging the agents in a shooting match is a productive solution, and neither do many of us. We survive by hiding our presence, not by goading them into a fight we cannot win. Are you going to be the one to defend our families when the agents come to find us?" This self-appointed leader of the opposition made no attempt to hide the contempt he felt, both for John's foolish decision to fight and for this foolish attempt to enrage the agency.

"And what will you do when these agents DO come to your doorstep? Will you fight? Will you surrender? Will you hand over your arms and bend to this tyrant? Or will you do exactly what I did when backed into a corner, sir?" John lashed out, careful to control his anger. He could not believe all these years later, he was still hearing the same pleadings. Obey the law, don't fight, don't resist, compromise. Compromise had brought them to this point, and this man and his kind would go on compromising all the way to the damned gas chamber so they could trade a dangerous life of freedom for a few more moments of life in captivity. John would rather face his mortality than live with a boot on his neck, and he was realizing just how alone he had felt all those years ago when he came to understand most people would rather the boot.

"We aren't engaging in a shooting match with these people just to satisfy you," the voice said with finality.

"I have argued with people just like you for years. People who told me to compromise, obey the law, tolerate a little more infringement, stop upsetting people. And those people will continue to compromise all the way to their demise.

If these agents come to your doorstep like they did mine this morning, they will not politely knock. They will come in and haul every one of you off to prison. No trial, no jury, no list of charges, no legal representation. No, sir, they will just come and take you and your families and your friends, and you can all share the same cell. The question is not DO we fight, it is when? Do you want to fight this fight now, while we have enough like-minded people still to push them back, or wait and let them pick us off one at a time? These people don't even realize the danger they are in, and we have an obligation to warn them. And if the consequence of issuing that warning is we have to defend ourselves, so be it."

"What you preach is madness."

"And what you preach is surrender. I refuse to surrender! Why the hell have all of you joined this movement if not to fight? Why did you hold onto your arms; why didn't you give them up? Why are you here if you aren't ready to lay it on the line for your beliefs? Either we fight this fight now, or we will lose it later. I'm signing off now so that I don't have to hear any more of this man's cowardice. In another three hours, we will have our answer. Who are the patriots who will stand with us at Lexington and Concord, and who are the Tories who will trade their brethren and their ideals for the false promise of life without freedom? People, you're either in, or you're out. Make your choice." John disconnected the transmission. He then stood abruptly and stomped out to the yard.

Kevin and Mark glanced at each other.

"Hell, after that speech, I'm ready to follow him into Hell itself," Kevin remarked. "He's right, the time to push is now, and if that leads to open hostilities, we are stronger now than we will be tomorrow. And that little prick from the city would sit there and do nothing until it was too late."

Mark nodded. "We always knew some of these people would not toe the line when the time came. He only echoed what many will think. But I think John just made the case for everyone, and I expect a lot of the other cells will join us. The ones on the fence will join in when they see everyone else. No one wants to be the cell that sat this out."

Mark turned to go talk to John when something caught his eye from the monitoring station they had set up to comb through news stories and press releases. They had it configured to hunt for keywords and phrases and to prioritize accordingly. What he was looking at was pictures of John and Rachel and the words *armed and extremely dangerous* in bold lettering above them. "Kevin, go grab John and his wife right the hell now."

John and Rachel came into the room, looking at their pictures on a large overhead screen. The news story being broadcast was damning. The Minutemen were named as a terrorist organization that had claimed to be responsible for the deaths of four "innocent" government agents, with the perpetrators identified but their whereabouts unknown.

"The pictures make these guys look like altar boys. Of course they don't want to show them all geared up for a raid, make them out to be some good guys just out doing their jobs when a couple of gun nuts shot them in the back. And of course they grab a picture from my service record. Two-for-one deal, cast a poor light on pro-gun people and military vets," John snarled. He had expected a government misinformation campaign, he had not anticipated it being so soon.

"John, this plays right into our hands. Once we bombard all the media and social media platforms with the evidence —"

"You're assuming we manage to. If everyone else doesn't follow suit, the message will go nowhere and we'll be hunted like dogs. Hell, my own mother would turn me in if she thought I was some crazy running around shooting people for no reason."

Mark could not disagree with John, only hold firm to the faith he had in his compatriots. "John, Rachel, this will work. We have to believe that."

Silence greeted him as John stared forward. His wife placed her hand on her husband's broad shoulder, and he visibly relaxed, if only a little. "Fine, we'll wait it out. About two and a half hours till we find out if our faith is misplaced," John said with finality.

Rallying Cry

That evening, what began as a trickle of posts on social media quickly turned into a deluge. Every platform was bombarded with a rapid-fire assault of posts and links to the information John and Mark had prepared. The information was damning to the agency, even damning to the government that had authorized it. Some saw this unauthorized press release as only further confirmation of the media's earlier characterization of the Minutemen as a terrorist organization, while many others were shocked at what they saw. That any agent of the United States government would act so aggressively to people who had not committed a violent crime was appalling, upsetting, and even enraging. More importantly, those gun owners who refused to surrender saw what waited for them. They realized the danger they faced was not the one they had faced years prior, in which you pay some fines or lose some guns. The penalty for their refusal to comply was now the safety and lives of themselves and their families.

Two things accompanied this press release. All across the country, gun owners pulled their rifles from the backs of their closets, from under mattresses, from out of attics; some even walked into their backyards with shovels. Guns were cleaned and oiled; magazines were loaded. For the first time in two hundred and fifty years, the spirit of revolution had awakened in Americans young and old. The fabled dragon had been awakened once again, the one that had prevented regimes from invading America for generations. There would once again be a rifle behind every blade of grass, only this time the threat was not levied upon Chinese or Russians or Mexicans or British. This time, the threat was for their government to respect the rights of its citizens. The people were ready to stand.

Simultaneously, there was a shriek of frustration coming from a mid-level supervisor working in a nondescript office somewhere in America. He was a program analyst tasked with screening social media platforms for libelous statements, hate speech, and anti-government sentiment. Years prior, the tech companies had finally ceded to the government's insistence that only they could be trusted with monitoring the internet, that last bastion of free speech. The ironic part was, the majority of people agreed only because of the tech companies' policies of censoring conservative speech. The votes were in to take this function out of the hands of the private-sector employees and place it in the hands of the bureaucracy that knew only its own interests.

"Can't you shut that down?!" he bellowed. They were working to scrub these unauthorized releases of information as vigorously as they were able, yet for every one they managed to take down, for every post they broke the link to, two more popped up in their place. It was as if his forty employees were impotent in the face of this onslaught of free speech. He would have taken little comfort in knowing that three to four people each in more than two hundred Minutemen cells were bombarding social media. The end result was simple arithmetic. The government regulatory arm simply did not have the manpower to stop them.

"Uh, sir, it isn't just on social media. I just got reports from the FCC they're hearing pirated AM/FM frequencies broadcasting this same information, including our own radio chatter from that day," a clerk warned his supervisor.

"What the...how in the hell are they doing that?!"

"I don't know, sir. The FCC said all of the registered stations are calling in on landlines, and it's locking up their switchboard. They all want to know where these transmissions are coming from too. It isn't localized either. California, New York, Washington State, Florida, flyover states, you name it—this is coast to coast."

The supervisor felt a bead of sweat roll down his back. "Well, how the hell do we stop it?"

"That's just the thing, sir, normally we would just call our men at the local stations and tell them to pull the plug. These stations aren't ours. We can't stop them. And they're on all frequencies. AM, FM, ham, CB, hell, even military frequencies. They are blasting every radio frequency but cell phones."

The supervisor could have opted to engage the internet kill switch, that oft rumored but never employed fail-safe. It had quietly been built into the system, its legislation buried in a thousand-page appropriations bill never read by the voters, to be employed in the event a cyberattack ever threatened to cripple or topple the government, and this seemed the perfect time to employ it. But the supervisor did not use his authority; as bureaucrats are apt to do, he reached out to his supervisor. And to his. And it would be hours before the unauthorized traffic was brought to heel by shutting off every internet service provider simultaneously. The internet, the last true method of free speech in America, was silenced.

Likewise, the decision was made hours too late to broadcast radio static on all available frequencies. They could not stop the pirate transmissions, but they could drown them out. The peer-to-peer sharing of pirate torrent files was a massive success, and once this spread outside the United States onto hard drives of military service members and families overseas, even the internet kill switch shutting down the US could not stop it.

All around the globe, people were seeing firsthand what a modern tyranny looked like, and they were shocked. The world media had all been led to believe the repeal of the Second Amendment was near unanimous, and the turnover of arms a peaceful one. What they were seeing was quite the opposite, something many nations would recognize from history books. Nazi Germany, Soviet Russia, communist China; many other nations would recognize a government's heavy-handed attempt to subdue its citizenry through the use of military or paramilitary assets. The global political fallout for the current presidential administration would be catastrophic and embarrassing. Not embarrassment at what had come, but at being caught doing it.

"Holy shit," John breathed. He had not dared believe this would be this successful. Only a handful of the Minutemen cells had refused to engage in their information war, and they would be severely marginalized by their fellows when this was all said and done. Their press release was nearly simultaneously released, across social media, P2P sharing, and radio broadcasts from coast to coast. The only variance in their starting times seemed to be the time their watches were set to.

Mark smiled proudly, but not smugly. "Told ya." In truth, he had held his breath for nearly two minutes after he had indicated to Kevin to start transmitting, waiting to see if his faith had been misplaced. Kevin's four-man team had prepared the radio broadcast equipment with a looped playback so it required no supervision, one man had stirred up the P2P sharing to get the torrent file into private hands as quickly as possible, and it spread like wildfire. Bulletin boards, forums, social media, everything but local church bulletins were trading the links to those torrent files, and with every download, the number of peers and seeds was growing exponentially. The attempts to track IP addresses were largely unsuccessful, as many people use VPNs (virtual private networks) to shield this activity from prying eyes, but some of the IPs traced overseas, which surprised Kevin. *Once they get on that side of the pond, things will just continue spreading like a virus*, he thought.

"What now?" John asked.

"Well, I'm going to keep out of Kevin's way and let him do what he does best. He's the IT guy here, used to work for one of the big tech companies in California before it got too liberal for him and he moved back to a freer state. I suspect we'll keep this up for a few more hours if our luck holds that long."

"What do you mean?" John asked.

Kevin answered, "Well, the way I see it is we have them on the back foot now. Sooner or later someone will get the balls to engage the internet kill switch and shut down all the ISPs. They might even figure out a good way to knock out our radio broadcasts. Once that happens, we're done, but by then it won't matter. We won the war, and they're still trying to fight the battle. If people react like we hope, the next time these agents put bootheel to front door, they're going to come face-to-face with one unhappy homeowner, not some pushover waiting for his turn at the detainment camp."

"And after that?" John pressed.

"Well," Mark replied, "after that we see what we can do to make more trouble for this agency. Sour the public perception of them enough, sooner or later the government will have to bring them to heel. That will at least stop the confiscations and detainments. That'll be some victory all by itself. Beyond that, we need to strategize in our own sphere what we can do to reverse the damage that has been done."

"I'll tell you what I'm thinking," John said. "I bet there's a lot of people stuck in that camp who would really like to see daylight again, and a lot of family and friends who would like to see them free. Remember I said the Minutemen were like Robin Hood? I think it's time to go bust everyone out of the sheriff's jail."

Every eye in the room swiveled to look at John, only to find the same stoic face they were becoming accustomed to.

The Game has Changed

Twenty-four hours passed while agents of the federal government's regulatory arm worked feverishly to remove the "libelous" statements that had blanketed social media platforms that afternoon. The pirate AM/FM stations ceased their transmissions once they realized the airwaves were being blanketed with radio static to the effect of drowning out their own signals. The Minutemen ceased their operation once they had drawn the intended response from the state, once they had provoked such a severe overreaction that the people had to take notice. The Minutemen were playing chess against a bureaucracy with near unlimited power that still wanted to play checkers.

The political fallout of that day was immediate and severe. Every international human rights organization condemned the house-to-house searches and holding of citizens without trial they had been assured was not happening. They saw with fresh eyes that the surrender of firearms was not universal, nor peaceful. And the rest of the world reacted with unrestrained alarm that the United States, once the bastion of free speech, had actually instituted and used a mechanism to shut down the internet in its own country that only totalitarian regimes had used prior. The most conservative elements within the House and Senate made quite a contest of who could lambast the presidential administration using the most creative language. Centrists and members of the president's own party were under such incredible pressure to publicly and officially sanction the president, they were unsure how to avoid such actions and stay in office.

Almost worse than the political embarassment was the sudden and severe impact on the United States' economy as a whole. The silencing of the internet ground bank transactions, large and small businesses transactions, personal and professional communications, indeed whole industries within North America to a sudden and obvious hault. The further trickledown effect had upon local power grids, utility services, even law enforcements' networked information systems hardly went unnoticed by the American public as a whole. The response from the American public was immediate, harsh, and very unhappy.

The full weight of public opinion had shifted, abruptly and irreversibly, in that afternoon, and the effects were only just becoming understood. Where before, the agency charged with regulation of social media had operated in near anonymity, now free-speech advocates and groups were calling for the agency to be shuttered and its leadership jailed for open violations of various privacy laws. The door-to-door searches ceased immediately. Not only were their communications severely impinged by the tsunami of radio static and transmissions crossing all bandwidths, but the information release had chilled relations between agents of the government and the citizenry. Rocks were being thrown; profanities issued. One search team had arrived at a residence to find the front door heavily barricaded and a note promising violence should the door be breached.

The game had changed.

"Give me a situation report. What are you doing to quell this insurrection?" the voice on the phone demanded.

Gary Shorts, station chief of the New Orleans detention camp, sat uncomfortably in his chair as he surveyed the reports in front of him. The four murdered officers were his men, this insurrection obviously began under his watch, and he was feeling the full brunt of indignation from his superiors. Fortunately, not being an elected official, he was much more difficult to fire than his bosses. The fat cats make the money, but he was safe from reprisal. Such was the nature of working for the government.

"Sir, we are currently combing the local area, talking to the subjects' family, friends and neighbors. We're trying to pick up their trail. So far all we know is they abandoned their home shortly after the murder of our agents and have not returned. They have not gone anywhere a networked security camera would have observed them; otherwise another agency would have reported back to us. They have not attempted to access their banks. They have turned into ghosts," Shorts answered.

"Well, you damned well had better find them and squash this. My boss is breathing fire, and even the president is getting heat from all of the information releases. Good God, man, you authorized your officers to knock people's doors down and drag them out? I said quiet search, weapons seizures, detain and prosecute. I did not direct you to reenact Nazi Germany, for Heaven's sake!"

Shorts bristled but held his tongue. He knew this was being said for the benefit of anyone who might be listening. He recalled his orders and the authority granted his agency under guidance from the Executive Branch: secure all illegal weapons, detain offenders until trial may be arranged, use all methods necessary. Period.

"Sir, I will handle this. And I will let you know if I need any assistance from further up the chain." Shorts briskly laid the phone on its receiver. "Agent Johns," Shorts called. In walked his second-in-command. "When will we have comms back up?"

"They're supposed to flip the internet back on tomorrow at 0800, same time they should stop jamming our radios. I get they had to stop these terrorists' propaganda, but it really shut down our operation in the process," Agent Johns groused.

Shorts replied, "Then tomorrow at 0800, start up the searches again. Same protocol as before, knock the doors down and drag people out. Anyone looks armed or puts up a fight, shoot on sight. Apparently these people aren't getting the message that we are in charge, not them."

Agent Johns grinned, and Shorts wondered not for the first time if he enjoyed his job a little too much.

It might have been easy for the casual observer to simply write off Gary Shorts as just another bureaucrat, but deep down he deeply believed in the work he and his men were doing. He had grown up the only son of two university professors, and hence had grown up in the ultraliberal environment only academia can foster. Gun control was an often discussed and fiercely defended idea, one his peers insisted must be instituted to stop the senseless slaughter of the citizens. All the more troubling was that racial minorities seemed to be the victim of gun violence far too often, which incensed Shorts and his parents. His convictions led him to this agency in an administrative role, then eventually to the post he currently held, and imbued him with the personality of a religious zealot.

That evening the target lists for the next seventy-two hours circulated. One agent, using a special app loaded onto his smartphone, sent an encrypted message relating the details of that list. He then finished his cigarette, crushed it out, and walked back inside to join his fellow agents. He was deeply conflicted, as he had always been, knowing that by staying in the agency and smuggling information out, he was helping the citizens on those target lists, but also endangering the officers he had come to know as friends. He often wondered how many friends of his, not shielded from these searches and detainments by their position working for the government, had ended up in detainment camps for standing by their beliefs. He wondered how many might be killed because they would not surrender.

Miles away the next morning, Mark, John, Kevin, and Rachel sat and discussed the past and future.

"So you two met while he was in Iraq. And you were literally sitting on your laptop chatting with her over Yahoo Messenger, a mortar strike would hit, and you'd have to haul butt to the shelter, and you'd come back and pick up the conversation like nothing happened? Does anything scare you?" Mark asked incredulously.

John shook his head. "Oh, don't misunderstand. I was scared shitless most days. I mean, you don't take a twenty-one-year-old kid out of a life of chasing skirt at college, ship him around the world, and shoot mortars at him every day, and it doesn't scare him. I just couldn't let it stop me. Every day, I'd have to wake up, shave, get my DCUs on, and go do my job right, or some poor bastards flying that Black Hawk would wind up dead because I screwed up. That's what kept driving me. I just didn't want someone to go on without their wife, husband, parent or child because I screwed up."

Rachel just nodded her head quietly; that was just her husband.

"But surely it got to you eventually. The stress, not knowing, being away from home," Kevin pushed.

"It gets to everyone in their own way. I had to spend my own time in counselling afterwards to decompress everything," John answered evenly. He had spent more than six months in counselling with a civilian psychologist after his enlistment. His symptoms were, in the words of his psychologist, severe but subclinical. In layman's terms, he needed help but did not need to be hospitalized. He exhibited severe anxiety, survivor guilt, mild depression, night terrors, and severe difficulty in sleeping. Rachel had stood by her boyfriend, now her husband, and encouraged him to get help. She had not abandoned him when he needed her, and for that, his loyalty to his wife was absolute.

"Onto other subjects." John shifted the conversation. "This morning it looked like everything came back online. Radio static cleared, which means our secure comms work again. Internet is back up, though I suspect the next time we try to bombard social media, they'll pull the plug a lot faster. We may have made a lot of progress, but we have to shift our tactics quickly or they'll catch up."

"You want to hit them directly," Mark stated. John had made little secret of his desire over the last few days. He saw the people held in detainment as prisoners of war, and his military mind demanded a rescue operation be mounted. He also saw this as a way to turn the tide of this battle they had entered into.

More gun owners out of jails would rally those not rounded up, and these people would see clearly they had no option but to fight and defend themselves. The support for the Minutemen's operation would grow exponentially. But the cost in blood worried Mark.

"John, hear me out…" Mark watched as a cloud hung over John's face. *Jesus, it's like he changes into another person when he's angry.*

"Mark, I agreed to throw in with your group here. You knew who you took in when you agreed to shelter us. You knew I wasn't going to sit here on my heels and send snarky emails to government officials until they have a change of heart. Those people could be living in squalor; they could be beaten and abused, maybe outright exterminated. The media isn't watching them, and you can't get any access via drone or you would have already gotten that information out. I can't agree to leave them there to rot," John replied coldly.

"John, I'm not saying we let them rot. I'm just saying assaulting a detention camp with our small force is a suicide mission."

"Then what about your intel of intended targets? Why not use that and assist them preemptively? I'll take a volunteer team out and secure people on that list, bring them back."

Mark shook his head. "I send a warning, the agents can assume they got tipped off. Too many of them vacate their homes before agents even show up, they'll know we have a mole in their agency and we'll lose our source."

"Then I take a team and hit them on sight. Dead men tell no tales," John shot back, irritated. "What do you want to do, sit here and play computer nerd and let this continue to go on? When are you going to get some skin in the game, Mark?!" John stood and walked out of the room.

Mark's head dipped. He was deeply conflicted about how to proceed. John was expressing what several of his men had expressed, while others were not in favor of a paramilitary campaign. The divide threatened to split his cell in two, and to attempt to appease both parties threatened to appease neither.

"On some level, you have to admit he's right," Rachel offered.

Mark looked up to regard John's wife. She had gentle eyes, green with a ring of brown, curly brown hair, and a natural beauty that took no makeup and little effort. Rachel had demonstrated over the last few days to be a natural manager and negotiator. Mark had garnered his cell together because of complementary personalities. With the addition of John, a turbulent force had been introduced, an aggressive type A personality that demanded action. Rachel was the glue that bound the disparate elements of this new cell together, able to mediate between all of them without being manipulative. She simply exuded calm and always sought balance and peace.

"It's not that I don't agree with him. I want those people out of there. I just don't know if his approach is the right one," Mark answered.

"What would you suggest?" Genuine question, not reprisal, no sarcasm, inquisitive. Rachel patiently waited for Mark to marshal his thoughts together.

"I think what we need to do is keep working the public perception. Eventually that will apply enough political pressure to change their—"

"And has that worked thus far?" She did cut him off, but even then it was gentle. Not to silence him, just to cut through to the truth.

"No. No, it has not," Mark admitted.

"Hear him out, Mark. You and my husband are committed to the same end result. Your methods may differ. The difference is John has little to no regard for the consequences of his actions if he feels they are justified. He wants those people freed, and he doesn't see your method yielding that result. Because of that, he has drawn the conclusion that direct action is the only course of action, and he will not let the possible consequences cloud his judgment. That's just the way he is."

"Even if that consequence is his death? Or he brings trouble back here and you and your child are killed? I mean, does he even think that far ahead?" Kevin sputtered, his patience run out. He was normally cool and collected, but this talk of assaulting a camp had him on edge.

"Let me redirect the question: do you think you can secure this camp against an attack without John?" Rachel asked. Mark heard something in her voice.

"We managed just fine before you and your husband showed up, trying to lead us into a firefight," Kevin retorted.

"Look down," she demanded. And Kevin and Mark saw it.

During the conversation, with two sets of eyes on her, Rachel had quietly drawn her Smith and Wesson Shield 9 mm, and it was currently pointed at Kevin. Her finger was off the trigger, and it was obvious she did not intend to shoot. No, this was a demonstration, not a threat.

"You two sat there and let me draw a handgun from my holster and never even saw it. You mean to tell me you are equipped to secure this cell from attack? I think you need to be honest with yourselves. John isn't here to lead you to your demise; he's a valuable member of this team. His methods are rough, that's just him, but in this case he isn't wrong. Politicking and phone calls aren't working. Your information release was a step in the right direction, but sooner or later someone has to set an example for these people to follow to resist their own capture and disarmament. My husband set that example; that's why we're here." Rachel reholstered her gun.

"You carry that everywhere?" Kevin asked.

"Yes, I do. So does John. Why?" Rachel replied.

Kevin started, "I just don't think it's necessary—"

"Neither did most of the citizens of your home state, where they pioneered disarming their citizens," Rachel chastised. "They were wrong then, and you are wrong now. NEED and NECESSARY are not the standard by which we judge our rights. Let's not slip back into old habits." Her tone began sharp but eased by the end of her making her point.

"Kevin, in light of the developing situation, I think it may be wise to have those members who feel inclined to arm themselves while here on the grounds," Mark replied, indicating the issue was settled.

Kevin nodded his head, still feeling the stinging reprisal from Rachel. She was right. In his home state of California, he had largely agreed with the more liberal aspects of the legislative gun-control agenda. However, he noticed the trend that further disarmament seemed to have little to no effect on violent crime. Gangbangers had no trouble finding weapons, and police seemed far more enthusiastic about denying firearm carry permits than they did about allowing law-abiding citizens to defend themselves. The problem worsened until it provoked Kevin to quit his job and move home. That day, everything changed...

'Almost home, just got to grab a change of clothes and a shower, then out with my friends.' Kevin lived in San Francisco and seemed to have figured life out at the age of twenty-five. He had an excellent job with one of the dozens of tech companies headquartered in California, had a nice studio apartment not far from work, he had friends, and he got dates often enough to keep him content. His daily routine was one of a bike ride to work, eight hours in the office, CrossFit after work, and an evening of leisure. Tonight, he was on his way to see some friends and a young woman he had recently met.

He had come a long way from rural Mississippi. He had left home when he was seventeen, graduated his small-town high school a year early, and accepted a scholarship in California. Over the course of his undergrad studies in information technology and computer science, he had been peppered with the politics and opinions of his liberal professors and classmates. He didn't realize it at the time, but the longer he spent in that environment, the more his ideals changed, and the more often he found himself arguing with family back home. Part and parcel to that was his constant disagreements about the right to keep and bear arms. His parents worried about him in the big city and encouraged him to have a firearm to protect himself. He thought the idea ludicrous.

"If I bought a gun, I'd just be a danger to myself," Kevin insisted.

"But, Kevin, you grew up around guns. Hell, you were shooting by age eight. I don't git where this is coming from," Kevin's father replied, exasperated. *Maybe all them liberals rubbed off on my boy*, he thought, not for the first time.

That evening, Kevin did not notice that when he turned the dead bolt on his front door, it didn't feel as though it were locked. He didn't notice the tool marks around the doorjamb. He did notice the two men inside his home holding guns and looking through his things. He froze and put his hands up. "Look, take whatever you want. Just please don't—" and a gunshot rang out.

He reflected later in the hospital, before and after his parents had arrived from Mississippi, that he had not resisted or threatened the criminals in any way. He hadn't acted aggressively. He had calmly offered to give up his property to prevent any confrontation. He had done everything his friends and professors and politicians had suggested to deescalate the confrontation…and he got shot. He would later reflect on how ineffectual the offered advice had been when his parents came to visit.

"Dad," Kevin whispered, "do you have your gun with you?"

"Of course I do," Kevin's father replied evenly. "Why wouldn't I?"

"Because you can't legally carry in California, much less in a hospital," Kevin explained, exasperated that his father hadn't realized this. He could go to jail for years if he were caught.

"Well, the way I see it is the cops haven't had any luck catching two guys who shot my son in his own condo. Odds are they won't have any luck catching an old redneck visiting from Mississippi. Besides, lot of good the law did keeping that slug out of your belly, didn't it, son?" The voice carried no tone of reproach, nor did it sound like a lecture. That was just his dad. He always saw things differently from most.

When it became obvious his son's interests did not lay in commercial welding like his father, Kevin's father hadn't balked or bullied. He worked hard, took on extra jobs, and did what he could to make sure the money was available to send his son to the best schools money could buy. He was the first kid in the entire county to get a personal computer. When he quickly outgrew that, his father put the money up to buy the parts to upgrade it, then completely replace it. He

66

understood little of his son's newfound world of computers, but he recognized talent when he saw it, much like in welding, and he was determined to encourage it. Not even the ribbing of his friends and coworkers, who referred to his boy as the "computer nerd," would sway him.

"That boy is going to make more of himself than a roughneck. He's got a double dose of brains, and I'm happy to see him use them," his father remarked to his friends once.

Now Kevin looked up at his father from the hospital bed. His father had big meaty hands covered with calluses and old scars. The tip of one finger was clipped a little short from an old oil field accident, but it never slowed him down. His face was lined and tanned, but his eyes were as sharp as his much younger son's. Kevin came to realize that his parents weren't uneducated rednecks or, even worse, conservatives (gasp). They were ordinary people who had worked hard to take care of themselves, and to that end his father had carried that handgun almost everywhere for most of Kevin's life. He had on occasion defended himself and his family with it and had never harmed a person under other circumstances. Here was a man breaking SEVERAL federal and state laws, who would be subject to years in prison were he caught, who had never hurt an innocent person.

Kevin's thoughts on the gun-control agenda he had so ardently supported wavered while he lay in the hospital. His father was right; the gun laws hadn't stopped the violence that pried itself into his quiet urban life. And the gun his father carried had not caused any additional violence. There was an incongruence in these facts and his belief system that he worked hard to rectify, and he eventually did. He had been wrong, his professors had been wrong, his coworkers and friends were wrong, and his politicians were doubly wrong. Their job was to guard the rights of citizens, not trample them. He applied for, and was denied, a concealed-carry permit. He purchased a handgun to keep in his home, only to be constantly irritated with the ever more stringent requirements for storage. (Seriously, how do you defend yourself with an unloaded gun locked in a safe, when the ammo is in another locked safe?!)

His permit was denied again. The appeal was denied, and the next, and the next. He had not shown good cause that his life was in danger even after several feet of his small intestine had been removed after being shot in his own front doorway.

He quit his job, packed his belongings, and moved back to Mississippi. He eventually found another job at a tech company in New Orleans and moved to Louisiana to be closer to work. He did, however, decide not to live in New Orleans with its more liberal climate and higher crime rate. The more rural area outside the suburbs was quiet and suited him, and the gun laws in Louisiana were infinitely friendlier. And then he met Mark at the local gun range years later, and the course of his life was altered...

"I'm sorry, Rachel. I think you and your husband have a point. Forget my earlier objections, please," Kevin pled.

Rachel waved her hand as if to indicate the matter was settled.

"Well, Kevin, I think we need to go settle the Incredible Hulk down so we can have a conversation with Banner about what we're going to do next," Mark quipped.

Rachel laughed. The jest was amazingly close to the truth.

A Step in the Right Direction

Mark found John in his usual spot. He had discovered over the last few days that John was a man of action, and as such he used any available task to take his mind off whatever was worrying him. His CZ was on the workbench, fieldstripped.

"John, I don't disagree with you. I just—"

"Mark, I get it. You guys aren't soldiers, and frankly, my soldiering days are long behind me. I'm just a chubby coonass with a lot of guns these days. But I am sick to death of sitting around, and I want to stop these damned raids," John stated. The effect was like an elongated sigh of exasperation.

Mark reflected on John's words and remembered how he had come to this moment in time, leading a resistance against the government's attempts to strip citizens of arms. One would be forgiven for seeing the comedy in Mark's decision to join the Minutemen and start up his own cell. He didn't even own a lot of guns; he wasn't a hard-core gun-rights advocate like John. Hell, if it weren't for Julie…

He had not been in favor of his sister moving to New Orleans. The crime rate was sky-high and getting worse every year. Another liberal, anti-gun mayor was likely to be voted in to replace the outgoing one. NOPD was historically and chronically corrupt and inept at curbing the violent element and gangs that roamed the city. But Julie had fallen in love with the city. "Mark, I'll be fine. I'm moving in with a couple of friends of mine to share a flat. It's two blocks from work, and it's in a nice part of town."

"That 'nice part of town' is a block away from the ghetto."

"Low-income housing area. Jesus, Mark, I love you, but sometimes you are so judgmental. It's not like every person who didn't grow up middle class is a gangbanger looking for pretty white women to—"

"Julie, I have seen the crime statistics. I don't care if it's a rich area or a poor one; the violent crime rates are high down there. Rapes, murder, drugs, theft, armed robbery, carjackings. I just don't want to see my sister end up on the six-o'clock news."

Julie's one acquiescence to her brother's worry was that she agreed to keep a handgun in her flat to protect herself and her roommates. They had all endlessly teased her and her brother for their paranoia, but Julie persisted. Mark wished his sister would get her concealed-carry permit so that she could have her handgun with her outside the home, but she argued she couldn't carry into any bar or club in the city, so there was little point.

Years later, when the courts changed their leanings and after Washington, DC, and other municipalities had disregarded the earlier precedent set by the Supreme Court and passed handgun bans in large metro areas, New Orleans saw an explosion of violent crime. Crime had always nagged at this city, with its rich history and vibrant culture, but now it was a biblical plague. Wait times for 911 calls quadrupled. Response for nonemergency (no imminent loss of life) calls was hours or DAYS. The rate of successful prosecution of violent crimes plummeted as the city prosecutor's office had far more cases to try than people to walk them through the court system. The outcome was that many violent criminals, ranging from sexual predators to armed robbers, walked simply because the legal system lacked the manpower and funds to prosecute them all. And what was a river of crime soon turned into a roaring torrent.

It was at that time, when the New Orleans Detention Camp was first being opened and the normal regulations regarding a timely arraignment and trial suspended, when Julie was forced to use that same handgun to defend herself. Her roommate's ex-boyfriend was a drunk, and an angry one. He had not reacted well to their unexpected breakup, and he had come to persuade his girlfriend to reconsider.

When the door did not unlock, his fists began to pound on the door and Julie got her gun.

"I thought those things were banned!" her roommate's exasperated voice demanded.

"Yeah, breaking into people's homes is supposed to be illegal too. Isn't slowing him down much, is it?" Julie demanded.

When the door finally gave, Julie fired three shots into the man's chest and he collapsed. That two women could have been seriously injured or killed by a man with a history of violence mattered not a bit to the responding officers. Julie had violated the New Orleans city prohibition on the ownership of handguns for any reason, and she was taken into custody. She was one of the first admittees to the detainment camp, hence Mark's efforts to determine what was going on in there...

John shook his head. "I'm sorry, Mark, I didn't know." The words were coated with genuine remorse and apology.

"I appreciate it. That's why I feel so conflicted. I want to see Julie out of there, like, yesterday. But I don't see leading this group into a firefight against impossible odds being a productive way to do it. I'm open to ideas," Mark replied.

"Well, Mark, what about a little intermediate step?" John asked.

"Depends on what you have in mind, John." Mark's curiosity was piqued.

"We get intel about impending raids. Why not arrange a couple of welcome parties for the agents? Test the theory that a show of force will back them down. That'll embolden others maybe."

Mark nodded. "And if they decide to push the issue?"

"Then I push back. Simple as that."

Mark considered this. It might prove messy, and their operational security would have to be airtight to keep their location secure and make sure no one followed them home. A drone or spy satellite could unravel the whole operation very quickly, to say nothing about the possibility the agency would call in close air support. "Let's sit down with a few of the guys and plan this out. We don't have any real hard-core tactical guys, and I get the impression your experience is less than extensive in that regard. But let's look at it."

"Let's start by looking over the target lists and doing some background checks. Maybe we can wheedle out the ones most likely to throw down with us rather than sit on the sidelines. Then we can stir up a little trouble for the agents. I take it you are amenable to inducting additional members?" John's tone was half statement, half question.

"I think that's prudent. We can house several additional families here. After that we'll have to figure something out," Mark replied.

"What about resources? I haven't even asked in the last few days how you feed everyone in this compound. You rob a couple of banks back in the day?" John needled lightheartedly.

Mark was relieved to see John's demeanor relax a bit. "We raise quite a bit of our own food out here on this homestead. Not one hundred percent self-sufficient but largely. If we bring additional people in, we'll find some way for them to be productive and continue to scale up. And we have a guesthouse out back we refer to as 'the barracks' that'll house a couple of families or two dozen single men. And your wife has been a welcome hand in the kitchen and around the garden. She and your daughter are fair hands at cooking," Mark complimented.

Rachel had always been at ease in the kitchen and never failed to put an amazing meal on the table. John was a fair cook in his own right, but it was his other talents and knowledge Mark sought use of right then. They sat down in the den and looked over the target lists, comparing them to the profiles Kevin had put together. And then it happened—a name jumped off the page at John.

"Aw, hell, this is perfect," John emphatically stated, jabbing the page with his finger. "Andy Bob, you're about to get a visit from an old friend."

"You know him?" Mark asked.

"Yes, sir, I do, and he is Old Testament Second Amendment. If I show up ready to party, he'll back me up. Hell, I'm shocked the agency picked him as a target. They must have an absolute death wish. If you had a list of people not to screw with about gun rights, Andy Bob is probably right there behind me on it."

They heard Kevin's chuckling voice. "Andy Bob? Where do you get a name like Andy Bob? Is it hyphenated?"

"No, it isn't, and I believe he was named by his grandfather. He's scheduled for a raid in the morning day after tomorrow. Let's get a tactical plan together, and I'll head his way tomorrow."

"Do you think you'll need to bring some people with you?" Mark asked.

"Not really. If I know this guy half as well as I think I do, he's got enough ordnance to assault a third-world country."

Old Friends

A knock on the door startled Andy Bob. He wasn't expecting visitors that afternoon. Everyone had been a little jumpy recently. Internet shut down, no news on cable or AM/FM, tons of weird static on his Ham radio setup. Then just as suddenly as everything went haywire, it went back to normal with some limp-wristed nonsense about a terrorist cyberattack. He, like many, had seen what had hit the internet four days prior. He couldn't say he was surprised, but he wasn't amused either.

He had always expected the government would become more heavy-handed in its attempts to subdue people's rights, he just didn't expect things to have progressed so quickly in his own lifetime. He could remember a time not long ago when going to the local range with your buddies was a typical afternoon. Nowadays that would get you sent off to one of those damned "detention camps." Like the whole damned world had lost its mind.

Another knock got him to his feet, and he retrieved his Smith and Wesson M&P 9 mm from its hiding spot. He approached the door, gun levelled as he looked out the peephole. "Hey, dickhead, you gonna let me in or what?" a familiar voice shouted.

"John?!" The locks started turning and the door flew open to see his friend standing there with a bag over each shoulder. "I got dropped off. Mind if I come in before one of your neighbors decides I'm worth the reward money?"

Andy Bob rushed him inside, then stuck his head outside and looked around to see if they had been watched. He didn't have many neighbors this far out of town, but he had a few. "John, what the hell is going on? You've been on the damned news, man. You and Rachel. People are saying you two shot a bunch of agents—"

"I did, Andy."

"Well, shit, I gotta hear this story."

John spent the next half hour filling Andy in on the last two days of his and his family's life, with a brief pause to answer a radio he wore on his belt. What Andy could tell from his end of the conversation was that John had been dropped off, and the other party wanted to make sure he was good before "heading home." "Yep, I'm good. Let my wife and Mark know I'm with Andy, and he isn't going to turn me in for the reward money," John joked, then resumed his story.

"So let me get this straight," Andy said incredulously, "these agents aren't doing compliance checks, they are straight up kicking down doors and dragging people off to goddamned camps like Stalinist Russia. You and Rachel jumped four of their agents when they tried to grab you, you are number one on the government's current shit list, and you have thrown in with the Minutemen, who half the country thinks is a terrorist group?"

"You forgot the part about you being next on their raid list."

"I was getting to that," Andy replied, exasperated. "And now you're telling me you have a mole inside their agency, feeding you the dirt on who they are hitting and when, and they're coming here tomorrow morning. And you stopped by just on the offhand chance I hadn't given up my guns and wanted to add my name to the most wanted list right behind yours and your wife's? Is that what I'm gathering?" Andy asked incredulously.

"Quit asking like you haven't already made up your mind." John tilted his head and gave his friend his best "don't bullshit me" look.

"Well, I need a drink and a cigar to digest all that." Andy stood, heading for his bar. John hauled out two cigars and offered one to Andy. How Andy had even come to know John was a story all in itself, much less how the two ended up almost neighbors...

Andy Bob Case had grown up in Michigan, quite a bit more than a stone's throw from Louisiana, where he ended up. He grew up in a family who certainly saw the value and utility in having firearms. He hunted, he shot targets, and he carried a gun both on his job and off the job for his protection. It was a twist of fate and a chance encounter with a like-minded person in Louisiana that altered his path. After years of friendship from afar, a job opportunity near John enticed Andy to relocate, which John happily welcomed. He hosted Andy in his home for several months while he got settled, until he found a place of his own. That was how he ended up on the New Orleans agency's list.

Andy had an arsenal that would make most gun owners proud. Among his items were several suppressors, which he had conveniently forgotten to hand over when the NFA was repealed and the mufflers for a gun's barrel rendered completely illegal for all but government use. He had no interest in handing over his property, nor did he when "pistols functionally similar to rifles" were made illegal, or when short-barreled rifles and short-barreled shotguns were banned. When the laws changed and limited how much ammunition you could have on hand, he laughed and ignored them. When the government required a background check to buy ammo, so they could track all the sales, he just started buying reloading components. Andy didn't just flagrantly violate the laws that had been passed, he actually took pleasure in it. He had never considered how deadly serious the government would take this business of taking his guns from him. He had brought the majority of his firearms from Michigan with him, but he had bought a few here and there locally and done a few transfers. Not that it mattered, every 4473 that ran through NICS had been catalogued, and the agency was expecting a nice high-profile arrest of a "gross offender."

"So what exactly do you have in mind?" Andy exhaled the smoke from his cigar.

"Pretty simple, actually. They're coming; they don't know we know they're coming. We lay a little trap for them with overlapping fields of fire and put them down," John stated flatly.

After years of knowing John, Andy read his face and voice like an open book. He was one of the few people Andy knew to never speak vaguely, and he meant every word of what he said. "Assuming they come in aggressively, I can agree to all that. The first move has to be theirs though, John. I don't doubt you, but I have to see this for myself how bad they've gotten. Question is what do I do afterwards? Not like I'm going to sit around here and wait for backup to show up."

"Join us, Andy. I'm biding my time till we can hit the detention camp in New Orleans and get everyone out of there. Till then, putting some fear into these agents so they quit coming outside the wire to snatch people is the priority. I could use another good shooter with me," John said.

Andy dipped his head and considered it. He could see the logic in his friend's words, and he had little doubt John would stand and fight even if he were outnumbered and alone. He and Andy would raise some serious hell in the morning, and the two of them together stood a better chance of surviving what John proposed. "I guess let's get a move on. If I'm leaving here in the morning, I got a bunch of shit to pack." Andy sighed.

John smiled. "You're saving some room for me in your Jeep, right?"

Andy fired back, "Hell no. You screwed up my whole evening. I'll strap you to the roof!"

The two friends had a laugh and finished off their cigars; then they began to pack. Andy was a prepper too, and before the night was over, Andy and John would load a covered trailer near to capacity with cans of ammo, freeze-dried food, and other essentials. That task accomplished, the boys sat down to arrange a welcome for their uninvited guests.

The next morning, three agents tried to get some sleep while the fourth drove. Comfort was not easy to find strapped into a surplus Humvee, wearing body armor. It was a skill they might have learned had any of them spent time overseas with the military, but they each rested fitfully. They had left at an unholy hour of the morning, necessitated by the distant proximity of their first target to their base camp.

"Why couldn't we have gotten one of the closer assignments?" one in the back groused.

"Cram it. Either try to get some sleep or sit there quietly so the rest of us can," came the reply from his supervisor, Senior Agent Johns, in the front passenger seat.

The four of them rode on in silence. Each was wearing their plate carriers, but now the previously optional ballistic plates were made mandatory, along with the cummerbund and side plates. The helmets hurt their necks, but there was no good place in the cramped up-armored vehicle to put them besides their heads. The full-auto M4 carbines sat between their feet. They had been briefed that a group of agents had been ambushed recently, and their rules of engagement had been substantially relaxed. This pleased the agents greatly, but now the other shoe had dropped, and the bureaucrats had demanded increased use of protective gear.

Andy Bob had spent most of the evening packing his Jeep and trailer with anything that would fit. Ammo, food, gear— it looked like the prepper version of the *Beverly Hillbillies* was getting ready to move out, he had stacked and packed his preps so tightly. He was sitting in his favorite chair, taking a few moments to relax and reflecting on the wild plan he and his friend John had hatched the night before. He had his plate carrier on the floor with his rifle and extra mags, ready to throw on at a moment's notice, but he waited impatiently. He nudged the radio on the table next to him, willing it to beep and give him an update from his friend John. It sat silently, the only indication of its function being the dimly lit indicator atop it.

Andy had not doubted John's analysis of the situation. Andy well knew the treasure trove of "illegal" guns he had refused to register and later refused to turn over as the laws became ever more restrictive. John had told Andy of the agency's aggressive posture, of the detention camps, and Andy came to the same conclusion John had years ago, which was only reinforced less than a week ago. The agents would not be bargained with, reasoned with, nor were they coming to collect overdue tax money or do a compliance check.

They were here to round up those citizens who disagreed with the government's assertion that they had the right to tear firearms directly from the hands of the citizenry, and apparently the heavier handed the tactic, the more it suited them. He did not doubt John, but he had to see for himself if things were as dire as his friend had indicated.

John was in the wood line next to Andy's home. He had taken a few minutes to build a hasty hide and had camouflaged himself well. He had no illusions this trick would work in all cases, but he saw an opportunity to get the upper hand on his friend's potential assailants. At roughly two hundred yards, his .308 Winchester bolt action would have about four inches of drop from point of aim. If he put his reticle on the target's chin, he would be putting rounds right into the chest cavity at this distance. A difference of fifty yards in either direction would change the trajectory, but not enough to stop the 168-grain boat-tail match bullets from doing their job. He had handloaded this ammo on his bench after judicious and repetitive testing to ensure the best possible accuracy. He knew to expect less than two inches dispersion at this range, a one-MOA, minute of angle, rifle and ammo pairing. The real question mark was what would the agents' reaction be to their recent antagonizing? Would they react with caution, or would they react more aggressively? The sound of an approaching vehicle caught his attention.

Andy heard the radio beep twice. John did not speak, and Andy knew he was keying his mic to alert his friend. He threw on his plate carrier and loaded his rifle, then made his way to the front door to look up the driveway. He saw a Humvee heading down the drive towards the front gate, which he had chained shut and padlocked. He figured he would know based on what they did at that gate what their intentions were.

Miles away back in the Minutemen's TOC, Mark and Kevin heard the rapid beeps too. Anyone listening in but not monitoring this particular set of frequencies for that signal would think it static, but Kevin immediately spun up their drone and got it into the air above Andy and John's location.

Its camera observed Andy's homestead, his Jeep parked behind the home, the long driveway with its gate closed, and the wood line where they knew John was hiding. There were elements of the plan, including the rules of engagement, John had neglected to discuss with Kevin and Mark over open radio, so they placed their faith in his judgment. They watched the video feed as the Humvee approached the gate, then accelerated.

"Ram the gate," Johns ordered. He had no intention of stopping and exposing his men on a dirt road in the middle of nowhere. The homeowner could file a complaint from his cell later about the cost to repair it. He had already ordered everyone to lock and load and to use lethal force at the first sign of trouble.

The gate flew open, and the chain shattered as the Humvee shot straight through it. "Well, I guess that's that," Andy said aloud. He pulled the charging handle back on his AR-15, released it, and fired up his red dot.

John saw the Humvee ram the gate. *Well, boys, I guess that settles the question that's been on everyone's minds. You guys aren't here to collect for March of Dimes after all,* John thought. He got his eye behind his rifle scope and tracked the vehicle as it drove up Andy's driveway at high speed. He had specifically chosen his hide to have a view of the front door but to make sure he wouldn't be shooting directly at the front door. He had little doubt his .308 would blast right through the walls, and he had reminded Andy emphatically to peel off to the left of his front door and not stand behind it or go to his right.

Andy looked down at the floor, at the tape markings John had left. "I give him one thing, his CDO does come in handy at times." CDO was what his uncle always called "OCD alphabetized." John had taken the time to lay duct tape on the floor with the words *SAFE* and *YOU GET SHOT* on it to remind Andy where John's line of fire would be. Andy retreated from the front door and took up position behind the prearranged cover he and John had set up.

Stopping, doors open. I see a ram, rifles, body armor.
Yep, same old agency. Well, you boys goin' to learn t'day,
John thought as he tightened his finger on the trigger. He
watched the four men approach the front door, taking up
positions on either side while the man with the ram had his
rifle slung and lined up on the front door. John watched the
ram come back, then rush forward, knocking the front door
of his friend's home inward off its hinges and through the
frame. His Ruger M77, a humble old hunting rifle he had
worked over into a respectable tack driver, thundered, and
the buttpad thumped back into his shoulder as the bipod
scrabbled for traction. John immediately flipped the bolt
handle up and back, using the knuckle of his right hand
rather than his fingers, then shoved the bolt forward and
down with his palm. He fought his eye back behind the rifle
scope and readied for his next shot.

Hours later...

"Johns, what the hell happened to you guys?!" Shorts
roared at the only remaining member of the team sent out
that morning. Johns had spent over an hour with the medics
before Shorts was permitted to debrief him. Several shards
of glass and wood had been removed from the side of his
cheek and neck. He had several broken ribs and had come
back covered in blood, though apparently none his own.

"Sir, we were set up," Johns started as he recalled his
morning.

Johns watched the ram come forward on the front door,
and at nearly the same instant saw the agent swinging the
ram lunge forward towards the splintering door. It would be
a few seconds before Johns and the rest of the team realized
he had been propelled forward by the 168-grain match bullet
hitting their teammate high in the back, just above his plate
carrier. The effect was immediate and predictable; the
agent's spine was shattered and his thoracic cavity
pulverized by more than two thousand foot-pounds of
energy.

"Contact rear!" Johns shouted. The men swung their rifles around to scan the yard behind them where the round had apparently originated, but could see no such firing position nearer than the wood line to hide. As one of the agents began to spray bullets haphazardly towards the wood line, the sound of another rifle erupted from behind them, coming from within the home as Andy poured .30-caliber rounds from his 300 Blackout AR "pistol" towards the front door. He had correctly surmised the agents were probably on either side of the door, and knowing his friend was clear of his own line of fire, shot through the drywall on either side of the door. At such short range, Andy eschewed well-aimed shots in favor of bump firing his AR from the shoulder, emptying the magazine quickly at the agents. All three agents were hit, but their armor was catching the rounds, while Johns grimaced at the flying debris peppering him in his unguarded face.

Johns suffered a moment of indecision, caught in a deadly and unexpected cross fire. Before he could issue the order to clear the porch, another .30-caliber round thundered out of the wood line. This one clipped a second agent just above their plate at the junction of his collarbones and neck. The unprotected human body proved little challenge for the high-velocity jacketed bullet, and three agents became two.

"Get back to the Hummer!" Johns yelled over the sound of another full magazine being fired behind them.

This time, judging by the flying debris and snapping sound, their closest assailant was taking more time in aiming and not only relying on suppressive fire. As they rushed towards their Humvee, Johns saw his driver take two rounds in the back and fall. His plates stopped the bullets, but as he tried to rise, he was shot three more times. Johns whirled around to face his attacker, coming face-to-face with none other than his subject, Andy Bob. "You son of a—" Johns snarled as a .30-caliber round slammed into his back and knocked him face-first into the dirt.

"You know, you could've hit me if that round would've gone all the way through," Andy remarked to his friend John.

"Yeah, but I didn't figure it had enough energy to get through Level 3 armor," John replied.

"And what had you so convinced they were wearing Level 3?" Andy retorted.

"Hey, sometimes you got a pair of twos, you just suck it up and play through," John said while shrugging his shoulders. The two men stood over the downed agent after they had disarmed him. "Now," John said, "what do we do with this peckerhead?" Hours later...

"You're sure it was the subject of this morning's raid and our mysteriously vanished terrorist?" Shorts asked Agent Johns, who emphatically nodded his head.

"Positive."

"And they just let you go?" Shorts asked incredulously. The tale Agent Johns told was remarkable, and one he scarcely believed. Two men had set a trap that four of his agents had stumbled into. Three had been cut down, and the fourth remained only so he could deliver a message.

"Sir, they said they want the searches to stop and for the detention camp to be opened and everyone released. Those are the terms they set," Johns replied, deadpan.

"And if I don't?!" Shorts roared.

"They said, quote, it will be open season on agents. Anywhere, anytime, no quarter. They also handed me this." Johns passed over an excerpt from the Bill of Rights, the Second Amendment.

*A well regulated Militia, being necessary to the security of a free State, the right of the people to keep and bear arms, **shall not be infringed**.*

Shorts crumpled the paper and hurled it across the room. "Johns, I want these bastards, I want them dead, and I want their hides on my wall. Am I stuttering?"

"No, sir," Johns replied evenly. He had been bested by these men and considered it a remarkably bad decision that they did not take him out when they had the chance. He would work hard to make sure they never got another.

The Pendulum

That evening, Andy and John sat with Mark, made introductions, and discussed plans. "I'm surprised you let one walk away, honestly," Mark said.

Andy nodded his head, having had that same argument with John hours earlier.

"It was a judgment call. I wanted them to know where we stood. Didn't figure they were bright enough to come to those conclusions if we didn't spell it out for them. That said, I haven't heard any reports of the gates being hurled open, so I'll assume they haven't had a change of heart. I say our next move is to garner some more support from the local population by genuinely making life hell for the agency in our local area," John explained.

"What exactly do you have in mind?" Mark asked.

Andy laughed and replied, "The short version, he wants to grab them by the nose and kick them in the ass until they get the message."

John smiled. "I believe what I said was to work to directly stymie their attempts to take more people into custody, enact those casualties we can while not exposing ourselves, and eventually, when we feel we have the upper hand, lay siege to their camp. The timing will be tricky though; wait too long, they'll reinforce with additional troops pulled from other locations. Hit them too soon, the odds are too lopsided. We need a plan we can enact on short notice when opportunity allows. And we need the support of the local area to help us carry through with this and shelter the people we release. If you want to get Julie out, that's what I think needs to happen."

At the mention of his sister, Mark started, "What do you need from us?"

"First of all, if they haven't realized by now they have a mole in their organization, they're bigger idiots than I thought. I would immediately advise your man to get himself out, like, yesterday. After that, we need a secondary source of intel. I know you can't get a drone over the compound, but we need a few in the surrounding area so we can pick up their movements. Also, I need to see how often they are restocking provisions and figure out that schedule. If we hit them right before they restock their pantry, that's sure to put additional pressure on them. Now, that said, what are the other cells doing?" John asked.

"Not as much as you are. I think they're pretty much waiting around to see what our next move is," Mark said. It came out as a sigh of resignation as he realized, not for the first time, that far too many of the Minutemen were reactionary in nature. John was out to fight a war; they wanted to be in the rear with the gear.

John nodded his head. "Fine, we have our own battles to fight."

Later, on the back porch, Andy prodded his friend. "John, you know I trust your judgment, but…"

"You think we should've smoke checked that last guy and left him for the critters to chew on," John answered knowingly.

"Hell yeah! Those guys busted my gate, knocked my door in—shit, they might have had it on their mind to perforate me for the hell of it, and you let one of them go?!" Andy emphatically shouted. His hands raised as if to insinuate a further question.

"Like I said, it was a judgment call. I want these guys pissed off or scared. I poked the bear; now I'll lay a trap for him," John replied.

"John, these guys aren't playing. How long do you think it'll be before they just send thirty or forty guys up here and burn us out?" Andy demanded.

"They won't know where to send them if we aren't here."

"You mean…"

"Yes, I mean we go outside the wire. Mark always said the Minutemen were modeled after a terror cell. The only thing harder to find than a cell are a couple of lone wolves. We spend a day collecting intel; then we start pecking at them. And once we start, we keep on till they start to crack. And, Andy, if you go with me, we are going to get bloody on this, brother. I aim to straight scare the hell out of those people, and I intend to take the gloves off doing it. We clear?" John questioned.

Andy looked at his friend, seeing the deadly serious expression on his face. "I'm with you, John, into Hell itself if that's where we need to go. I trust you," Andy said evenly.

John took a draw on his cigar and thought, *The only tricky part is figuring out how far to push this pendulum before it swings back in the other direction.*

The next morning John discussed his plan with a very unhappy spouse. "I can't decide if you're crazy or suicidal sometimes," Rachel spat. "We could pack up and head out and walk away from this. This isn't our war."

"Honey," John replied evenly, "it became our war the day they invaded my home with guns drawn."

"But what we did then was self-defense. What you're planning is cold-blooded murder."

"That's the same charge levied against every terrorist group in the world, but if they are victorious, they rewrite their history to infer some righteous cause. Ask the men who fought in the American Revolution."

"Uh-huh. A lot of them died on those fields." She looked at her husband.

"And they died knowing that life without freedom was no life at all. You and everyone here will be in danger if we keep coming back here. If we go outside the wire and limit our return trips, they won't have a trail to follow," John reasoned.

"You had better come back to me, John, or I swear to God I'll never forgive you," Rachel said through tears.

"With my shield, or on it." John quoted the old Spartan axiom. He would come home the victor, or not at all.

John walked down the hallway to find Mark, Kevin, and Andy digesting the intelligence they had collected. The agency's schedule was consistent to the point of monotony. Any vehicles heading out for raids left at the same time, usually between 0700 and 0800. Earlier departure times were uncommon but did happen. Return times were more varied. They were still surveying the facility to determine their supply times.

"John, we've been looking things over. I wish you two would reconsider what you're planning. If you get hung up out there, you'll both be sitting ducks," Mark related.

"But if we keep coming back here, sooner or later this cell will be discovered. No dice. If we go out alone, we can hit and disappear and keep the pressure on them without them having the larger target of this cell to come after. If you keep feeding us intel, I'm sure we can crank up the pressure on them and check in often," John replied.

"You sure just two of you? I could send a couple of my guys along," Mark started.

"Yes, Mark, I'm sure. Out there in the bush, I can't afford the liability of bringing tourists or amateurs. Andy is neither. He's one hell of a good shot and an experienced outdoorsman. Besides, I have a little homework for you and your other cells while we're outside picking a fight," John said. "I have a list of names and hometowns—some guys I bet may be sympathetic to our cause. You would have to convince their local cells to find them and make them an offer, but if you want to turn this organization from a bunch of computer nerds to door kickers, then we need to bolster our ranks. These are people who will move the Minutemen in the direction they need to move in."

"Okay, leave me the names and any information you can give me. I'll transmit it around on secure comms and let you know what comes of it. You two please be careful."

"Yes, mother," Andy replied, rolling his eyes.

The House of Cards

"Shorts, what in the hell is going on down there?" his superior roared. Shorts was becoming accustomed to these daily ass chewings, made regular by the near constant harassment of his agents by these insurrectionists. The ass chewings were then summarily passed along to Johns, for all the good it did.

"Sir, we are trying to ascertain the whereabouts—"

"I don't want to hear what you're trying to do! I want this brought to heel right now!" Then the line went dead.

In the past month, his camp had suffered numerous injuries and casualties. Sniper fire, IEDs (improvised explosive devices), ambushes. The mounting pressure being placed on the camp was having its effect on the morale of the men, and all of their efforts to capture or kill their assailants had amounted to nothing. They struck from cover and disappeared like ghosts afterwards.

Shorts thumbed through the reports from the previous thirty days.

Four agents in Humvee ambushed en route to their target. No casualties, multiple injuries.

Four agents assaulted while entering target residence with small-caliber rifle. Agents sustained moderate injuries, no casualties. Subject was killed in exchange of gunfire.

Four agents in Humvee struck by roadside bomb en route to their target. No casualties, multiple injuries.

Four agents in Humvee ambushed. All deceased.

One agent on exterior wall patrol, single gunshot wound to head from a large-caliber rifle. Agent deceased.

Four agents living off-site victims of explosive devices set at their residences. All deceased.

Four agents received sniper fire while entering a residence. Subject was killed in crossfire, no injuries to agents.

One agent ambushed during off hours with bladed weapon. Agent deceased.

Two agents in guard tower, single gunshot to each from large-caliber rifle. One agent deceased from gunshot to head; other severely injured, gunshot struck chest plate.

Shorts was sorting these reports into two piles. One pile was obviously the work of opportunists observing their neighbors being raided. Casualties among agents were rare, injuries superficial. The assailants were amateurs, and the damage was troublesome but not alarming.

The other pile was stacking up to be the work of the core group of the insurgency. The attacks on agents were obviously preplanned, well rehearsed, and intended to cause casualties or injuries of agents as they went about their duties or after hours. The most troubling of these were the sniper attacks that had begun to occur directly against the detention camp. Shorts had requested additional personnel be brought in to replace his wounded and deceased, but the orders had to crawl through the massive bureaucracy that was his organization before he would see any relief.

The other danger Shorts was battling was the tumbling morale of the men under his command. Three and a half weeks prior, his post had lost their second team to a vicious assault by this local terrorist group, with only Senior Agent Johns surviving. Since then, their casualty list and injured list had grown daily. Dissent among the men was increasing, and Shorts feared an all-out revolt if something did not give. Shorts had also quietly accepted the resignation of one of his veteran agents right after the second team went missing, who gave no official reason, only stated he refused to continue working for the agency.

At the rate these attacks were occurring, it would not be more than a week before his camp was below critical strength. Almost more problematic were constant reports of attacks now coming in from other stations around the country.

Hundreds of miles away, another so-called "gundamentalist" from John's list was being dragged into this insurgency.

John, you crazy bastard. I don't think anyone else could've sold me an idea this nuts, Matt thought. Over three weeks ago he had seen his friend from New Orleans on the evening news, along with his wife, proclaimed for all the world to be domestic terrorists. Then, a few days later, another friend of his in the area, Andy, had the same charges levied against him. Matt had known both men for years and knew there had to be more to the story than what the media was releasing. John and Andy were both hard-core gun-rights and free-speech advocates, but Matt also knew them to both be honest men and ardent patriots. That either of them would randomly become a lone-wolf killer left more questions than answers, until he got his answers from a very unlikely source.

An unaddressed letter showed up on his doorstep. It contained a short message purportedly from John and Andy, explaining their actions, and a method of contact. The people who picked up on the other end of that phone call were a local cell of the Minutemen based close to him, with an offer to join them before the searches and confiscations inevitably came to his doorstep.

Matt had pondered this. He, like many people, did not willingly hand over his guns on the government's word. *Give me a break. You guys want to take all of my guns, can't take all the criminals' guns, then you won't give up yours?! Do I look stupid?* he had thought at the time. With the rumors growing more frequent, the videos and audio files that had flared across social media, and now this personal and direct message from two men he trusted, it seemed the time to get in the fight was now. Matt, heeding the prudence and caution urged by John, slowly reached out to the Minutemen, then began recruiting men in the local community he knew held the same beliefs as he did. The ones who would not outright join he left with a warning to ready themselves for a fight.

When the day came that the black Humvee showed up at his door, in much the same fashion it had shown up at John's and Andy's doors hundreds of miles away, Matt made the only decision a man in his position could. Matt fought back and defended his family. The result was several dead agents and another family displaced from their home. Matt rushed his family from their quiet suburban home to the uncertainty that awaited them. The resistance, the Minutemen, the insurgency—whatever you called them, these men and women were just like Matt. They were people pushed to their practical limit by a government intent on taking that which was not theirs to take. They were people who banded together and said No More.

Like Matt, all over the country, people were fighting back. Some rushed to join their local Minutemen chapters. Some fought as individuals when their homes were directly threatened. Some went on the offensive much like John and Andy were, harassing their local detention camps and individual agents with any and all means available to them. In every case, the message was clear: the Minutemen wanted these camps closed down, and they wanted their people released. Right now.The pendulum had swung in the other direction. After years of unchallenged supremacy, the federal government had pushed the people to their breaking point, and the people were in near outright revolt. What had begun as a localized problem in the New Orleans area was spreading. The ranks of the Minutemen were being bolstered, and even those cells previously hesitant to join the fight were now so overwhelmed with support and the demand to fight back they were acquiescing to public opinion. The resources of a nation-state are limitless, but so far they proved unable to quell this rapidly growing insurrection.

Poking the Bear

"Wolf's Den, this is Wolf checking in," John called into his radio after checking to make sure they were on the secure net. Much like the military employed, the radio network the Minutemen maintained was able to rapidly "frequency hop," jumping across a set of preselected radio frequencies at set intervals. Any radio set up with these frequencies and synced with their timing had unrestrained communications. Anyone trying to listen in on any one of the frequencies would hear nothing but static with occasional blips and clipped sounds. It was not impenetrable, but it was as secure as they could manage, and based on his military experience and training, John had urged the importance of destroying these synced radios if capture became inevitable.

"Wolf, this is Wolf's Den. You coming home for a little while?" The voice was not Kevin, as John was expecting. Rachel was apparently taking a shift on the radio. She had picked up the particulars of being a radio operator quickly from Kevin and was fortunate to be on her shift when she heard her husband's voice on the radio.

"Yes, Wolf's Den, we're inbound. ETA unknown. Keep a plate out for us." John's way of saying they'd be back by dark/dinnertime.

"Roger that, safe travels. Wolf's Den out." Rachel had worried endlessly with John away. Just to have him close by brought her calm, and for him to be away and in obvious danger was a constant source of anxiety for her. Kay likewise had missed her father terribly. While Rachel had experienced John's bouts of absence for military service and his previous careers, he had been a near constant fixture in their home since Kay was born, and his absence was very conspicuous to her.

"They're on their way back in?" Mark asked, walking to the console.

"Yes, should be here by dark," Rachel answered.

"I'll try to talk him into staying a few days. I'm pretty shocked how much havoc they've been causing. Surely if they lay off for a couple of days, it won't undo the progress they've made," Mark offered.

"Progress towards what?" Rachel asked bitterly. "Why is everything always his responsibility? It doesn't matter if it's a job or politics or anything. He always takes everything upon himself, and no one else can be expected to hold up their end." She lashed out, frustrated that she had to sacrifice her husband while other wives spent quiet evenings at home with theirs. The stinging words were felt most by Mark, who had quietly dealt with the pangs of guilt that these two men were taking on so much of the burden of the mission they had set for themselves.

John and Andy had, according to assorted radio traffic, either killed or wounded over a hundred agents in the past thirty days. They had picked at so many of the supply convoys (that they now knew were arriving weekly on Saturdays) they were being escorted by armed guards when available personnel could be spared. The tensions inside the camp itself were at an all-time high. Every guard had to be saying a prayer every time they climbed into a guard tower or walked the wall, expecting the evening silence to be shattered by the sound of John's or Andy's rifles. Shorts, Johns, and the rest of the camp leadership were at their wit's end trying to find these two men, not realizing just how small a force was managing to cause them so much trouble.

Similar campaigns were being waged around the country, with varying degrees of success. Even outside of these coordinated attacks, the random lone-wolf attacks by common people were causing the agency a phenomenal headache. Calls for replacement personnel went unanswered simply because there were no longer any replacements to send. The president had even been asked to send in the National Guard or the Army to quell the insurrection, which he refused, afraid the sight of military troops in the streets would only promote more resistance.

He set the problem firmly back on the shoulders of the agency he had directed to locate and confiscate all contraband firearms and deal with those who flagrantly flaunted the new laws.

The longer the insurrection went on, the more it bloomed, the louder the whispers of a full-blown rebellion grew. Local news stations were heavily regulated and unable to report outside of news the state had approved, but international news and bloggers across the internet had no such qualms. What was once a few isolated stories was growing into trending news.

BBC news: Reports continue to surface from various locales around the United States of sporadic acts of violence targeting government officials. A White House official statement indicates anti-government extremism at work, but unnamed sources point to the recent repeal of the civilian right to keep and bear arms as the culprit. If the report is to be believed, what we are witnessing is the beginnings of a full-blown rebellion in the United States over gun rights.

Reuters: Attacks against government officials in America continue to mount, and the group known as the Minutemen is claiming responsibility. They assert that their violence is constrained to officials of the governmental arm responsible for seizing civilian firearms and jailing those who refused to surrender their firearms to law enforcement. Press affiliates in the US media refuse to comment, only to reiterate the official statements released to the White House press corps.

AFP: It was not long ago we welcomed the United States into the modern age as it finally took meaningful steps to curb its gun violence epidemic. Now it would appear the country is not as united as we once thought in this endeavor, as gun violence has exploded all across the country. Despite significant governmental resources allocated to locate and seize these contraband firearms, there appears to be no end in sight for the escalating violence that has racked the United States.

The independent bloggers were doing a much better job of reporting the actual issues. They were actively reaching out to the Minutemen through bulletin boards and forums, pleading for interviews and conversation. They were all too happy to report what the Minutemen were after: Stop the seizures and detainments, release all prisoners, restore the Second Amendment to the US Constitution. Or else.

But all of this unfurling on the world stage meant little to a worried wife and mother wishing for her husband to come home. All she could think of was raising a daughter alone if something happened to him. Yet she understood that he could not be dissuaded from this course. When he had left, he told her he would return "with his shield, or on it," an old Spartan axiom for he would win, or he would die. The best she could do was to support him and pray for his safety.

Several hours later, the two weary men were sighted coming up the road in Andy's Jeep. As they pulled down the long driveway, they each waved to the lookouts on each side. They were greeted by Mark, Rachel, and Kay. John could see his daughter running towards the Jeep even before they came to a full stop.

"Daddy!" Kay yelled. He was nearly bowled over by her, but her embrace was cut short as she pulled back, and her face betrayed John's marginal hygiene. "You stink," she loudly announced.

"Well, princess," Andy retorted, "not a lot of opportunities for a good shower when you live in the woods for a week."

They all grabbed gear while one of Mark's men pulled the Jeep around back in the barn, and went inside. Everything was unceremoniously thrown on the floor of the shop, and John and Andy retreated to their rooms for much-needed showers. John stood under the stream of scalding hot water, just barely at a tolerable temperature, and let the grunge and grit of a week living in the field run off him. He and Andy had been reduced to "GI showers" for that time, and a hot shower with soap felt amazing.

He exited the shower into his room to find his wife. He couldn't read her expression: worry, relief, anger, contentment—every emotion mixed together was draped across her face. "What is it, honey?" John asked, braced for the worst.

"I can't decide if I'm happy you're home, or pissed off at you for putting your life in danger and leaving us here," Rachel replied honestly.

John sighed. "Honey, we both know that the morning we shot those four agents there was no going back. The only way I see to put things right is to force a change."

"I know that," Rachel said, her voice softening, "but it is how I feel. I want my husband back, and I wish I knew who to resent—him for leaving so willingly, or everyone else for not doing what he alone feels compelled to do. You always seem to be the one trying to do the right thing when no one else will."

John stared at his wife, wrestling with the words. "I'll stay for a few days, honey; then I have to see this through. If I'm ever going to have a normal life for my family, this has to end on our terms, not theirs. If we give up before we finish, they will just come hunt us down and probably put me up against a wall for all the trouble I've caused them."

Rachel closed her eyes, nodding, a tear escaping the corner of her eye. "I know, John. I know. I just want you back when this is over. Don't make a widow of me yet."

Later that evening, John and Andy sat with Mark and Kevin for the debrief, trading intel from the field for that which they could only get from Mark's surveillance apparatus.

"You two have made quite a bit of trouble for the local supervisor," Kevin began. "Guy's name is Shorts. I've been listening to the ass chewings he's getting from on high, and they want his skin. He's getting most if not all of the blame for the little campaign you two have waged. He also caught hell when you guys hit their storehouse and stole back all those confiscated firearms. Why did you guys do that, anyway? We had plenty of guns and ammo already."

Andy looked to John.

"We do for now. Call it planning ahead. I concentrated mostly on handguns, smaller carbines, but I've got a plan. For now, let's just clean, oil, and function check them and load the magazines, then store them away for a rainy day," John explained.

Kevin looked to Mark and shrugged his shoulders.

"The interesting part is that the attacks have begun to spread," Mark said. "Illinois, Michigan, East Coast, hell, even in California and New York. People are taking notice and fighting back."

"Casualties?" John demanded.

"Some, but that's unavoidable. John, you said it yourself, the choices are to fight or surrender," Mark replied.

"I know what I said, doesn't mean I don't have to wear it on my conscience." John sulked. No one, other than perhaps his wife, understood how a man could so callously slaughter a man one moment and feel such deep remorse and responsibility for another death the next.

"Regardless of how you feel about it, it's working. World press is starting to report on it. The bloggers and alternative media have picked up the stories, and the government can't seem to get them to shut up about it. Some of these guys even moved their blogs to servers outside the country to keep the US regulatory arm out of their business. The focus isn't just gun rights anymore; people are outright pissed off about the invasion of privacy and the surveillance. Hitting the internet kill switch a month ago bought our government more bad press than anyone could have predicted. People from every walk of life were furious they couldn't pull money from their banks or even go shopping for that day, and a lot of people got sent home and lost a day or two of pay. That and scrubbing social media after everyone had already seen it. Free-speech advocates have been working three shifts protesting for weeks, and they show no signs of stopping. John, we are winning this fight," Mark said emphatically.

"The fight isn't over till they yield. Those camps are still there. The searches have certainly scaled back a lot, but if their ranks get refilled, they'll be back at it. They haven't gotten the message yet, 'cause they haven't changed course," John stated flatly.

"What do you suggest?" Mark asked.

John looked him squarely in the eye. "I think the time has come to stop poking this bear and stab him in the eye."

A Chance Encounter

Johns, like nearly all of the agents working out of the New Orleans detention camp, had lived on the premises even before the attacks began. Free room and board left him more expendable income for leisure was his way of viewing the situation. With attacks on agents nationwide becoming more and more common, his leisure time had become constrained to the camp. The only rub was the crimp that put on his social life, as visitors were strictly disallowed. That meant if he wanted to visit his girl of the moment, he would have to go to her.

Johns, unlike the citizenry of the surrounding community, was fully authorized to carry a firearm concealed or openly. That privilege had been suspended years prior on a city level by many more liberal mayors, then nationally later. Working for the government, however, had its privileges. Johns wore his holster inside his pants up against the skin, with his Glock 19 under his shirt. He drew the keys from the motor pool for an unmarked car, wrote into the log some BS about surveillance and countermeasures, and left the base. He was not off post fifteen seconds before Mark and Kevin's drone picked him up. What they could not ascertain was WHO they were following and vectoring John and Andy towards, only that it was an agent travelling alone in an unmarked vehicle.

While John and Andy worked towards his position, Agent Johns absentmindedly drove towards his destination. Jody, Joanne, what the hell was her name anyway? He decided to stick to "honey" to avoid screwing up a good piece of tail. He stopped at a stoplight, and another vehicle pulled up behind him.

As he sat there impatiently waiting and daydreaming about an evening in a real bed with a warm body, he failed to take notice of the person in the vehicle behind him.

While the agent's vehicle might not have been marked, it wore government plates and was the make and model nearly notorious for being used in government motor pools. The driver of the other vehicle was no one of note, just a retired firefighter named Randall who had grown tired of a government grown too big for its britches. He drew his old Smith and Wesson revolver from his glove box. It had been a gift from his friend, who had worn it on his hip for decades as a local police officer. The same firearm those pinheads had sent a letter demanding he hand over when they decided civilians couldn't be trusted with handguns. He had tacked that letter up to the backstop on his range and used it for target practice. The last straw was when they came for his friend...

Two years ago, the two of them were at Randall's private range. It was so far out in the sticks no one would bother them. They were just doing a little plinking with their AR-15s. When they finished up, they loaded their cars and headed home. Randall didn't get the call till later that evening from his wife that his friend had been pulled over, the firearms found, and they'd actually taken him to the detention camp and turned him over. No trial, no charges, just off to the camp. And it was HIS OWN department that picked him up. Didn't matter how many favors Randall tried to call in from guys he knew; even the damned DA wouldn't budge. They hung him out to dry.

Randall had to wonder at that point what would have happened if they had picked him up instead. He'd spent thirty years of his life serving people in this city. Would an officer he had worked with on a scene hand him over to the damned gestapo just like that? What was happening in this country when people's rights could be taken away by a vote, and then the people suffered the further indignity of having their right to trial by jury suspended too.

Well, son, not sure who you are, but I wager you're going to question your career choices here in the next few minutes, Randall thought. He sat there with his revolver in his lap; the light turned green. He contented himself with following the man to see if another opportunity arose to exact revenge for the loss of his friend's freedom. Two intersections later he saw a yellow light, pulled into the lane next to the unmarked car, pulled up alongside while rolling down the window, and raised the revolver.

Agent Johns just barely glanced to the left when the window next to him shattered.

"John, we have a situation," Kevin radioed John while watching the drone feed. "Someone pulled up next to your subject and is shooting from his vehicle towards the subject's."

Agent Johns slammed the gas pedal to the floor and shot through the intersection, nearly hitting crossing traffic. He was damned lucky not to have been shot, the window was blown out, and he was sure he'd be doing paperwork on all the damage done to the motor pool vehicle. He swerved left at the next intersection, abandoning his rendezvous and heading back to the safety of the camp.

Randall cursed his shaky hand, rolled up his window, and went about his business. "At least I screwed up his plans this evening, little shithead," gruffed the old man to himself.

"Okay, John, reverse course back the way you came. Subject is moving at high speed directly to you, heading back to the camp. His assailant is proceeding on his way like nothing happened," Kevin said into the mic.

"Disregard assailant; focus on subject. Give us a vector so we can set up an ambush," John ordered. "Andy, flip a bitch, he's coming straight at us."

Andy stomped on the brakes and wheeled the Jeep around in an abrupt 180.

"Step on it. We need to get enough gap to set up on him before he overtakes us."

They chose a spot as close to the camp as they dared, and rocketed up the back road to open the gap. Fortunately they found some concealment on the roadside for the Jeep, dismounted, and readied for their ambush. A raid on a local supply yard had yielded a set of "spike strips" like police used for stopping speeding vehicles, and now seemed a perfect time to try them out. On this dark road without streetlights (one shot with Andy's suppressed .22 took care of that), the speeding vehicle would never see the danger in time to stop or swerve.

Johns sped down the road, following his GPS back to camp. He took a moment here and there to brush the glass shards from his collar and shirt, cursing whoever it was who had taken a shot at him. He also cursed that he hadn't taken the time to shoot back. Because his mind was distracted from the task at hand, he never even saw the spike strips when he hit them at sixty miles per hour, deflated all four tires, and careened off the road, struggling for control of the vehicle barely half a mile from the safety of the detention camp. He exited the vehicle and saw the small straw-like metal tubes impaling both tires on the driver side of the vehicle. "Aww shit," he said aloud.

He drew his firearm just as he noticed the two men approaching him. In the dark he could only make out the rifles they carried, and he raised his handgun to fire while he backpedaled. At a range of seventy-five yards, three times farther than his agency trained its agents to shoot at, his shots were woefully off target, but even a broken watch is right twice a day. One of the men was hit and dropped down to a knee. The other raised his rifle and fired two shots, both of which hit Johns. The shot in the shoulder knocked his handgun from his grasp, while the one in his stomach crumpled him.

"Shit, John, you okay?!" Andy shouted, grabbing for his friend's plate carrier. John was down on one knee, his right hand on his rifle to keep it out of the dirt while his left hand felt inside his carrier for anything wet indicating the round had penetrated. "I'm good. Plate caught it. Motherfucker, that hurts," John groused. John rose unsteadily to his feet, and he and Andy approached their prey.

John held his rifle covering Agent Johns as Andy rolled him over, and all three discovered familiar faces. "You two," Agent Johns sneered.

"Well, well, if it ain't the one that got away," Andy singsonged to the downed man. "John, I take back calling you a shithead for letting him go."

"You never called me a shithead," John replied.

"Not to your face," Andy quipped.

The back-and-forth provided just enough distraction for Agent Johns to fish his backup gun from his belt and raise it to fire.

Rook Takes Knight, Check

Hours later at Mark's home, a very sore John sat in a chair while Vicky wrapped his ribs. "Easy." John grimaced. Vicky surmised that John probably had several bruised ribs, no apparent fractures, no punctures to his lungs. He was sore and suitably grouchy, but he would be fine. As she wound the Ace bandage around his rib cage, the intense pain made him wonder how badly he was wounded.

"What happened?" Mark asked. Rachel stood to her husband's side, thankful he was alive and anxious at the obvious danger he had put himself in.

"Hell," John retorted, "I was going to ask you the same thing. Plan was to zap this guy when he reached his destination. All of a sudden some rando takes a shot at him and he comes hauling ass straight in our direction. We had to improvise."

"That's exactly what happened," Kevin offered. "The target was in an unmarked vehicle, but whoever pulled up behind him must've noticed the government plates and had an axe to grind. At the next red light, he pulled up next to him and shot two to three shots through his open window at the target vehicle. Target floored it through the intersection then turned in your direction, heading back to camp."

John wondered at the turn of events. They had managed to stir up so much anti-agency sentiment that a random citizen, with no support from the Minutemen and apparently purely on the spur of the moment, had decided to attack someone he merely *suspected* to be an agency man. At a red light. In traffic. In the middle of town. He couldn't decide if he was bearing witness to incredible bravery or pure foolhardiness.

104

"Well, regardless, we realized we had to improvise, so we backtracked and set up on him in his path. We used the spike strips we borrowed from that local agency supply depot to stop him cold, and they worked like a charm. When he exited the vehicle and saw us walking up on him, he got a lucky shot off on us, and I caught one in the plates," John stated flatly. "Andy zapped him, and we walked up on him to finish it."

"And that's when..." Rachel started.

"And that's when the shithead pulled a backup gun and took another shot at us," John finished. He was pissed at himself, not Rachel. He couldn't believe he'd let his guard down in that moment. He of all people knew how easily a dead man could still kill someone, lashing out in his last moments with a hidden weapon. It was a lesson he should have learned already, and one Andy would never forget. "He missed, thankfully. Andy and I put about three rounds each into him and he was done. It was the same guy we turned loose when we set up on Andy's house the morning of his raid."

"You still don't know who you got, do you?" Kevin asked. "Agent Johns was the second-in-command of the detention camp, Shorts's right-hand man. Airwaves are lit all the way up with the reports of him being KIA, and the agency is pissed and scared. They're talking about putting out a bounty on you guys."

"Well, we said we wanted to get their attention," Andy said matter-of-factly. "I guess we got their attention." He looked to John, his face betraying no emotion.

John held his friend's gaze as his mind replayed what happened.

People always say time slows down, and their life flashes before their eyes right before they die, or when they come close to dying. It was a phenomenon John had experienced himself during the close calls he had seen in his life. The gun, a little Glock 42 380 ACP, came out of Johns's waistband from under his shirt. He cocked his elbow, raising the gun, pointing it at his assailants.

John had just registered the danger and lunged back when the shot rang out, the bullet narrowly missing John and the powder burning his jeans. The next shot snapped right between Andy's shoulder and his ear, the force felt so clearly he initially thought he had been shot. John brought the barrel of his AR down decisively as he began tapping the trigger. At this range, he didn't even need the sights.

Three shots from his rifle silenced Agent Johns, followed by a few more from Andy out of pure reaction. The two men stood there on the verge of hyperventilating, realizing how close they had come for the second time that night to being shot. Andy reached up to his face, feeling for a trace of the blood he knew must be there, while John shined his light down on his pants, looking for holes. Both men brought their heart rates back down to double digits and collapsed down to their butts in the dirt.

"Andy, if I ever do that shit again, you be sure to slap the hell out of me." John's voice rang out. He could only hear the pulsing of blood in his ears, making his own voice sound as though it were underwater.

"Do what?" Andy inquired.

"I let my guard down, and that motherfucker damned near shot both of us. I should've known better." That was John, always taking the blame for everything and always taking the blame alone. Andy knew there was no point arguing with his friend, who felt responsible for the safety of them both.

"What do we do with him?" Andy asked, motioning towards the body next to them.

John regarded the body of Agent Johns and spoke with absolute cold fury. "I say we send the camp a message they can't ignore. Hope you don't have a weak stomach."

"I still can't believe you two did that," Vicky intoned. She had happened to be near the radio when Kevin was listening to and transcribing the reports of what Andy and John had decided to do to "send a message."

Mark looked from his wife to John and Andy. He found it hard to argue with Vicky's assessment of these two men as being "barbarians." After shooting Agent Johns multiple times, the two of them had dragged his body behind the Jeep back to camp, written a note, tied it around Johns's neck with a piece of string, and sat his dead body up against the front gate of the camp while rigor set in. He was found shortly after by a patrol, and the radio traffic was graphic. Vicky had asked her husband what kind of men he had thrown in with, and he wondered himself.

"I'm not questioning your judgment, but this is pretty bloody, guys." Mark tried to make his voice sound soothing, not wanting to provoke a confrontation with these men. It was not fear that motivated him, more of a quiet respect. These were the men who had won more ground in this fight with the agency in a month than his group had won in years, and he desperately wanted to keep this partnership together, but even he had to question this provocation.

"It isn't like we cut his head off and stuck it on a pike or anything," Andy retorted. Andy, always with the sardonic sense of humor and sarcasm, and always ready to back John no matter how bad things got. It was easy to see why the two of them had become fast friends.

"I'm not saying you were wrong. Just give some of us a minute to come to terms with the reality of leaving dead bodies in plain sight as a way of getting a point across," Mark seethed.

John stood briskly, his knees knocking the chair out from behind him. "Now you listen here. Every time we called here for intel, every time we reported 'mission accomplished,' every time we came back here and locked ourselves away in the shop to reload ammo, what in the FUCK did you think was going on? Were we out selling Girl Scout cookies? Collecting for the American Red Cross? We have been killing these guys every night, everywhere we can find them. Hell, I quit counting so I wouldn't have to wonder how many of them have wives and kids. I have to sleep with what I've done every night, and I have to keep reminding myself we are at war, and war involves casualties. I'm sorry, Mark, that you suddenly noticed a few drops of blood on your own hands. I can't see the drops anymore 'cause I'm covered in it."

"John, I—"

"Fuck you, Mark! You want your turn outside the wire? You want to wake up at two in the morning with bugs crawling on you, picking ticks off Andy's ass every morning so we don't end up sick? You want to tell your wife 'sorry, honey, got to go shoot people in the face for a few weeks. See you later'?" John's eyes flared, his fists clenched, the cords in his necks and arms pulled tight.

"John." It was Andy's voice that spoke. John's head craned in the direction of the sound, to see his friend at the back door, holding two cigars. He angrily stomped towards the door, snatching one of the cigars on his way past his friend.

"Mark, I wouldn't suggest you come out this door for a few minutes if you like chewing your food. Take that as a friendly suggestion," Andy said seriously as he closed the door.

The room was silent. Even Rachel, normally the peacekeeper, was deeply conflicted. She found little to argue with that John and Andy's methods were brutal, but she was incensed at Mark for his reaction. "I suggest you do some soul-searching, Mark. If you want us out of here, just say the word. But John is right, he is the one out there doing what no one else wants to do. He is fighting this war while you watch it from the comfort of a computer monitor. It isn't fair that he comes back after almost getting shot twice in one night to have you and your wife unload on him. You don't get to send him out there into danger just to 'Monday morning quarterback' him afterwards." She left the room to check on Kay and George, then joined her husband and Andy on the back porch.

"What do we do?" Vicky demanded of her husband. "Those two aren't men, they're animals. How can they kill a man like that and feel nothing?"

"That's just the problem, Vicky," Mark replied. "I think they do feel something. Andy may hide it with sarcasm, John may rationalize it, but they both see the face of every man they've killed. And I just threw it right back in their faces."

"Damn that man." John fumed. His friend stood just out of arm's reach. "Where does he get off questioning me? He sits here in his ivory tower, eating home-cooked meals and banging his wife, while we sit out there smelling our own shit, risking our asses every night! And then when we come back, I've got a hole in my plate carrier and a bruise the size of a fist, both of us scared to death we almost got shot, and he has the freaking nerve to say 'hey, guys, little over the top.' I got half a mind to go punch his lights out for his trouble."

Andy just stood there, toasting the foot of his own cigar while regarding his friend. He was not given to the same brand of explosive anger his friend was, but he understood the reaction. John was a man of action, and he understood intrinsically the only way to end this fight was through violence. Anything less than that would only prolong the fight and invite casualties he did not want to incur. What John was really wrestling with was his own conscience, not wanting to be reminded of the body count they had already caused. "Look, give him a few minutes, and I'm sure he'll come out here with his tail between his legs," Andy offered.

"Until the next time. Then I'm going to have to chew his head off all over again. What did he think, we'd just send the government a politely drafted email and they'd realize the error of their ways? Did he think this little insurrection wouldn't balloon into a full-scale shooting war? He knew what he was getting into; he just doesn't like the feeling of the blood being on his own hands," John spat.

The sound of the door opening sent John's head swiveling around. He was sure it was Mark and was readying a dizzying array of profanity to hurl in his direction when the sight of his wife walking through the door greeted him. "At ease, boys, I come in peace," she said, half joking. "Has he found anything to throw or punch yet?" Rachel asked Andy.

"Nope, think Mark smartened up and started nailing everything down," Andy said through a grin.

John's shoulders slumped, the humor working to defuse him. He took another pull from his cigar and looked back at the house. Once a refuge from the ugliness he was seeing daily, now it just looked like judgment to him. He saw recriminations, reminders of his past deeds. He saw the questions and the looks.

"Rachel, I can't do this." John sighed. "I can't stay here and work with these people if every time I come home, I get dragged across the coals. This is just like Iraq, when someone would grease a guy and the damned Army wanted to try him for war crimes. Put a soldier in a situation where he practically has to get his head shot off before everyone wants to clear him to shoot. And with two on a thousand odds, we don't have the luxury of waiting for our enemy to fire the first shot."

"John, I understand what you're doing. The reality of it is shocking even to me, but I understand. Where do you think the disconnect is between you and Mark?" she asked.

"I think," he answered, "he was under the impression the good guys act like good guys. He wasn't prepared to be the villain in this story. Good guys don't desecrate bodies and shoot people in the back."

"They don't?" Rachel prodded.

"Shit yes, they do, they just write the history books afterwards and clean up the finer details. When we talk about the first Thanksgiving, everyone talks about the Native Americans and colonists breaking bread together like old friends. No one talks about the smallpox blankets and the ambushes, the murders and rapes, the turf war over land. This country is not unique in its history. The victor always writes the history books to present themselves in the best possible light. I can assure you, if the Germans won World War Two, you wouldn't have read about a single Jew walking into a gas chamber. The bombs fall on Hiroshima and Nagasaki and the Japanese Imperial Army wins anyway, you never read a word about their prison camps and GIs being starved half to death. That's just reality." John's words came out in a rush, his mind racing. "Mark's problem is that he sees what we're doing for what it is. We are mounting an insurrection and behaving as insurrectionists.

We are operating a terror cell, fighting against a technologically superior force with vast numbers and near unlimited power."

"In other words, we're acting like ISIS," Rachel summarized.

"Yes and no, some of their methods are so inhumane even I won't be able to face myself if we used them. More like the kinds of tactics employed by the colonial militias against the British before the Revolutionary Army was raised. These men weren't soldiers, they were farmers and outdoorsmen. They didn't stand in a field lined up nice and pretty to be cut down by British muskets, they hid in trees and used their rifles to shoot officers off their horses. And trust me, there was plenty of backstabbing and assassination to go along with that, it just never made it into the history books. Even we wanted to portray ourselves after the fact in the most righteous light possible," John explained.

"So how do you get that across to Mark?" Rachel asked.

John looked at his feet. "I guess shithead just needs a history lesson. 'Cause from here, things are going to get a lot uglier."

A History Lesson

John sat with Mark, just the two of them, as they wrestled with their words to communicate. They were just realizing just how different their worlds had been the last month of their lives, and Mark just how detached he had felt from all of the violence John and Andy had wrought upon the local agency personnel. For the first time, Mark questioned the methods employed by John and realized just how deeply personally John had taken that questioning. "John I'm——" he started.

"Shut up for a second and listen." John clipped Mark off midsentence. His eyes bored straight into Mark's, as Mark wondered whether he had come to talk or just to throttle the life out of someone. "I left here a few weeks ago pretty sure you and I were on the same page, and it has just come to my attention we are not. So let's you and me put our cards on the table. What the fuck do you want?" The words came out of John's mouth dripping with venom.

"John, I want what you do. I want these camps emptied out, and I want the searches to stop. I want our government to back off," Mark said evenly, careful to choose his words.

"I want the same thing. The problem seems to be my methods are a little too brutal for your liking, so please tell me how you propose to accomplish your goals without me and Andy getting our asses shot off. I can't go out there, knock on the front door of their compound, and ask to speak with Mr. Shorts to work out this little misunderstanding we seem to have had. They will take about six seconds to put me against a wall and blow my damned head off. I likewise don't have the luxury of waiting for a dozen of them to start shooting at me and Andy before we start shooting back. The disparity in our numbers just makes that impossible.

So spit it out. What's on your mind?" John's voice was simultaneously a demand and a challenge.

Mark saw himself for the first time as John's adversary, and the reality frightened him. He saw what all of those men must have seen before they met their end. He saw a man simultaneously in control and on the verge of losing control, like a train barreling down the tracks, going too fast to stop before it flew off the rails.

Mark sighed. "John, I was wrong. I shouldn't have put you on the spot like that. The news was shocking, and I let it get the best of me. I apologize."

"That's it?" John snapped.

"What else do you want from me?" Mark fired back. "Jesus, John, look at yourself. You walk into my house with blood and mud all over the two of you after you just executed a man while looking into his eyes and sat him up against the front gate of his compound for everyone to see like some kind of gruesome scarecrow. You've bombed people, shot them, ambushed them; you guys are out there acting like terrorists—"

"Motherfucker, what do you think we are?!" John roared.

Mark's speech was stopped in mid-word.

"You said the Minutemen were modeled after a terror cell. Well, bubba, I got news for you, we ARE terrorists. Go grab your dictionary and look up the word; tell me what it says. We are using violence to enact and force political or social change, straight out of Webster's. What, you thought the good guys didn't do that shit? We always fought fair? Hell, son, you're a pretty smart guy, but you're the most ignorant person I've ever met," John lectured. "I'm going to go grab a shower, and I'm going to bed. Between now and tomorrow morning, friend, you do yourself a favor and open up a history book and start reading. The American Revolution was a bloody war. Every war is. If you question my methods, you do some homework and have a look at how the game is played before you start questioning the rule book."

John turned and saw Kevin standing there, his hand on the butt of his sidearm. It occurred to him he hadn't even realized till now that Kevin and several others had started carrying sidearms around the compound. His eyes grew deadly serious. "Kevin, you want to take your hand off that gun, or you want to see if you can outdraw me?"

Kevin looked down at his right hand, unaware he had even reached for it, and slowly moved his hand away. "I just came to see what the yelling was about."

"I didn't tear your boss's head off, if that's what you're worried about." He walked past Kevin and down the hallway to his room. Rachel and Andy came in from the back porch.

"Well, that went well," Andy quipped.

"Agreed. Mark isn't dead, and my husband is going to get some rest. See everyone in the morning," Rachel said nonchalantly as she followed her husband to their room.

Andy sat down by Mark, kicking his boots up on a footrest without regard for the muddy condition of his footwear. "So have you figured it out yet?" Andy asked. His tone was halfway between chiding and a genuine question.

"Figured what out?" Mark asked, emotionally exhausted.

"That we aren't the good guys this time?" Andy said levelly. "That's what John said outside, we aren't the good guys. No such thing in a war. There's just people looking out for their own interests. We want our rights, not just guns but all of them, to be respected. The government, with the backing of some of the population, disagrees. They are willing to use force to accomplish their goals, so are we. The difference is, they are at peace with their decision and you don't seem to be. Why is that?" It was the longest sentence Andy had spoken to Mark since he had arrived at his home.

"I'm not a soldier, Andy. I don't kill people. I don't shoot them. I'm not like you and John."

"Rachel overheard what Vicky said about John. He isn't what you think he is. Vicky is wrong; he isn't an animal or a barbarian. He actually places such a high value on human life he wrestles with taking one every single time. That's why he takes it so personally when you question what he's doing. He and I have known each other a long time, and we've spent a lot of time out there in the woods together.

He is, on a very deep and emotional level, haunted by every life he has taken, but he won't stop," Andy explained.

"Why is that?" Mark pleaded, looking for the key to unravelling John.

"Because," Andy explained patiently, "he is at peace with his decision. He knows these men must die, not because they are evil men, but because what they do is evil. To take another person's freedom or free choice or property, that is all evil. If they serve the will of a government that engages in evil, then they must be sacrificed to bring that evil to an end. I kinda wish you hadn't pissed John off, he could've explained this a bit more eloquently than I am."

"Why do I seem to constantly piss him off?"

Andy sighed. "Believe it or not, it isn't you. You and your wife just dredged up the same argument he's been having with himself and caught hell for it. Tomorrow morning, after a good night's sleep, he'll probably come out of that room with his tail between his legs and apologize for tearing your heads off. You don't know, can't know, what it's like to be out there doing what we do every day. But do not mistake the fact that you all screwed up. You let that man go out and do the dirty deeds you don't want to do, or can't, whatever. You cannot turn around and throw him to the wolves of his own conscience after he has shed blood on your behalf. Like it or not, no one is innocent in this fight, whether you pulled the trigger or you told him where to go to pull the trigger. You may not be a wolf like John, but you aren't sheep either."

Andy hauled himself to his feet. "Think long and hard about what we just talked about, and take some of John's advice. Crack a history book, because that man certainly has. He is such a nerd in a library, reading history and philosophy, that you'd never believe what he's like in a fight. A savage fighter with the intellect of a scholar. If you want to understand him, try understanding where he's coming from. Try to understand what it means to wish for peace, but resign yourself to viciousness to achieve it."

As Andy turned his back on Mark and walked to his room, Mark did just that. He walked to his study and started looking for a book on the American Revolution. By the time he fell asleep with a book on his chest, he had indeed come to understand John a little better. That was incidentally where John found Mark the next morning.

He gently shook Mark by the foot, well outside the reach of his arms. It was an old habit born from the military, to wake a man out of his reach so you couldn't be struck by a jumpy person. He needn't have worried, Mark woke gingerly and peered over the top of the book on his chest at John. With a fresh cut to his beard, trimmed hair, and thoroughly scrubbed face, he looked like a different person. "Listen, Mark..." he started, the remorse obvious in his tone.

"No, don't you dare apologize to me." Mark's words came out as a sigh, not an accusation. He raised the book to show John the spine. "I took some of your and Andy's advice and read several history books. Then I read a bunch of old Army field manuals about unconventional warfare, guerilla tactics and such. I don't know what I was expecting you to do, but I never really stopped to ask either, and it was insensitive of me to second-guess you after the fact. Insensitive and unfair." Mark sat up and looked at John. The usually intense eyes were merely blank this morning, exhausted.

"You are doing what is necessary. It is bloody and ugly, but necessary. I don't know if I could do what you and Andy are doing, and I don't really want to find out. I don't think I'd sleep for a month if I'd seen the kind of violence you two are seeing every day. All I need to know is what you need from us so you can end this."

"Define end this," John asked.

"I mean end this. Look, I've read so much military history and philosophy since you put me in my place last night, I have a whole new perspective on warfare. The longer this war, and that is what we are engaging in, lasts, the bloodier it will be. The faster we end it, the fewer people will die," Mark explained.

"There is some merit to that ideal," John agreed. "On the other hand, since we are engaging in an outright insurgency, possibly precipitating an all-out rebellion, brutality constrained to our target without collateral damage has the effect of frustrating our enemy. If he lashes out and harms civilians, it pushes more people to our cause. If he measures his strikes, he fails to stop us because we will engage him where he may not engage us."

"How did you learn so much about this?" Mark asked.

John smiled. "Part of it I watched with my own eyes in Iraq. The rest I read in books. Vietnam, Afghanistan, Iraq, the French Resistance, the Warsaw Uprising; history is littered with examples of numerically smaller forces stymieing larger and better armed forces. But in order to accomplish that hat trick, you have to fight dirty. And that is what we are doing, fighting dirty."

"Andy told me last night you said we aren't the good guys. That really shook me," Mark replied.

John sighed. "We aren't. We aren't acting like good guys. We aren't standing up in a field across from the redcoats for a fight with honor. We're sniping their officers off horseback just like we did two hundred years ago. We're playing dirty because that's the only way we win this fight. And we will continue to do so until I get the result I want."

"Which is?" Mark asked.

"Until I have broken that camp down enough to tear it open. Until I have broken their will to fight. Until I have breached the door of that little peckerhead's office and stomped on his neck with my boot. I will continue until I beat them, or they beat me. Your job is to keep them off my ass and keep my family safe. You fight the information war; I fight the war out there. If you hold up your end, I'll hold up mine. Anytime you want to switch places, you say the word," John said matter-of-factly.

Mark shook his head. "No, John, you've made your point. I can't do what you do, and I won't question your methods outside this property again. Just tell us what you need, and let's get this over with."

"What I need right now is intel," John said. "I need to know how much we've weakened them, and I need some idea of the layout of that camp. I desperately need to know where the prisoners are so I don't breach a wall and kill them in the process. A rough schedule of the guard changes or patrols would be awesome. After that, I need to see if we can drum up some support from the local area."

"What kind of support?" Mark asked.

"To pull this off, I'm going to need supplies, vehicles, and maybe a few extra hands. If we manage to take the camp, there are going to be refugees looking for a place to hunker down. And the reprisal from the government very well may be extreme, but we can't predict that. I'm no Rambo; I can't assault that camp alone or with just two of us."

"Okay, John," Mark answered smoothly, "let's see just how much goodwill you've won in the local community. Judging by the reports we've been intercepting, you and Andy won't be the only two raising hell out there."

Healing Wounds

The next several days saw a flurry of activity from all parties involved. The reaction at the detention camp bordered on panic. A late night patrol had discovered the body of Agent Johns, shot multiple times in the chest and face, apparently dragged behind a vehicle, and propped up against the front gate with a note on his chest proclaiming:

"Release your prisoners and walk away, or you all die. No quarter shall be given."

Shorts tried mightily to suppress the information, but it rocketed throughout the camp. Several agents resigned on the spot and walked out the front door. Reprisals and threats of jail time had no effect. Some even refused to surrender their government-issued firearms, demanding they needed to protect themselves and insisting the agency could not protect them whether they stayed or left. The agency assets in the New Orleans area were on the verge of complete mutiny. None of this information escaped Mark and Kevin's information-gathering apparatus.

"I can't believe this, Mark, over two dozen agents apparently turned in their immediate resignation and walked out the door. All because of the 'message' John and Andy sent. It may have been heavy-handed, but it's working," Kevin gushed.

Mark nodded his head somberly, recalling the conversations of the previous evening and that morning. He and John had come amazingly close to blows, all because he had been unable to see the logic in what John did. John saw the goal, and in his mind the end always justified the means. To desecrate a body and leave it for all the world to see was barbaric, an act no less deserving of the label "terrorism" than anything John had seen in the Middle East.

But Mark was forced to admit that in the dangerous game they played, you didn't gain ground by playing by the rules. Sometimes, it paid off to be the villain, and the agents in the detention camp were justifiably terrified of John and Andy in a way they had not felt since they feared monsters under their beds as children. Those two men had become the face that waited for them in the dark of their nightmares, and the effect it was having on their will to fight was immediate and pronounced.

"So the time is nearing to end this." Mark sighed, feeling relief. He longed to answer the question of whether or not his sister, Julie, was safe or even alive. He longed for some peace, even a temporary one, to return to his home. He did not delude himself that the war was over, but hoped that at least this victory would win the battle. But there was much work to do, and he had so little precious energy left. "We need to start putting together supplies and people, get a tactical plan together. John wants to hit the detention camp directly, and the time has to be drawing near."

"What does he have in mind?" Kevin asked wearily. He had learned over the past month of his life that where John was concerned, he should expect a fine mixture of ingenuity and brutality.

"I haven't asked yet. We both needed coffee, and he needed some time with his family to decompress before we could process all that. We may get started this afternoon or tomorrow. I'm done trying to call the shots. We are in John's world now," Mark replied wearily.

"Mark, I didn't join this cell to follow John. I joined because I put my trust in you," Kevin replied uneasily.

"Then put your trust in him, Kevin, because I am. Every step of the way, that man has proven to be able to act decisively at precisely the right time to advance our goals. His methods are...brutal, to say the least. The devastation he leaves in his wake is hard to stomach. But it is working. In the last thirty days the local agency assets are on the verge of scattering, and in the past two years we barely managed to save a dozen people from these bastards. We weren't winning the war by ourselves, we were waiting for him.

It took me some time to see that, but now I do," Mark said confidently.

"He's no George Washington," Kevin replied sarcastically.

"Funny you should mention that, Kevin. I have a book for you to read," Mark said with a rueful smile.

In the backyard, John and Rachel sat with Vicky, watching Kay and George play. "John, I said some things last night that I need to apo—"

"Forgiven." John cut in with his usual deadpan tone. "What I did is going to give me nightmares for a few days at least. I hope it isn't longer. I understand how it looks to people not accustomed to it."

"But I could have been a bit more tactful," Vicky insisted.

"Yes, ma'am, you could've been. But to be fair, you've never had men in your home who do the sorts of things Andy and I have been doing, and I can sympathize with the shock it caused. Like I said, all is forgiven. I do not make a habit of holding grudges post apology. It just isn't how I was raised," John replied with a tone indicating the matter was settled.

He gazed out across the yard, watching his daughter, seeing glimpses of the happy, carefree child he once knew. The sight of the dead bodies in the doorway of her home had shaken her badly, as had the new surroundings. His leaving for weeks at a time hadn't helped either, but with his return, she seemed to have suddenly found her old self. He reflected on this with guilt at the thought he would soon be leaving again.

Rachel squeezed his hand and he glanced over at her. She could read the trouble on his face as if he were an open book, familiarity born from time spent together. "I know you have to go eventually. She does too. We'll manage till you come back."

John nodded, feeling a hole in his chest that must match the one he left behind in his own family when he left the compound.

"Morning." Andy yawned, walking out onto the back porch. "Please tell me someone has coffee brewed."

"Pot is behind you," John replied, smiling. His friend's coffee addiction was nearly the equal of his own. There would be no productivity had from Andy until his blood-caffeine ratio was corrected. Andy filled a mug sitting by the carafe and gingerly padded out to the edge of the deck to join everyone.

John looked up to his friend's bleary eyes and asked, "So, what exactly did you say to Mark after I went to bed last night?"

"I gave him some perspective, John. You know, and I know, the dangerous game we are playing, and the rules. He doesn't, or more accurately he didn't. He does now," Andy said simply.

John nodded. Mark seemed to have rapidly altered his way of thinking overnight in a way John could not fully attribute to the brutal ass chewing he had doled out. He had gone to bed that night silently cursing himself for losing his temper, though Rachel had accurately pointed out if he really had lost his temper, someone would've needed medical attention. Regardless of what had precipitated the shift, John welcomed it. He finally felt like a member of a team, and the work that was about to be undertaken would require the combined efforts of an entire team.

"Andy, I'm not sure what you're thinking, but I could do with a day or two here to get some wind back in my sails and heal up before we go back out again. Let these ribs heal and remind my family they have a husband and father."

"I kinda figured. I could do with a few hot showers and cigars myself. And I would sell a piece of my soul for some whiskey," Andy replied, deadpan as usual.

"You know, if you guys ask nicely, I know where Mark hides the booze to keep the kids out of it," Vicky volunteered.

John and Andy both regarded her with a smile. John replied, "I accept as long as you aren't still trying to apologize for last night."

Vicky shook her head. "Already issued and accepted. I told your wife weeks ago you three—four were a part of our household as long as you stayed. I'm trying to be a good hostess—when I remember my manners," she said with a thin smile.

"Accepted," Andy replied. Andy turned on his heel to head towards the house to retrieve the whiskey and raid his and John's dwindling cigar stash, walking right by Mark.

"How is everyone this morning?" Mark inquired.

"Fine, Mark, just enjoying a little family time while I can get it," John replied easily, holding his wife's hand.

Mark noted the distinct differences in John's personality. With his wife and daughter, he was an incredibly gentle, eminently relaxed person. Right before and immediately following an operation, it was as if he were a completely different person: anxious, alert, focused. Mark reflected on the effect being around his own family had on himself, and came to understand a sizable portion of the stress John was feeling spending a week at a time out in the field. John's family was his comfort, more than any creature comfort his home could offer. The real hardship he felt was not being out in the woods fighting for his life, it was being away from the two people he loved more than life itself.

"John, I think we can spare a day or two for you and Andy to get some rest. I think we'll need that much time to get organized for the next phase of our operation, but I did want to share some intel with you later this afternoon when the two of you can spare some time," Mark said.

John nodded his head. "We're thinking along the same lines, Mark. Andy and I have some work and healing to do before we go out again, but we don't intend to rest on our laurels. Say after lunch?"

"Sounds good. Is Andy on his way to raid my whiskey and cigars?" Mark questioned.

"Actually," Andy replied, walking towards them, "I raided your liquor and my cigars." Andy passed one to John and offered one to Mark.

"What exactly do you have in mind, John? I'm guessing our next move is to hit the camp directly?" Mark asked.

John scratched his chin, a habit he indulged when thinking of how to phrase his words. "When we hit the camp depends on what we can scrounge together, and the layout of the camp and our manpower. We may have to chip away at them a little while longer. One problem is I need to know where the prisoners are and how many other hands I have available before I can really put pencil to paper. You make any headway on that front?" John asked, hoping for positive news.

"Yes and no. Since you've caused so much chaos in the camp, we've managed to get drones much closer and get a good layout of the camp. The holding area for prisoners is dead center in the middle of the camp, flanked by barracks for the agents and the admin offices, where we believe Shorts is. Based on his movements, we're guessing he has a private room in there, that or he's sleeping on his desk. There's only one thing that worries me."

"You got to wondering why the camp was so small for a metro area?" John asked knowingly.

"Yeah. Don't know why it didn't hit me earlier. We estimated peak strength was about two hundred, maybe two fifty personnel. Based on the size of the holding area, even if they're stacked up four high in bunks, they can't be housing more than a hundred people, and that's really pushing it. Probably more like half of that," Mark rambled. "But in this area, there's no way they only grabbed that many people since the searches started. The numbers don't add up."

"Which means one of two things," John started. "Either this isn't a final holding area, or they aren't actually holding prisoners."

"What are you saying, John?" Rachel asked, her mind racing. What else were they doing with the people they grabbed if not imprisoning them.

"I'm saying the scale of this camp, based on the potential population of detainees, follows about the same proportions of either a temporary detention center, or Auschwitz," John replied flatly.

A collective gasp was heard, but it was Vicky who spoke first. "You can't seriously believe they are just executing people."

"No, actually, I don't. I think those trucks we mistook for supply trucks aren't supply trucks at all. They are prison transports. Which means tomorrow when it shows up, I need you to track it one way or the other to wherever it goes. Wherever they are bussing people, that's our next target after we put this detention camp out of business." John looked up at Mark. Mark could almost see the thoughts dancing behind those eyes. John had a hunch, but not one he cared to volunteer without evidence.

"Got it. We'll get 'em. To answer your other question, I have a few volunteers from the local area. Small world, one of them is our random hitter from the other night," Mark said, the humor obvious in his voice.

"You're shitting me," Andy exclaimed.

"Nope. We know him, kind of a friend of a friend. When we reached out to him and some other guys, he told us about what happened. Imagine his surprise when he found out someone finished the job he started," Mark explained. "He's in, all the way. He's kind of a loner, old-school prepper, lives on a homestead out in the sticks. He was a local firefighter for decades before he got sick of the fed trying to involve local LEOs and first responders in reporting and seizing firearms, so he told them to cram it and retired. Friend of his was a retired police officer who got nailed after doing some plinking at his private range. That's why he took a shot at your guy last night."

"Well, if we can count on a couple of willing hands, then I have one hell of an idea. Is there a Tractor Supply or similar in the local area?" John asked.

"Our neighbors are pretty well outfitted. Anything else we need I can get in town. What're you planning, John?" Mark asked, his curiosity piqued.

"Remember the Oklahoma City bombing?" John replied, grinning.

Later that afternoon, John, Andy, Mark, and Kevin sat in the living area discussing the plan that was brewing. Mark had gone into town, scoured used-car lots, and found a well-used fifteen-passenger van for peanuts, being sold without title for parts, then brought it back to the compound for Andy and John to look over.

Even without registration or any paper trail tracing the van to them, they still opted to take a chisel and hammer and stipple every VIN and serial number they could find throughout the entire vehicle. They then jettisoned the seats and most of the interior; then John put some of his woodworking experience to use and built a wall behind the driver and passenger seats. This they reinforced with sandbags, and they securely glued and screwed several inches of plywood to the floor, walls, and ceiling of the vehicle, and added more sandbags and more wood to hold it all in place.

Mark and Kevin kept out of their way, only volunteering tools and muscle for some of the heavier tasks. It also became apparent John would have to add some helper springs to the van's rear suspension to cope with the additional weight. A visit to a nearby farmer netted sufficient fertilizer to fill a sizeable portion of the van. After adding a few items, John had constructed a sizeable enough portion of ANFO to suitably breach the compound.

"Do I even want to know where you learned to make this thing, John?" Kevin asked hesitantly.

"Sure, the internet," John replied with a humorous smile. "Don't believe me, Google it. The information wasn't exactly a state secret after Tim McVeigh pulled this same stunt. They don't exactly teach this sort of thing in the Boy Scouts."

Kevin shook his head, surprised at the inventiveness of John and Andy. He knew by now he shouldn't be surprised when John dredged up some piece of history to provide the solution for a contemporary problem, but his near encyclopedic recounting of historical trivia still took some getting used to. "And the sandbags?"

"To direct the blast. I'm trying to keep this blast from flattening small structures and busting windows in the local community as much as I can. I want all the bang to go straight towards the wall," John explained. "That, and I'm thinking we hit the compound in one of the corners. Just in case we underestimated the scale of this package a little too much, we'll be a little farther away from the prisoners in the center.

Puts us right by the searchlights in that corner and the guard tower, but I'm sure Andy and I can keep them occupied to give our driver a little cover."

"It's pretty audacious, that's for sure," Kevin remarked.

"When is the question. What's going on in the camp?" John asked of Mark.

"The camp is in near full revolt. They're down to fifty or sixty people, best we can gather. Their guard towers are so hunkered down, when they can convince people to actually man them, they aren't even shooting at our drones anymore. Shorts has only ventured out of his office twice since Agent Johns showed up on their doorstep. We sighted the 'supply truck' entering the camp, and you were right, they are loading up prisoners. We'll track them and see where they're going. We're also relaying what we're learning to the other cells; we figure the same setup is in place nationwide. What they do with that information is on them," Mark said. It was apparent by his tone he had mixed feelings about the organization he had so readily thrown his support behind.

The Calm Before the Storm

That night, John sat with his wife and daughter. Dinner had been a welcome change from Andy and John's improvised rations, a mixture of MREs and Mountain House, or energy bars when they couldn't spare the time or risk smoke or a flame to cook. Rachel and Vicky had put on quite a spread for everyone at the compound. John had to think, but it sure seemed as though the ranks sitting down to the table had swollen over the past few weeks. Mark correctly guessed his thought.

"We've been adding to our numbers. Seems your and Andy's campaign against the local agency has garnered us a lot of support and emboldened a lot of people. I owe both of you a lot of credit for what you've done. It's been far more effective than I could have imagined," Mark offered genuinely.

John nodded his head, looking down at his plate distractedly. "I'm just doing my part, Mark. If it weren't for you, I probably wouldn't have made it this far."

"What's wrong?" Mark asked.

John's eyes turned up towards Mark. "Just a lot on my mind is all. I'll be fine by morning."

Mark opted not to push the issue. After dinner John had insisted on helping his wife clean the table and kitchen. Just a day after nearly losing his life in the altercation with Agent Johns, he did seem to be moving around with less soreness. One had to question how much of that was simply John being John, not wanting to let the discomfort deter him from any task he had set for himself. No one but John knew the agony he felt was less in his ribs and more in his heart.

John and Rachel sat on the back porch with their daughter, watching the stars and ruminating with their full bellies. John's hand held Rachel's firmly, as if he was afraid she would slip away while Kay sat in his lap. When the mosquitoes started biting, Kay went inside, leaving John and Rachel. "I want this to be over," John said somberly.

"I know, love, I do too," Rachel replied. She had struggled mightily with her emotions when John was away. As much as she calmed him, he calmed her. Their being conspicuously absent from each other's lives was something neither of them tolerated well. "Will taking down the camp end it?" she asked.

"It will end a battle. I doubt it will end the war. We have to find where the rest of these prisoners are. Mark's drone operator should have something for us any minute, but based on their direction, I'm guessing Angola," John said.

"I can't believe they would put people in there. Wasn't the ACLU lobbying to have that place shut down years ago. They called it a violation of human rights to subject people to that sort of treatment," Rachel emphasized.

"They did shut it down, but I suppose they don't consider gun owners to be people anymore," John said hotly. "Rachel, I'm afraid what I've done is going to destroy more lives than I can live with. Mark and Kevin were filling me in on the operational reports from other cells. Have you been following them?"

"Only what I've overheard," she replied.

"All around the country, people are openly shooting at and resisting agency attempts to confiscate firearms and arrest citizens. A month ago, we must have looked insane to do what we did. Now, it's like we were just the spark to set fire to the whole forest. This little insurrection is turning into a civil war, and most people don't study enough history to really respect just how bloody that will be. Neighbors are going to turn on neighbors, family on family; hundreds of thousand will die. That, or the people in power realize the price isn't worth paying and they do an immediate about-face and call this off. It's gotten to the point even if we shut down and stopped our assault, this wouldn't end.

It's grown bigger than us." John's words tumbled out, the pain in his voice obvious.

John, history nerd, Army veteran, prepper—he knew what was coming. The civil unrest would spread across the country, grinding society to a halt. Open hostilities would shut down public services and private businesses alike. Grocery stores would not restock; workers would not come to work; utilities would struggle to provide for the public. The end result of every civil war is that the citizenry suffers, and as society breaks down, the death toll always supersedes those lost from direct hostilities. Accounts of the Bosnian War and Sub-Saharan Africa provided a good portrait for what life in America could become in the very near future. This reality caused John such sadness he did not know the words for it. He had lashed out at four men trying to harm his family, and now innocent people would lose their lives because of it.

"John, what happens is not your fault. It is the fault of the people who sent those men to our home that morning. They set men like you on a collision course with their agents, they are responsible for the end result. You can't take all of this on yourself." Rachel's voice plead with her husband, not wanting to see him torture himself with guilt.

John nodded absentmindedly. He knew his wife was right, but he still felt incredible sadness for what would come next. That night, sleep was hard to find for John, but sleep did find him eventually. Rachel stayed up, holding her husband tightly to her. She knew any day could be his last, and she cherished every moment she spent with him. She fell into a fitful sleep huddled up against her husband's back, with her arms wrapped around him. Her dreams were of war, death, and loss. The war her husband had alluded to played out in her subconscious; the gunshots sounded incredibly real.

It was the sound of gunshots that she awoke to, to find an empty bed. A moment of anxiety gripped her before her waking mind reminded her of her husband's proclivity for being an early riser, and she quite the opposite. She dressed in the bare minimum to keep from flashing her current housemates and sought her husband.

She found him on the back deck of the house, crouched behind his bolt-action rifle. To his left was Andy, to his right was Kevin, all three down in the prone on shooting mats, peering through magnified optics on their long-range rifles. Far in the distance, she could just make out what looked like some sort of metal cans. Another gunshot rang out, startling her, and one of the cans jumped.

"Kevin, you shoot like you never stopped," John remarked to Kevin. It was just the night before Kevin had surprised John and Andy with the news that he had been a competitive F-Class shooter years ago. Based on Kevin's relentless ability to make hits on small targets, he hadn't lost his touch.

Kevin smiled to himself. "Thanks, John, you two aren't half bad yourselves. I can see why the agents in that camp have been having such a rough time. Looks like you both shoot right around one MOA."

John nodded behind his scope. "Yeah, but it's obvious you shot F-Class. That paint can out there isn't even giving you a challenge." John sat up on his heels and unloaded his rifle, taking a break and stretching his back. He glanced behind him to see his wife. "Hey, honey. Did we wake you?"

Rachel smiled and shook her head. Of course the sound of three rifles blasting paint cans off the back porch woke her up, but she couldn't bring herself to be aggravated with him. She saw a relaxed grin on his face she hadn't seen in weeks. He wasn't shooting people with wives and kids this morning, he was just out with his buddies doing some target shooting like he would have been years ago. He didn't have a care in the world, and for a brief moment she was thankful for that. She blew him a kiss and retreated into the house in search of a cup of coffee.

John returned his attention to the range just as Andy fired his 6.5 Creedmoor, solidly connecting with one of the paint cans at the other end of his Vortex optic. He drew the bolt to the rear, leaving it open and exposing his empty magazine. Kevin fired his last round and likewise left his bolt open. With all three rifles unloaded and safe, the men stood to stretch. "I tell you this much, the older I get, the more it hurts to lie down on a shooting mat," John groused.

Kevin smiled. "I can imagine, you two have a few years on me. I'm going to head into the shop after breakfast to load some ammo. I could use a hand if you don't mind. That and put a dry patch through the barrel. I don't want to mess with it much so I won't need a fouling shot later." The three collected their rifles and moved them to the shop, then headed off to the breakfast table.

Mark had silently watched the shooting exhibition from the window for a few minutes, wondering to himself how they had come to the point that even normally pacifist Kevin was ready to head off to battle. He questioned, not for the first time, why other men went off to fight while he stayed behind. Then his mind drifted to the news he had just learned: the final destination of the prison transport they had been surveilling. That was what he was pondering when John caught his glance.

On his way back to the house, John noticed a very worried look on Mark's face. John motioned Mark towards the workshop and led him through the door, gently shutting it behind him to give the two of them some privacy.

"What's wrong?" John asked.

"The prisoner transport just pulled into Angola. I'm sick to my stomach at the thought they actually reopened that hellhole and are putting people in there without trial. It's unconscionable." Mark's words just ran out of him.

"It makes sense though—plenty of room to house prisoners. It's away from the public eye; most people probably don't even realize it's come back online. And in the past decade or so, there's been tremendous pressure on these old maximum-security prisons to close down, so there's plenty in every state," John reasoned.

"That's the maddening part, John. All these bleeding hearts lobbied to have the max-security prisons declared uninhabitable, to crank up the regulations on prisons until no maximum-security institution could possibly operate, which forced their closure and pushed those prisoners into less secure prisons. Then they became overrun and overpopulated, which forced almost every state in the country to massively decriminalize nonviolent crimes.

I always looked at that as a victory, but the less secure prisons are wholly incapable of controlling hardened and violent criminals. Escapes became frequent; violence against guards soared; hell, the inmates run those prisons not the guards," Mark spat. "And now, after our criminal justice system has been stripped to the bone, after all the legislative grandstanding and screaming about poor living conditions and overcrowding, they are cramming tens of thousands of everyday citizens into those same cells because the government demanded they give up their rights or else, and they DARED to say no."

John hadn't seen this side of Mark. He was passionate, angry, and distraught. John questioned in his own mind how much of the idea of the man's sister sitting in a cell with three or four other people weighed on his mind. "The people you're referring to, Mark, they've proven on every other issue to change their stripes at the party's insistence. Criminals in jail cells bother them, but we are worse than criminals. We dared to question the eminent brilliance and righteousness of the state, and for that we deserve any punishment we get," John said, his sarcasm as evident as his disdain. John was an ardent Libertarian, some would even accuse him of being an anarchist. His ideal was not one based on an absence of rules, but the absence of rulers. He had always feared that the state would one day amass enough power in the name of "fairness" that it would regress into the same tyranny the colonists had fought. He was saddened at the realization that it had come to pass in his own lifetime.

"Mark, let's you and me sit and have a really frank conversation." John started lighting a cigar. He unholstered his sidearm, which he now made a regular habit of wearing, unloaded it, and started to disassemble it for cleaning. "We both agree we have to hit that detention camp. That's our current end goal. We have nowhere near the numbers to pull that off, and we need an intermediate step to bolster our force and demoralize theirs. I'm figuring taking one of their prison transports ought to accomplish both if we can pull it off. Maybe then we'll have a fighting chance at taking the camp itself without getting our asses shot to pieces."

Mark's eyes flitted up to John's, the look bordering on panic.

"Now settle your nerves. I don't think we're going to meet our maker; I'm just realistic about what could happen. We may not all come home; none of us may. That's just life. If things look bad enough, I'll call full retreat and we'll scatter and return here. What I'm asking you is what then? The natural progression seems to be we go shut down Angola after this local camp, get those people out of there. That's an operation we have nowhere near the manpower for, and we need a lot of support to even consider it. Maybe more than all the Minuteman cells in the whole state. But even if that isn't our next move, what is?"

Mark pondered John's question. He had never considered what their next move was. Truthfully, he hadn't expected them to get this far. John and Andy had cut a swath through the agency's local assets, making a run at the camp an actual possibility. But John was right, to go after Angola with its high walls and guard towers with what they had was absolute suicide. "I don't know, John. Hadn't gotten that far," Mark said with resignation.

"Well, do some thinking about it. I hate to break the band up when we have some more concert days ahead of us," John said easily. His CZ was already cleaned, just a little wipe down and a few drops of oil on the moving parts was all that was needed, and he began reassembling. The double *click* of his handgun sliding into the holster and the active retention being engaged snapped Mark's attention back to the present from his musings. John turned on his heel and headed for the door.

"John, what would it take to hit Angola? To have a legitimate chance at tearing that place down and freeing those people?" Mark asked.

"We would need a goddamned army, Mark," John said as he passed through the doorway.

The Hunter Becomes the Hunted

John found his wife and daughter sitting down for breakfast with an empty chair and full plate between them. He sat, drawing an arm around his daughter's shoulders and dropping a hand to his wife's thigh, then turned his attention to the bacon and eggs that set his mouth watering. Vicky, George, and Kevin joined them. Several men filed through the kitchen and took plates out towards the barracks, while one gentleman older than the rest lagged behind. "Mind if I sit with you folks?" the newcomer asked.

John couldn't get the words out through a mouth full of food, but emphatically waved to an empty chair. Once he got his mouth clear, he asked, "Would you be the gentleman who took that shot at our agent the other night?"

"Yes, son, that was me," Randall said evenly. He was average height, with white hair and a handlebar mustache. He hardly had the look of a man who would take a shot at a stranger he'd never laid eyes on before, more like your favorite uncle.

John nodded his head. "I'm sure Mark or Kevin already told you we got him later that evening. We were actually on our way to get him when you took a shot at him."

Randall nodded. "Don't know what came over me. I saw that guy with government plates on his car and thought of my friend. He spent thirty years of his life protecting this area, and some of his own trainees hauled him off to that damned camp. I guess I'd been holding a grudge," he said simply.

It was that moment Andy made his way to the table, his eyes searching for coffee. John slid him a cup, which he filled from the pot on the table. He nursed it gingerly as his eyes slowly opened to regard the newcomer to the table. "Do I know you?" he said questioningly.

"Nope," Randall said simply.

After breakfast, John retreated to the workshop to help Kevin load some match ammo to replenish what they had shot that morning. John had, upon his first trip to this room, immediately noticed the small desk in the corner with the reloading gear. The press was a simple green RCBS single stage, not unlike the one John had at his own bench at home. Kevin had apparently been slowly processing brass for several days, getting ready for the day it would all need to be loaded.

"I couldn't get enough matching head stamp brass to do a lot of load tuning for everyone else's rifles, but I did go through them and cull the ones with drastically different internal volumes. I'm loading 168-grain Sierra MatchKings in all of them over 42.5 grains IMR 4064 since a lot of our guys are shooting .308 Winchester," Kevin explained.

John nodded. "Same load shoots under a minute in my gun. I've got about a hundred loaded if you or your guys want to take them with you. They're loaded on damned near the same equipment you have here, and all the same headstamp."

"I'll take you up on that, though I could use a hand loading the rest if you can spare some time," Kevin said.

While he and John worked to convert the box of bullets and bucket of brass into useable, match-grade ammunition, John asked Andy to spend some time loading magazines for their rigs. Per John's request, he wanted one magazine with twenty-eight rounds for his rifle (he always liked to download a magazine two rounds to keep loaded on a closed bolt), three magazines for his plate carrier, and one more for the speed holster on his battle belt. That satisfied, plus Andy's magazines loaded, he then set about loading every spare magazine he and John had to store in assault packs for the two of them. Normally, the two of them would be carrying a fair amount of ammo, but balanced against the need for shelter parts, food, water bladders, etc. Indeed, the two of them typically carried a medium rucksack each and dropped them hundreds of yards back in the woods before they would resume their antagonization of the camp.

136

This time, they were carrying much smaller packs filled almost exclusively with loaded magazines and spare medical gear to supplement their IFAKs. The idea was if they were stuck there long enough to need food or shelter, they were both dead already.

John took note of a third set of equipment on the bench where Andy was working. His puzzled look caught Kevin's eye. "I hauled that out of my footlocker in my room. Figured just in case, I'd better check it out and get loaded up." John was looking at a FAL, a nicely built one apparently off a demilled parts kit, sitting on the bench next to a body armor set similar to his own. The FAL shot 7.62 NATO, and while it lacked ammo commonality with more ubiquitous AR-15s, it gained a sizable range and power advantage. "You've got good taste, Kevin. Now I see why you keep stocked up on . 308 brass."

Meanwhile, in the wood line east of the Minuteman compound, the lookout gazed west through a high-power spotting scope down the road. Traffic was a rarity this far out of town, but it had been drilled into them over and over the importance of acting as the cell's early warning were a raid to come to their doorstep. The tripod-mounted spotting scope's 60X magnification lent a considerable advantage to the spotter in this endeavor. A speck on the distant horizon could be easily seen, a distant vehicle identified, and precious minutes of advantage given to the cell if he spotted a potentially hostile vehicle. Most days went with him calling in an approaching vehicle, obviously civilian, and listening to the lookout on the other side confirm it did not stop nor double back towards the compound. He reflected on how he came to this moment, sitting in the woods swatting at bugs while his friends were all out chasing skirt at the local state college.

He had been barely a teenager, but unlike many teens, he didn't want video games and the latest electronics. His home was littered with mounts and trophies from his father's long hunting career. Richard Senior, called Jack by everyone in creation to distinguish him from his son, had spent time overseas as a professional game guide before returning to the United States to continue the trade. That was barely two years before hunting game became so heavily regulated it was impossible to make any kind of a living helping people hunt. His father didn't take too kindly to the intrusion into his career and personal life by the government, but being close to retirement age anyway, he made do. Growing up the son of a lifelong hunter, what Richard really wanted was a rifle of his own. Not the little 10/22 he had shot for years, on its third barrel already, but a big-boy centerfire rifle like his dad's .308 or .30-06. It was with phenomenal irritation then that his father had to explain that such firearms could not be simply bought and given to "children," as had been common years prior.

"What do you mean I can't have a rifle? I've been shooting since I was eight," Richard asked emphatically.

Jack sighed, thinking this would be difficult to explain to a reasonable person, let alone a thirteen-year-old. "Son, the government passed laws making it so you can't own any centerfire rifle till you're twenty-one. Even then, you got to apply for this crazy-ass license, and I hear a lot of people are getting turned down. Even the ones who have been hunting for years."

Richard's face betrayed pure puzzlement and outrage at the idea. "But don't you have a LOT of those rifles already? What about those?"

"Son, if you take one of those rifles out of this house with your own two hands, you may be arrested. I don't mean like the sheriff will bring you back here, or I'll have to go pick you up at the station, I mean straight to prison because you are in possession of a centerfire rifle without a license. Maybe when you're older we can get you licensed, but right now, it just isn't possible. I'm sorry, son."

It wasn't two years later the rifles Jack owned weren't just heavily regulated, they didn't just require a license, they had to be registered, just like "assault weapons" years prior. Jack trusted his government about as well as many people did, and refused to. Richard was not with his father when he was stopped at a checkpoint in town and his old lever-action rifle discovered behind the seat of his old pickup truck.

From friends of his father, he heard that he had been arrested for being in possession of an unregistered centerfire rifle and had been taken to prison for it. Jack had never cheated on his taxes, never harmed a person, Richard didn't think he'd ever heard his father have a cross word with anyone. Just having a damned rifle made him a criminal.

He had just returned his eye to the spotting scope after a stretch and rubbing his sore eye when he could just make out an approaching vehicle far off in the distance. "New York calling on channel." The decision had been made months prior to assign call signs of New York and Washington to the roadside lookouts, along with Cali and Florida to the wood line sentries south of the compound to disguise their relative locations. "Vehicle approaching. Cannot identify yet. Over." He heard the distinctive double clicks of someone keying the mic twice to confirm receipt, then returned his attention to the eyepiece. The vehicle was dark colored, probably a truck based on height, but he couldn't be sure till it approached closer.

Then the lookout on the other side called in, "Washington. I see a second vehicle behind the first, following very close."

As the seconds ticked by, New York and Washington came to the same conclusion almost simultaneously, which sent their hearts into their throats. "New York. Hostiles inbound. I repeat, hostiles inbound!" The east side lookout had just identified two agency Humvees, painted black, closing on the compound at high speed. He prayed and willed them to continue on their way and not stop, until he saw the front bumper of the lead truck dip and the rear truck slow to match it.

In the workshop no one had a radio, but John heard the flurry of activity in the main room and stuck his head out the doorway. "What's wrong?" he asked of the first person who ran by.

The man's wild eyes and fear told the story before his words could. "Agents, they're here!"

John whirled in place, almost running full steam into Andy and Kevin. "Grab your rifles!" he bellowed to them. The three men launched themselves at the kits Andy had just been prepping, throwing on body armor and loading rifles. John ran into the main area, grabbing a radio and turning up the volume. "Two trucks just turned down the main drive heading to the compound. No air assets apparent. I count at least three or four guys per truck."

"Sonofabitch!" John exclaimed to himself. His thoughts immediately turned to his wife and daughter. He didn't see them in the main room, nor out the back door. In the moment his indecision got the best of him; should he make ready to defend the compound, or run to his family's aid? Could he even find them before the agents hit the front door? "Cali and Florida, any report?" John yelled into the mic.

"No report, all quiet down here," came the reply.

"New York and Washington, if anyone goes to flank the building, you two had better let us know in advance. Hold your position. Be our eyes." He didn't wait for a reply. "Andy!" he yelled.

Andy turned the corner, walking quickly but unhurriedly, rifle at low ready, armored up for a fight. The weeks spent with John outside the relative safety of the compound had worn a kind of quiet confidence in situations like this into him, and John couldn't see an inch of panic on his face. Only resolve.

"I need you and Kevin to hold that front door. If you hear guys coming around the sides of the house to the back door, you all collapse down that damned hallway. You can't let them hit you in the nose and the ass at the same time, you'll be cut to pieces."

"Where you going?" Andy asked. No reproach, all business.

"I have to find Rachel and Kay." John's eyes communicated the panic his voice did not.

"Go, I got this," Andy said. He began directing traffic, barking orders. A month ago, his harsh voice and profanity would not have been received well. Today, with agents on their doorstep, suddenly everyone appreciated having their own tamed wolves in the henhouse.

Everyone cleared the living area, retreating to the back of the house, while Andy and Kevin stacked up behind cover, aiming at the front door.

John raced down the hallway to the bedrooms. "Rachel!" he called out.

When Mark ran into the hallway, he was nearly thrown clear through a wall by 240 pounds of armored freight train carrying a rifle. "John, I've got them. They're with my family in a safe room. We're good," Mark said emphatically. He recognized the mental state John was in, and it took a second for the realization to hit him.

"Then get a rifle and stay with them. Anyone but us comes through that door, Mark, you burn them down, no hesitation." John turned and ran rapidly back to the living room as the sound of a wooden doorframe being struck with a battery ram sounded through the house. John thanked himself for insisting that door be reinforced as a precaution.

John had taken the liberty, and hadn't really asked Mark for permission to modify his house, of heavily reinforcing the front and back doors. The cheap hardware-store screws securing the doorjambs, frame, hinges, and strikers had been replaced by three- and four-inch deck screws. John would've preferred more invasive strengthening, but settled for less obtrusive but still effective. It must've worked reasonably well since the ram bounced off the heavy wooden door rather than simply knocking the frame in, but John saw daylight and knew one more strike would send the door in. He shouldered his rifle, brought the red dot to bear on the front door, and waited.

Beep, beep. "Two runners heading around back!!!" sang the radio.

John's attention turned from the front door to Kevin and Andy on the other side of the living room. They had taken up positions to shield themselves as best they could from the front door, but they were sitting ducks to an attack from the back of the house. He yelled as loud as he could for them to fall back to him, but it was too late. The front door came off its hinges.

John immediately turned his attention to the two agents running in behind the falling door. At ranges inside a typical home, aiming was not a time-intensive nor careful chore, and it was not now. John's rifle tracked right to left in pursuit of the black-clad men from the doorway. Every time his glowing red reticle struck one of the men, his finger began a rapid staccato tapping of the trigger, sending 55-grain full-metal-jacket rounds sailing across the room towards his targets. He struck each man several times in the side, neck, and arm. As the first two men fell, he tracked back towards the door in search of more targets. This entire turn of events was not consciously contemplated by John, nor by Andy or Kevin on the other side of the room, it was simple training put into action. They did not have to burden their minds with additional time spent sifting through the faces looking for foes or friends, anyone coming through the open doorway after it had been knocked in was by definition unfriendly.

John's mind just barely registered the sound of the back door being shot off its hinges, apparently by a shotgun meant for breaching doors. As the door sagged inwards, time slowed to a crawl. The rifle in John's hands felt unnaturally heavy and sluggish to turn, but turn it did towards the back door. Andy and Kevin were laying down fire on the front door while shielding themselves from return fire, and neither could afford the seconds to confront this threat to their rear. John assumed two assailants, but could not count on the odds only being that lopsided. He placed his reticle on the chest of the first agent, tapped the trigger twice, and the third time was not greeted by the feeling of recoil and the flash of a round being discharged. He felt and heard nothing but an empty rifle.

As the first man fell, his partner raised his rifle in John's direction. John dove to the floor, knowing the drywall corner he hid behind would offer him no cover from the incoming fire. The sounds of gunfire rang out as John released his grip from his rifle and moved to unholster his sidearm. With a practiced movement, his thumb came down to disengage the active retention of the Blade-Tech duty holster; then he firmly pulled upwards toward his armpit to unholster the gun.

He rolled to his side to bring the gun into a two-handed grip, extended his arms, placed the front post on his assailant, and pulled the trigger just as the agent had finished swinging his rifle to his left to fire at Andy and Kevin.

John's first shot went wide, barely missing. In John's haste, he had not accounted for the fact that handgun sights are calibrated to be fired with the handgun oriented vertically, and with the gun held sideways in John's improvised position, the sights required correction. He adjusted and tapped the trigger twice, dropping the agent. He rolled in the other direction to check the front door, seeing no more movement there, then stood and approached the agent he had just shot to find him writhing on the floor. He stomped heavily on the wrist of the man's arm that was holding his rifle, crushing the small bones and causing the hand to go limp. He then produced a small knife to cut the man's sling and disarm him. He likewise removed his sidearm.

"Kevin, Andy, you two okay? Anyone outside check in!" John shouted into the mic while scanning the home. He counted one dead agent at the back door, one he was holding his handgun on, and six by the front door. He hoped that was all of them. "Kevin, Andy, answer me!"

Mark entered his once quiet living room, his AR-15 held at low ready, and his face fell. Andy was on his back, with Kevin working feverishly to get his body armor off.

When Luck Runs Out

"That lucky son of a bitch," John said to no one in particular. He was sitting on the back porch, smoking a cigar with a clenched fist while trying mightily not to crush it. Rachel sat next to him, holding her husband. She had not felt fear like this since the day their own home had been raided, and she had allowed herself to believe Mark's compound was a place of safety for her and her daughter. She now realized how incredibly naive that assumption had been, both hers and everyone else's. There was no safe place anymore.

When John threw himself to the floor, the agent had incorrectly assumed he had struck his target and moved to engage the two men to his left. John's first shot missed just as the agent fired his first shot from his M4 at Andy, striking him in the side. Kevin immediately recognized the danger and swiveled his rifle towards this new threat, but there was no way he would beat the agent to the shot that would kill him. It was with mingled wonder and mercy, then, that John's next few 9 mm shots rang out from his CZ, striking the agent and knocking him down. John, knowing 9 mm had no chance of penetrating any Level 3 armor the agent was likely to be wearing, hurried to the agent to disarm him and ensure he was really out of the fight. It was at that moment Kevin looked down to Andy's prone shape on the floor and saw the blood running out from under his armor.

Kevin had immediately flipped Andy onto his back and began unfastening his armor, fearing the worst.

"Motherfucker, watch it!" Andy bellowed. He hadn't decided if he was hit or not, feeling the pain but not the impact of the agent's shot. Right at that moment, he felt a searing pain in his side that was greatly exasperated by Kevin's rough handling.

"Hold still, dammit!" Kevin shouted to Andy as he cleared his armor and yanked up his shirt. Kevin discovered the round had creased Andy's side and just grazed him. A few inches one way, he would have had a punctured lung and almost certainly have died. A few inches the other way, the agent would have missed entirely. Life in a firefight was just that way.

John reflected on the last ten minutes of his life, on how fast their luck had changed TWICE. He now worked to calm his nerves and steady himself for what had to come, when Rachel spoke. "I thought we were safe here."

"So did Mark. So did I. I feel foolish for that now, but I admit it." John sighed. "Not that this changes anything."

"THIS doesn't change anything?!" Rachel nearly screamed. "Your friend got shot, you almost got shot again, and eight agents just ripped our only safe haven wide open! What hasn't changed?!" Her eyes searched the side of her husband's face for some clue as to the insanity that had gripped her husband.

"Nothing. We were going to hit that prison transport tonight, and we still are. If we don't keep these agents off balance, I promise you those eight agents will be followed by eighty tomorrow. Then five hundred next week. What do you think would have happened if we'd sat in our home waiting for the next round of agents instead of retreating here? Well, honey, this is the Alamo. There is nowhere else to go. Either we keep fighting, or we abandon the fort and scatter. We've come too far for that," John explained.

Rachel's mind raced. She could not immediately decide whether to hug her husband or strangle him. She couldn't figure out how a man who had just seen a friend shot and who had murdered a half dozen men could maintain such control of his emotions. He barely looked upset by the events. Then she realized worryingly, she couldn't read his emotions at all. Before she could form her thoughts, Mark poked his head out the back door.

"John, we stripped him down to his boxers and zip-tied him to a chair in the shop," Mark reported. Those were the orders John had left everyone with right after he hollered to Kevin and Vicky to tend Andy's wound.

"And you're sure he can't wiggle his way free?" John asked.

"Not a chance. Kevin was so enthusiastic with the zip ties, I'd be surprised if he can feel his fingers and toes," Mark replied without hesitation.

"Post a guard, with a sidearm, with strict instructions not to talk to or even look at that asshole. Let him sit there for an hour and sweat before I go in there and ask him a few questions," John said. His voice did not waver, but his tone indicated he had far more than questions in mind. Mark's stomach turned as his mind contemplated what John planned.

John stood to go in and check on Andy. "How're you feeling, peckerhead?"

Andy glanced up at him, grimacing. "Alcohol ain't for pouring into open wounds, it's for drinking. I'm sure that's why this hurts so bad."

"Quit your bellyaching. If your wound gets infected, you're a dead man. You're lucky that agent rushed the shot," John said good-naturedly. "I do wish I'd caught him with my first shot; you wouldn't even have had a scratch," he said seriously.

Andy grabbed John's arm hard. "Don't you sit there and feel sorry for me. We won; that's all that matters. I'm alive. You got the bastard before he shot me again and killed Kevin. Don't fall on your sword, 'cause you can't save everyone."

John nodded his head, patted his friend's shoulder, and turned to leave. "Vicky," he started.

"I've got him, John," she replied sincerely.

He nodded his head and went to the TOC to find Mark and Kevin.

"What's the radio chatter saying?" John asked.

Kevin looked up from his terminal. "Lot of chatter about their missing team, even their lead guy, Shorts, is demanding they check in. I'm not sure if they're that shorthanded he's answering radio calls, or that frantic they aren't answering."

"Any indication if they know this cell is here? Was this a random hit, planned? Did they act on a tip?

We need to figure out really fast if we've been made." John voiced the same worry everyone at the compound was feeling.

"Haven't heard anything, and honestly, John, the way these guys operate, if they knew this cell was here, they would've sent every agent they had. Or called in the damned Air Force to stick a bomb through our roof. They're not that incompetent," Kevin reasoned.

John couldn't argue with his rationale, but he worried about what conclusions they would draw now that eight armed agents had failed to return from their raid. The natural conclusion was that whatever resistance they had encountered was substantial and merited an overwhelming response by all agency assets that could be brought to bear.

"Alright, let me know if anything changes," John said, turning towards the shop.

Mark looked up. "What are you going to do?"

John's eyes darkened. "I'm going to start with a bucket of water and a towel; then I'm going to go ask some questions. And I had better get some answers that make sense. Or I'm going to get a blowtorch and some pliers, then ask those same questions again."

Mark struggled to hold John's smoldering gaze. "You're going to torture him?"

John just glared at Mark. "No, I'm going to make him a glass of warm tea and wrap him in a blanket. Maybe rub his shoulders. Hell, I might just strip down and spoon with the bastard before I politely ask him what's on my mind."

"John, you can't seriously—" Mark started before he realized he was looking down the barrel of a handgun and listening to the sound of a hammer being thumbed back.

"You going to stop me, Mark? Or do you want a piece of what that agent has coming to him? You just say the word, 'cause it makes no difference if he sees Jesus today by himself or has some company." John's diatribe wasn't angry, it was cold. His eyes were not clouded in emotion, they were like the eyes of a snake staring at prey. Mark felt his heart skip a beat, and he finally realized who and what John had become.

All the men's lives he had taken, all of the blood, all of the violence. John had turned from a friend into a pure predator, and he was trying to figure out if Mark was his equal or his prey.

The room stood silent. No one even breathed. Mark could feel sweat dribble down the back of his neck. "John, I am not your enemy." That sounded lame even to Mark, but it was all the command of the English language he could manage at that moment. The fear he felt was incredible.

"John," Rachel's voice called gently.

John's face softened, but the gun did not waver. His finger might have eased its pressure on the face of the trigger, but it did not move.

"John, this isn't the way. These people aren't your enemy. Your enemy isn't in that shop either. He's waiting at that detention camp. He is whoever sent them all to hunt us." Rachel's voice soothed.

"Then why do I feel like I have to fight a war out there, then come back here and fight another war? Why should I listen to the pissing and moaning of these people? They aren't wolves. Wolves do not care for the opinion of sheep," John spat.

"You are not a wolf, dear. You're a sheepdog. Sheepdogs do not tear the throat out of sheep, because that is not who they are. You are not a wolf." Her voice was patient, but firm.

John's shoulders dropped ever so slightly.

"Love, you've been fighting so long you're forgetting why you started in the first place. You killed the first man to protect your family, not for the sake of killing. You've killed dozens, maybe hundreds, but you aren't a killer. You are not a wolf."

Seconds dragged by, feeling like hours to everyone present. Then a click was heard through the room and everyone flinched. John had hit the decocker on his sidearm. He holstered the gun and lowered himself to the floor, taking a knee. Everyone held their breath as Rachel walked forward to put her hand on the back of her husband's neck.

John felt the stinging of the first tear slip past his eyelid. His emotions rushed out: shame, fear, remorse, guilt, anxiety, depression. He had almost lost control of himself. He had actually drawn a gun on Mark, a man who had saved him and his family. Even he couldn't put into words everything that ran through his mind right then.

The tears came, and everyone in the room sat or stood silently and watched John's shoulders heave. Mark had come within fractions of an inch of dying, and all he could think of was the stress this man must have been under to cause such a drastic change in his personality. An hour ago, he had been good-natured, lighthearted. He had been eating breakfast with his wife and daughter, content with his life for that moment. Then he had changed once again into a vicious fighter and was finding it so difficult to change back, he had very nearly killed another man who had not threatened him. Mark wondered not for the first time if his luck would run out, and this man would be the death of him or someone else.

Rachel looked up to Mark, her eyes saying what her words could not. She knew her husband was hurting, but she felt the remorse that he felt for his actions. "Give me a few minutes with him, please."

Mark could only nod his head, and she gathered him to his feet and led him out of the room. Mark caught himself thinking for just a moment how childlike John's mannerisms were at that moment. How scared and incredibly sad he looked, how his wife drew her arm around his broad shoulders to comfort him, and how he clung to her. It was like watching a man come apart at the seams and hold onto someone else for their very life.

"Holy shit," Kevin said in a whisper. "Mark, he's even more on the edge than I thought."

"Kevin, he's more on the edge than I think any of us thought," Mark agreed.

"What do we do?" Kevin asked, looking to Mark.

What do we do? Mark thought. *Like I know what the fuck to do.* Mark ushered everyone else back to work while he wondered how to deal with one of his men pointing a loaded handgun at him. He of all people knew time was running out, and one of the most important pieces of their plan was on the verge of a mental breakdown.

Shattered

Andy charged down the hallway, only wincing in those moments he pulled on the bandage around his side. He was heading for John and Rachel's room after he had heard someone say John had almost shot Mark, and he felt incredible urgency to reach his friend. He lifted his hand to knock, stopped for just a moment to soften what was sure to be a heavy fist against a door, and gently rapped his knuckles on the door. A few seconds passed, and he was greeted with the face of a very worried Rachel.

"What the hell happened? Someone said John almost shot Mark," Andy said in a loud whisper.

Rachel motioned him in and shut the door, for him to come face-to-face with his friend sitting on the edge of the bed, looking down at the floor, completely unresponsive. He stepped forward to grab his friend, but Rachel's grip on his arm was savage and insistent.

"Andy, I think he's had a psychotic break. He won't talk. He doesn't answer to his name. He's gone," Rachel said, a thin shade of panic on the edge of her words.

"What happened?" Andy repeated.

Rachel looked from the worried face of a good friend to the blank face of her husband, and she wondered the same thing. John was not sitting on the bed, in a room with his wife and close friend. John was in his own mind, reliving weeks of violence in gruesome detail...

John was sitting in the improvised blind he and Andy had constructed earlier from a bush they'd hacked the center out of and layered with additional branches and foliage. It provided them fair concealment from every angle but directly behind them and allowed one man to crawl forward into a makeshift firing point, while the other stayed behind them to defend their unprotected back.

John would normally be firing his .308 Winchester bolt action off its mounted bipod, but the position he was in precluded that. Instead, he rested his rifle in the crotch of two branches and peered through his 12X riflescope at his target. He watched a man tell some joke to the other man in the guard tower and meander around aimlessly; then the man jerked as if someone had struck him in the chest with a sledgehammer as John's 168-grain Sierra MatchKing struck him high in the chest. John had been lining up his shot, increasing the pressure on the trigger between breaths, and hadn't even realized the rifle was about to fire until the rifle jerked and bellowed.

John and Andy had collected intelligence on a group of these agents for a few days. Unlike many of their counterparts, these had rented a local house just off the compound and preferred the relative luxury. The tricky part about dealing with these four was the house's proximity to noncombatants, and John desperately wanted to prevent collateral damage. He also understood they would only have one bite at this particular apple, so eliminating all four... targets was a requirement. A bomb of sufficient scale to ensure all four deaths would, by design, be large enough to severely damage neighboring homes. Too small, and the men's dispersion throughout the house would allow survivors. John opted for multiple bombs, command detonated via a throwaway cell phone.

Eight small bombs were attached around the doorframe, little more than pipe bombs and ball bearings wrapped in duct tape, hooked up to a common detonator. Two more were placed in a cabinet in the kitchen, a cabinet in the only bathroom, and one in each of the beds of the house. That evening, when the last man had walked through the doorway, Andy and John rapidly dialed each of the predetermined numbers and listened to the irregular banging noises emanating from the home as the devices detonated around the house. Andy saw one man, bloody from head to toe and looking like the world's biggest shotgun had hit him, stumble screaming out the front door before John silenced him with his rifle.

Hitting supply trucks was ridiculously easy, since they ran on a constant schedule and on the same route. John wondered if the supply convoys that had run to his post in Iraq were this dim-witted, or if they had actually given the insurgents some sort of challenge. Once Mark had figured out the weekly schedule and rough timing and related that to John, John picked a section of rock and shelled road off the main highway leading to the detention camp and, under cover of darkness, had buried an IED directly in the path of the truck. Cribbing from history, a pressure cooker filled with black powder, buried only a few inches below the surface, would suffice to stop the truck in its tracks.

The next day, when the truck came along and ran atop the device, it was remote detonated by a waiting John and Andy. The device, true to John's predictions, was insufficient to disable or destroy the truck, but was more than sufficient to shock the driver and grind the truck to a halt. He was immediately confronted by two men with rifles standing in front of his truck. "Park it and get lost," came the order, with the rifle providing the "or else." He did as instructed while Andy shot the lock off the back of the truck and hurled a Molotov cocktail in, immolating the contents.

One agent, apparently enjoying an evening off, was followed to a local movie theater. John picked the seat directly behind the agent and patiently waited for the few other attendees to become absorbed in the movie while he put on a pair of nitrile gloves. John thanked his lucky stars this was an unpopular movie and there were fewer potential witnesses as he drew a knife from his pocket, leaned forward, and quickly ran it across the right side of the agent's neck, severing his jugular. The man jerked and reached for his neck, only for John to repeat the motion on the other side, then drop the knife and walk briskly towards the emergency exit.

Andy sat outside with the engine running in the closest parking spot he could manage. When he saw John, he shifted into drive and quickly pulled up to the curb as John shed his gloves and jumped inside. The two were leaving the parking lot within seconds, disappearing into the night.

One afternoon John and Andy went back to John's home to survey the damage and see if John could recover any of his cached gear and preps. The men shoved the door, left knocked off its hinges, out of the way and entered to find a house torn apart. Whether by the agents' hands or vandals afterwards, there was little left of John and Rachel's once happy home. John was able to recover some additional ammo caches he had buried in the backyard, and several weeks' worth of Mountain House freeze-dried food stored in the attic away from prying eyes. John tried to salvage what pictures and keepsakes he could for his wife, but much had been damaged or was missing. John's anger at the reminder of this intrusion flared, and he quickly hatched a plan.

He and Andy cleared the house, sealed up all of the broken windows, propped the door back up in its frame and taped it shut, cracked the gas lines for several large appliances, and attached a homemade incendiary device to the front door. They then walked out the back door and called in an anonymous tip...on John's own home. For added effect, John racked off a full thirty-round magazine in the backyard, guaranteeing lots of calls from panicked neighbors.

When two teams of agents arrived, anxious to discover the source of the gunfire and make an arrest, and reached the front door, the result was immediate. All eight men were engulfed in the hellish inferno. The two who were far enough away to escape their immediate death were shot by John from the tree line. Damage to neighboring houses was unavoidable, but John felt abandoned by these people who hadn't lifted a finger to help his family and cared little.

John and Andy had identified one man, a "field supervisor," and made note that though he drew a vehicle from the camp's motor pool, it was always the same one. His job, as best John could tell, was to drive around and find shady spots to recline his seat and take a nap. It was during one of these moments of slumber that John low-crawled to his vehicle and quietly attached a device to the bottom of his SUV directly under the driver's seat. The magnets ensured it would not be dislodged; two pounds of ANFO and miscellaneous screws and bolts provided the punch.

John worried the device would not penetrate the floor (he had experience overseas with armored Humvees and knew about the armor they wore on their undersides, though he couldn't be sure this SUV was so equipped) and came to a solution. They followed this supervisor to his next stop, waited till he exited his vehicle and had both feet firmly on the ground less than a foot from their homemade claymore, and detonated it. He survived the immediate blast but would almost certainly lose the use of both legs for life if he managed not to bleed to death.

After the Minutemen had lost their man inside (they told him now would be a good time to resign, for his own safety) they began tracking and vectoring Andy and John towards agents on confiscation missions via drones stationed around the camp. John and Andy preferred to set up complex ambushes for the agents, with good cover and predesignated lanes of fire, when possible, but occasionally time did not allow. On days like today, they resorted to that favorite tactic of terrorists everywhere and set up a simple ambush.

With the drone feeding them heading and location information, John and Andy did not have to tail the vehicle. They simply set themselves on an intercept course, pulled over, and popped their hood. John's CZ was sitting on top of the Jeep's engine, Andy's AR-15 sitting in the hatch. When the agents pulled up to the stop sign and stopped, both men jumped into action. Twenty-one rounds of 9 mm Parabellum were fired through the front windshield of the SUV at the two agents there, while Andy emptied a full thirty-round magazine of 5.56 at a glancing angle through the vehicle to get to the agents in the back seat. Neither saw movement as they reloaded.

On another such occasion, John had improvised a more daring tactic when they did not have a route to get ahead of the agents. They had secured two twelve-gauge pump-action shotguns, loaded with one-ounce slugs, and when the agents were stopped at a red light, they pounced. Both men jumped out of the vehicle, rapidly approached the agents' SUV from behind, and emptied both shotguns full of slugs through the back window directly at the seated men.

The noise was deafening, and the effect both brutal and to the point. None of the four men even had time to take the safety off of their weapons.

Towards the end of their campaign, when the guard towers were only sporadically manned, John began using a . 22 rimfire rifle with an improvised silencer to start knocking out the searchlights. It became obvious very quickly the camp did not have many spare bulbs, as they stopped coming on at night. John was unsure if this was to prevent further harassment, or a lack of parts, but either way gave John the result he wanted.

He quietly crept up to the front gate of the compound one morning, with a large backpack on his back. The pack contained a large quantity of black powder John and Andy had made from saltpeter, charcoal, and sulfur. Also in the pack were several ziplock bags full of gasoline to which they had added a quantity of gelatin. The ignition device was a simple friction device hooked to a pull tab that John affixed to the gate opposite the one the pack was secured to.

The next morning, when the first vehicle went to leave the camp and opened the gate, the agent was greeted by a cacophony of noise and a hellish inferno that quickly set the front gate ablaze, to say nothing of the vehicles and the agents. Three men were burned critically, two more suffered severe smoke inhalation, one Humvee nearly destroyed by fire, and an entire day's worth of operations scrubbed tending the damage caused.

Living in the field, or out of Andy's Jeep, was taking its toll. The men struggled mightily to keep their hygiene acceptable and prevent any infections. Blisters were a constant struggle as well because of the humidity, sweat, and often wet environment they operated from. Ticks and mosquitoes were plentiful, making Andy wish for the cold and snow of his home state, and despite John's intense distaste for snow, he almost agreed. Showers were via baby wipes, blister care was duct tape, and meals were whatever they had packed or scrounged. Beards grew wild on their faces. For all their efforts to take care of themselves, the constant effort, walking, and marginal nutrition caused them both to lose a little weight.

It was a welcome reprieve for them to head back to Mark's for a few nights of good meals, reloading, planning, and bomb making in the shop.

The killing was awful. John felt as if he lost a part of his soul with every life he took. He wondered where the line between freedom fighter and terrorist really was. It was during these moments of reflection he questioned so many things he had thought he knew so well when he was younger, when he was on the other end of a very similar insurgency demanding they stop acting like cowards and come out to fight. And now, he was sneaking around, bombing and shooting and stabbing and hiding and sniping, because that was the only way to fight back against the overwhelming odds. The mosquito cannot fight the elephant, but a hundred can encourage the elephant to move elsewhere. Equally awful was the frightening realization that he was beginning to feel more at home out here, murdering people by the dozens, than he did at the compound in relative safety with his family and the Minutemen...

John's head tilted back, and he looked up to his wife and his friend. They both looked down at him silently, willing John to return to them.

"Honey?" Rachel's voice prodded.

John focused on her. "I...I don't know what I'm doing," he said simply. He could feel the struggle in his mind, as the near constant stress had finally stretched him to the breaking point. "I don't know what I am anymore."

"What do you mean, John?" Rachel asked.

"I don't know if I'm a soldier or your husband. When I first went out there, those first nights in the woods, I barely slept. I had nightmares about what we were doing. Every time we came home, I was relieved. Then one day I didn't feel relieved when we came back, and I felt anxious to go back. Now when I'm here, it's like I'm lying to myself about what I am. I feel like I'm losing myself." John's words tumbled out of him.

Rachel looked at Andy, and the look on his face told her everything. Even he had not realized the mental strain John had been under. That was John, he would take everything on himself, never ask for help, and not want to worry anyone. Later, Andy would recount to Rachel that contrary to John's earlier statements, it was John who had taken the overwhelming amount of the sniper shots. John had done much of the killing. John had worked hard to shield Andy from the worst of what they were doing. And at that moment they were realizing that John had pushed himself over the edge.

A knock at the door caused Rachel and Andy to jump, but John's reaction was what concerned them; his hand swept down to his holster and disengaged the active retention. His eyes darted up to the doorknob, his muscles tensed. There was no doubt what would happen if that door opened.

"Andy, get the door, and don't let anyone in," Rachel barked as she threw one hand on John's shoulder, the other on top of his holstered pistol.

Andy reached for the doorknob and stuck his foot just behind the door, allowing him to open it but preventing it from opening farther than he wished. He was looking into the eyes of Mark…and Mark was carrying a handgun.

"Move, Andy," Mark said simply.

"Mark, you need to step back and let us deal with this," Andy said simply. His voice was steady but forceful. Mark could not see Andy's M&P 9 mm in his hand behind the door, angled roughly at Mark's chest. He had no intention of standing aside for whatever Mark had in mind.

"That man pointed a gun at me, in my home. He has to answer for that." Mark's voice wavered just slightly. Andy heard it.

"Mark, listen to me really carefully. John had a psychotic break. Rachel and I need a minute to get him back to himself, and you and he can talk it out to your heart's content. But if you try to push your way into this room now, he is probably going to blow your damned head off. And if he doesn't, I will." Andy's voice did not waver. He didn't blink. He was, emotionally, back in the woods with John watching his back while the whole world tried to kill them.

158

He was standing over John when that agent had shot him. He was protecting his friend, and he would cut a hole through anyone who tried to hurt John.

Andy nearly shot Mark through the door when he felt a large calloused hand land softly on his shoulder. He craned his head to look over his shoulder and was looking into the brown eyes of his friend.

"I got this, Andy," John said simply.

"You good?" Andy questioned, careful to keep one eye on Mark.

"Yeah. Thank you for watching out for me," John said genuinely. He turned his head to his wife, forced a smile, and mouthed the words *I love you*, then turned to the opening door and his very upset host. Mark's holding a handgun did not escape John's attention.

"So, you want to talk, or go ahead and try your hand at killing, Mark?" John asked, deadpan.

Mark read John's face. The man who had retreated, both emotionally and physically, to this room with his wife was gone. He was back in control of himself, which did not immediately make him any less dangerous in Mark's estimation. "We need to talk. Right the fuck now." Mark turned on his heel and walked swiftly through the hallway.

Andy chuffed to himself. "I think I just heard his balls drop."

Even John had to laugh to himself. "Go easy on him, Andy. He has a right to be pissed at me," John said.

"Maybe, but I still say if the little peckerhead takes a swing at you, you'd be well within your rights to bend him over and paddle him in front of the whole household," Andy said, only half joking.

John found Mark on the back porch, pacing back and forth. John just stood quietly and waited.

"I have half a mind to tell you and your people to take a hike," Mark said hotly.

John stood quietly.

"Say something, damn you!" Mark hollered.

"You didn't ask me a question. And truthfully, I've had the same debate. Whether we should cut you loose and go our separate way," John said simply.

Mark's pacing changed course, on a collision course with John. John stood his ground and continued to stand it even as Mark loaded up a punch and aimed it at his jaw. John easily dodged the blow, sidestepped, and dropped Mark to his knees with one solid punch to the solar plexus. He stood over Mark, unholstered his sidearm, and tossed it to the porch while he listened to Mark work madly to suck breath into his lungs while his diaphragm resisted the intrusion mightily. Mark felt as though he might pass out, but he concentrated on keeping the blackness at the edge of his vision at bay.

"Feel that? That fear? Knowing I'm standing here over you, you're on your knees, unarmed? I could snap your damned neck if I felt the urge. Shoot you. Stab you. And you can't do a damned thing to stop me. THAT, you little shit, is what I have lived with for the last month, knowing my life hung by a thread. And the only way for me to survive another five minutes was to kill. Twenty, fifty, a hundred. How many lives can you take, how many times do you trade a human being for a few more minutes of life before it's all you can think of? Kill, live, kill, live, KILL, LIVE!" John's speech rose in volume and urgency.

John sat heavily next to Mark and looked into his eyes. "I'm sorry. Asshole."

Mark blinked, trying to comprehend what he had just heard.

"I lost control, and I apologize for pointing a gun at you. I will not apologize for saving your ass, or Kevin's, or your family's, or greasing six or seven guys in your house today who would've happily hauled you off to fucking Angola. Nor will I apologize for what I am going to do to that agent you zip-tied to that chair. I'm not going to light him on fire for fun, but I will interrogate him, and anyone with a weak stomach doesn't want to be in attendance. Mark, you aren't my enemy, but I need you to stop being an impediment to me. Do you understand?" John said all of this with incredible patience, trying hard not to let it sound like a lecture.

160

Mark wrestled for the words as he worked himself to a sitting posture. "John, I am grateful for everything you have done for these people, but I can't endorse torture. Nor can I say I'm very comfortable with a man obviously on the edge walking around armed."

"Well, Mark, you're going to have to make peace with a few things. Because like it or not, you guys need me if you want to get this done, and the longer we go on together, the more obvious it is you don't have the stomach for what's necessary. I'll hold up my end; you hold up yours," John said simply, in a tone that made it obvious he considered the disagreement to have been cleared up. He stood, retrieved Mark's handgun, and offered it to him.

Mark looked up, past the butt end of the handgun to the man offering it to him. John's face betrayed no worry that he was handing a loaded firearm to someone who just moments ago had tried to harm him. Mark couldn't decide if it was indifference or trust that motivated John. Mark reached for the gun and placed it back in his holster as he rose.

Heating Up

Gary Shorts was lying in bed in his private quarters, hoping for an afternoon nap. He had converted one of the spare offices into a small bedroom when the attacks started, preferring to stay on post for safety's sake but unwilling to lower himself to sleep in general quarters with the rank and file. He regarded the ceiling in the darkened room and wondered how things had gone so wrong. His appointment to this post was a career maker and promised him great promotion potential after all of the illegal firearms and criminals were rounded up in this area. And it all started that day one of his teams went missing...

"Chief Shorts, we have a situation out here," Agent Johns voice rang out.

"What is it, Agent?" Shorts demanded.

"One of our teams went silent. They reported they have arrived at the residence on their hit list and were preparing to breach the front door, now nothing. None of them are answering on the radio," Johns explained hurriedly.

"Get another team over there and find out what's going on," Shorts ordered, returning to the report he was preparing. Last week, thirty-two arrests had been made, 157 illegal, banned, or unregistered firearms had been confiscated, and nearly two tons of ammunition confiscated. All in all, not a bad week though Shorts intended to offer some sort of incentive for additional arrests and seizures. He was sent to produce results, and he intended to please his bosses so that his future promotions would be forthcoming.

"Sir, you need to come and hear this yourself," Johns called to Shorts from the radio room.

Shorts rose, irritated at the constant interruptions, and made his way to Johns.

162

"I've got four agents down, multiple gun shots to all four. Three look like they got shot up by a firing squad, holes everywhere. The fourth one has a gunshot to the forehead execution style. Subjects are all gone, gun safe has been cleared out, and it looks like they took everything. Only thing they left behind was a couple of kid's BB guns," the agent on the radio reported.

The hair on the back of Shorts's neck stood on end. Four dead agents! How in the hell had four of his men, with their armor and training and weapons, been overtaken and killed? And where were the subjects? Shorts's eyes trailed to Agent Johns, who was equally confused by this turn of events and equally unsure how to proceed.

Then that damned unauthorized information release he had caught so much hell for started. Then the attacks on his camp and on his agents whenever they were away from camp. Finally, a few days ago Agent Johns's body had showed up on their front doorstep, shot to pieces, dragged behind a vehicle, with that damned sign hanging around his neck. He thought all of his agents were going to walk off that day. As the situation stood, he was down to forty-seven active personnel, himself and the cook included. If this apparent antagonism turned into an outright rebellion, it threatened to cut his numbers even more. Morale was bottoming out.

Today, their hit list had included the name of one Mark Thompson. Mark Thompson, according to the NFA and NICS records searches, did not own any banned firearms. He apparently had shown proof during the amnesty period that he owned no firearms at all. Yet Shorts had received a handful of reports over the past week of people hearing gunshots in the area, so Shorts had approved a few teams to go "knock on doors" in the area and see if they could turn up anything.

The two teams had not found anything and had opted to stick together in light of the constant attacks on agents, especially when they were in the process of conducting a raid. They had reported they were heading to the Thompson residence, there was one quick report of "taking fire," then nothing.

163

All attempts to contact the team were unsuccessful, and it was too late in the evening to send another unit to establish their whereabouts.

Shorts had already briefed two teams to head that way first thing in the morning, armed to the teeth. They even mounted a belt-fed machine gun in the turret of one of the Humvees just in case. Shorts did not know what the other eight men had run afoul of, but he intended to fix the problem whatever it was.

Unable to nap, Shorts was still awake with his radio turned on to low volume when he started to hear the chatter.

"Prison transport heading northbound out of town, we are approaching some sort of roadblock."

Shorts's eyes snapped to the radio. There should be no roadblock, certainly not one in the path of that transport. He reached for the radio and keyed it up. "Shorts to transport, say again. A roadblock?"

"Yes, sir, looks like an old beater pickup truck parked across both lanes of traffic," the voice replied.

"Drive around it on the shoulder. Continue along your route," Shorts ordered, putting the radio back on his nightstand. *What next?* he thought.

Andy was crouched behind the truck, waiting for a call on his radio to indicate whether the truck would hit the shoulder or the oncoming lane to bypass the improvised roadblock. He stood at the ready with the spike strips they had procured from an equipment depot, and equally ready to make a run for it if the bus did something unexpected like ramming the truck. "Sunrise," came John's voice on the radio. They were going east, or to the truck's right. Andy wound up and deployed the strips as he heard the bus approach.

The driver had no time to react. Every tire deflated, forcing the bus to an abrupt stop. Andy shouldered his rifle and rushed to the bus's side to prevent any guard from getting a sight line on him. John and Randall approached from the front in Andy's Jeep, stopping the vehicle quickly and making their exit with guns drawn.

They weren't sure how many guards they would be facing, but the disabled bus would not be a good position from them to negotiate or fight from. Kevin pulled up behind the bus and keyed the mics on the radios sitting on the seat to his right. Andy and John had had the idea to modify some ham radios to transmit on military frequencies, and Kevin's experience with electronics made that a quick, if not highly illegal, job.

"You know the FCC would have a coronary if they found out about this," Kevin had remarked with a grin. Kevin currently had three different radios, each tuned to different frequencies in intervals to spread out the number of frequencies they could jam, hooked up to three directional antennae mounted hastily on the roof. The effect was a tsunami of radio noise directed at the bus, guaranteeing they would not be making any troublesome calls back to the camp for help. This fact the guards immediately became aware of.

"Shut that thing off, Jesus!" the guard shouted to the driver over the shriek of the radio. He reached for the radio and tried different frequencies, only to find the same result, an ear-bleeding screech on any frequency they attempted.

"What the hell do we do?" the driver shouted back. He was looking through his windshield at two men with body armor and assault rifles approaching from the front, sighted squarely on the two of them. "Man, all I got is a peashooter. We don't have a chance."

The guard made a spur-of-the-moment decision to reach for his sidearm, a decision that halved the number of armed guards on that particular transport as Andy reached the driver's window, assessed the situation, and fired three shots through the window at the guard before his handgun could clear its holster. The driver reacted predictably, grabbing his ears in response to the intense noise, his eyes shuttling from the guard to the source of his demise.

"Your hands drop below your eyeballs, you don't go home tonight. We clear?" Andy's voice was clear but detached as he struggled mightily to rein in his emotions. This was hardly the first life he had taken, but every one hollowed him out.

It felt like he was selling a piece of his soul to pull the trigger. The driver's wild eyes and obvious terror indicated he had gotten the message.

John pounded his fist on the door. "Open up, dickhead, before I shoot this door open!" The door hissed, then opened. John motioned to the petrified driver with the muzzle of his rifle. "Out." No sooner had the driver dismounted than John dropped his rifle to hang on its sling, shoved the driver roughly against the side of the bus, disarmed him, zip-tied his hands behind his back, and shoved a cloth sack over his head.

He looked to Randall, careful not to use names. "Stuff this guy in the back of the Jeep. We'll take him back and pump him for info, see if it matches what the other agent told us." He then shook the driver to get his attention. "I swear if you piss in the back while we're driving, I will personally tie a rope around your neck and drag you where we're going." He then shoved him into Randall's open hands, who led him off to the Jeep.

Kevin pulled up closer in the Ford Econoline and angled his head out the window to shout to John, "Other van will be here in five or less. Lookouts all report we're clean."

John nodded, five minutes to pickup and no hostiles inbound. They had pulled the op off perfectly. He entered the bus as Andy followed closely with two pairs of bolt cutters. They sheared the lock and entered the prisoner compartment. They were faced with two dozen adults, in orange jumpsuits, with their hands cuffed to eyebolts on the floor in front of them. The garb was that of a common criminal, but the eyes that greeted him were a mixture of scared and angry. These people were outraged at what had been done to them, and were trying to figure out where John and Andy fit in.

"Everyone, listen up. I am going to cut you loose from your restraints, and I am offering you a chance to get off this bus and find your freedom. If you come with us, you will be fugitives. If you stay and wait for the agents who will come to find their property and captives, you will be slaves. The choice is yours," John stated.

166

Andy and John efficiently cut the chains securing the two halves of each pair of handcuffs together, thereby releasing them from the floor. As they passed, each person made their way off the bus. John noted some were obviously waiting for a spouse on the same bus. He was relieved they had not been separated, but he worried about where the children these people might have had ended up. That would have to be addressed between him and Mark when they got back to the compound. When John and Andy got to the back of the bus and freed their last captive, they noted with satisfaction that not a single person opted to stay. People unwilling to give up their rights and property were apparently people unwilling to place themselves back into bondage without a fight.

Andy stepped off the bus first and readied a Molotov cocktail as John dismounted too. John just saw the second van pulling up to load the last of the freed captives when Andy hurled the flaming device into the bus to set it ablaze. John signaled to Kevin.

Kevin grinned, he had rehearsed this with John a few times to make it believable. John had insisted it also be suitably gory. Kevin keyed the mic, with the antennas aimed back toward the detention camp.

Shorts sat up so abruptly he thought he might have injured his back when the screaming sound shrieked from his radio. He thought it was a malfunction until he realized the sound was a human voice screaming.

"Help! HELP! They're burning us! We're on fire!" the voice wavered.

Shorts snatched the radio and keyed up. "Report, who is this? What's going on?"

"They shot my guard and took the prisoners! Now they're burning the bus! I can't get out! I'm on fire!" And the radio went silent. Shorts nearly lost control of his bowels and bladder. Someone had just hijacked his prison transport and burned his guards alive. And every other person in the camp within twenty feet of a radio just heard it.

John and Andy rode with Randall back to the compound in the Jeep. John's mood was jovial, what most would consider odd in other company considering they had just committed a dozen felonies, killed a man, burned a bus to the ground, and had a hostage rolling around in the back of the Jeep. Having a dark sense of humor was a common coping mechanism among a certain sort of person, like military veterans and first responders. "Those guys back at the camp are probably trying to figure out whether to pee their pants or crap their shorts right about now," John said with a smile.

Andy nodded his head somberly, not relishing the task ahead of them. Their last captive had met his end after an hour-long interrogation that included several broken fingers and waterboarding.

When John unholstered his pistol and shot the man in the head, Andy's shock was obvious. "Andy, he knew who we are. He knew where we are. His life would have endangered all of us."

Andy could not argue with John's simple rationale, but he was not accustomed to shooting an unarmed man with his hands tied to a chair. Mark was in the TOC when John and Andy stepped out of the shop. He regarded John with a look. "Mark, I need a shovel, if you have one handy."

"For what?" Mark asked.

"To bury that body. I couldn't let him live, but I don't have to let him rot aboveground either," John said simply.

Everyone in attendance struggled mightily to rectify the kind of man who killed an unarmed person then wanted to give him some semblance of a decent burial. John walked out back, prepared to undertake that task alone, when Andy and Randall walked up.

"Many hands make light work," Randall started.

"I appreciate it, guys, but you don't have to do this. My responsibility," John offered, trying to spare the two of them the unpleasantness that lay ahead. They responded by kicking the ends of their shovels into the dirt, and the three dug in silence.

Andy wondered how many more holes were going to get dug before this was over. He also wondered if he would be digging a hole for a friend. He couldn't decide if John was genuinely capable of reading his mind or just his face when he answered Andy's fears.

John whispered, careful not to let the bound agent hear him, "Don't worry, we'll pull over someplace on the way back to the compound and sweat this dipshit then let him loose. He doesn't know where the compound is, and he's too damned freaked out not to spill his guts."

Andy breathed a sigh of relief.

A Growing Pack

The rest of the day was spent hacksawing the handcuffs off the prisoners and debriefing them. John was concerned that in a group of this many people, certainly some of them had to have children. He couldn't imagine the anxiety these people must feel having their families separated. He took a personal hand in talking to as many of them as he could, wanting to hear their stories and accumulate more intel.

"The agents kicked our door in, held us at gunpoint. They handcuffed us right in front of our son, then marched us out the front door. One of the agents grabbed him by the arm when he tried to run after us. I saw a van with DCFS on the side of it. Some woman took my eight-year-old boy after he had just watched his parents being carted off in handcuffs."

"They shot my dog. He was an old thing, never hurt a fly, but he sure did bark a lot. He was standing by the front door with his hackles up, barking like crazy. That agent knocked the door in, took one look at him, and shot him right there on the spot. I just reacted. I rushed towards him 'cause he was hurt and crying. They shot me too then, left me there bleeding while one of them kicked my dying dog. Sons of bitches shot that little Jack Russell like he was gonna do something besides snarl at them, and he never meant anyone any harm."

"The state took my fosters a few years ago. I had two boys who came to live with us because their mom was a dope head. These poor kids came to us with nothing but a garbage bag with a couple of days' clothes in them. They weren't even washed. I brought those boys into my home with my wife, and we made them family. They spent four years with us, great grades in school, good well-mannered kids who would've never had a chance if they'd stayed with their momma.

Then when we ran into that trouble with our registration paperwork, state said the serial on one of my forms wasn't clear. They claimed I was trying to cheat the registry, so they sent DCFS by to take my boys. All because some shithead paper pusher didn't think my handwriting was up to his standards. Then a couple of days ago these four gestapo assholes show up, shove me and the missus to the ground, and haul us off to prison like criminals. Getting to be I don't even recognize my own country anymore."

"I don't care what they say, I wasn't giving up my damned guns. I fought in Desert Storm, Somalia, and went back to Iraq AGAIN, all so my own government can tell me I can't be trusted with a couple of scary black rifles! Hell, what do they think we were shooting while we were over there?! So yeah, I told them to fuck off. You could've knocked me over with a feather I was so shocked when they showed up, blew my lock off the front door, and hauled me out."

"My husband didn't make it. He was…a lot like you guys, I guess. We always joked he was a gundamentalist. He just believed in individual rights and the Constitution. He didn't think the government had any business telling good people what they could do on a daily basis. That day, I was in the back room when they knocked our door in. He kept carrying his handgun concealed, even after the state took away everyone's concealed-carry permits. Even after they passed a law making all handguns almost impossible to own. He always said, 'I'd rather be judged by twelve than carried by six.' When they kicked in our front door, he didn't know they were feds, he just saw a guy with a rifle storming into his home, and he shot the guy. The next one through the door shot him dead. I came around the corner just in time to see him fall, and I went running to him when another agent knocked me to the ground. They were tying my hands behind my back while my husband died ten feet away, and I couldn't even reach him, those bastards."

Vicky and Rachel worked mightily to serve up a decent meal to everyone. Several of the ladies, fresh out of handcuffs, quietly walked into the kitchen and offered their help, which was welcome.

Soon, a half dozen women in orange jumpsuits and the two unofficial den mothers of the Minutemen were whipping a simple but filling meal up for everyone while Kevin worked out sleeping arrangements for their new guests.

Mark offered his help, but was more in the way than a help with this many capable cooks in the kitchen. He found Andy instead. "Where's John?"

"He's out back, Mark. And before you go out there, he's shook up, man. All this talk of people's spouses getting shot and kids getting taken has him in the kind of mood that makes a man skin someone alive and roll them in salt. I don't know whether to tell you he's mad or just plain upset about all of this. I know how he feels. What I've heard this afternoon is almost worse than I imagined," Andy replied, the fatigue in his voice evident and overwhelming.

Mark knew what he meant. He had been almost unable to keep his head above water, swimming in the grief of these people and imagining how many more had already been captured and shipped out to Angola. How many lives had been shattered by this agency and the government's crusade to stomp on the rights of good people? How many lives had been lost? How many families torn apart? Mark nodded his head, steeled himself, and walked out the back door.

John heard the back door, but did not turn to greet his guest. He was fighting hard to will the tears away. All he could think about was his own wife being killed, or his daughter being taken. The thought, just the possibility, was eating him. He was also convinced, for possibly the first time since he had shot that first agent in his doorway, that he was right to do what he had done. If he hadn't, he would be with these people, his wife in handcuffs, his child taken from him, or, worse, one of them dead. He was still pondering this as a cigar entered his peripheral vision.

"I come bearing gifts," Mark offered, trying to lighten an impossibly heavy mood.

John accepted the cigar and reached to his pocket for his cutter and torch. He clipped the end of the cigar off for an easy draw, toasted the foot for a few seconds, then started a slow and steady draw to finish lighting his cigar.

172

The chore taken care of, he offered his tools to Mark, who accepted them. The two men sat on the porch and smoked in silence for a few minutes before Mark started. "John, I've already had more than half these people ask if they can join our cause. They are angry as hell. I can't decide if their motives are revenge or wanting to put things right."

"What does it matter?" John replied, deadpan. "Motivation is a private thing. It's what fuels your engine. What matters is what you do with that fuel. If they want to throw in with us and shut these bastards down for good, I'm happy to have them."

Mark nodded. "Well, Kevin has been on the radios and the drone footage since you guys got back. He said he's seen no less than two dozen agents walk out. Apparently, that transmission Kevin put out impersonating an agent lit on fire was convincing enough. They can't have more than thirty people in there, based on what we can tell. With what we have on hand, plus these folks, I think we can make a run at the camp."

"Good. 'Cause right now, I want to bathe in the bastards' blood who did this. Did you hear some of these people? Shot their dogs. Shot their HUSBANDS. Beat up their kids. Mark, this isn't just a three-letter agency run amok, this is full-scale NAZI SHIT right here. And it's our government. OUR OWN GOVERNMENT! I'm so fucking ashamed to have ever fought for this country under that flag I'm sick to my stomach." John's anguish poured out of him.

"Then let's get a plan together, and let's end this. After that, we'll figure out our next move," Mark said confidently.

"Mark, our next move after we hit the camp is to find these kids. I don't know how yet, I don't know what resources we can leverage, but we have to get these people their kids back. If it was George, what the hell would you do?" John asked.

Mark blinked and nodded. The thought had crossed his mind; what would he do if his wife and child had been taken from him? After having his own door kicked in by these agents, he had a little more insight into John and his mind, his reactions, and his anger. Mark was beginning to feel pretty damned angry himself.

"Right now, Mark, we need to get our shit together and hit that camp. The longer those walls stand, the longer those men are there, the greater chance they will either get the reinforcements they've been begging for or decide to come in here with everything they have left and burn us down. Burying that agent only stopped them from confirming what they suspect. It does not stop them from coming to their own conclusions," John explained.

Mark looked at him. "Then let's get going. We had eight guys, you included, before today. I figure we're closer to thirty now, including the people you freed. They aren't soldiers, but they are willing, and it seems every last one of them is a hard-core gun-rights activist and well trained with firearms. At this point, that's who the agency is rounding up. All the casual gun owners surrendered years ago, all that's left is people like you."

"No, Mark, not people like me. They're angry and scared, and sure, they know how to shoot, but they aren't like me. I'm the guy who's been offing government employees like there's no bag limit and it's open season. I'm not sure I can depend on these people to put foot to ass when the time comes," John said, openly voicing his fears. He well knew there was a lot of difference between punching holes in paper at the range and walking into a government facility with the intention of killing every breathing person. A month ago, he would have doubted his own ability to follow through with that course of action. Today, he doubted everyone else's.

"Well, John, you need the extra hands no matter how low their manpower is. I would venture a guess that you can leverage their anger to motivate them. Lord knows, you and I have had our disagreements, but you've been right every step of the way. I am putting my faith in you to know what the right way to get this done is," Mark said evenly. "When?"

Such a simple question, if only simple on the face of it. John knew the answer had to be the next evening. Darkness gave them an advantage, as long as the agents didn't have night-vision equipment. Nighttime, when the agents were hopefully mostly asleep, gave them the advantage.

And the sooner they finished this, the less the chance their cell would be found and torn apart. "Tomorrow night, and we have a shitload of work to get done between now and then."

Mark nodded. "Tell me where you need me, and maybe I can keep from pissing you off so bad you try to kill me." He said it in jest, but there was a little truth in every joke.

John looked to Mark. "I'll do my best, Mark. Just try to keep in mind, once we start this, this is not a democracy. We do not vote on what happens, whether or not someone dies; we do not debate. I intend to release any prisoners we find, annihilate that camp, and kill every living person in it. I am not going to take prisoners or make arrests or bargain or negotiate. We are going to be the right hand of vengeance, and all of them must die. We clear?"

Mark's head nodded as he held John's gaze. "I hear you."

"Good," John replied. "Then let's go figure out who's in this fight, and who needs to be moved to a safe house, and let's do that right now. Because everyone left in this house once we start laying plans is in it whether they like it or not. I have to know who's got teeth and who doesn't."

Some Lessons You Learn the Hard Way

The evening had been spent in the main living area, and a very frank conversation had with all in attendance. Not only were the recently released captives given their options, but also the various volunteers Mark and Kevin had attracted while John and Andy conducted their campaign against the agency personnel and the camp for the previous four weeks. John and Mark, in equal parts, laid out what they had in mind. Details were sparse until it could be determined who was in and who wasn't, but John spared no vocabulary communicating exactly how bloody the coming night could end up, that injuries were a foregone conclusion, and casualties certainly possible.

After their impromptu briefing, fourteen of the twenty-two fugitives volunteered along with all eight of Mark's volunteers. Anyone lacking the courage, or the motivation, to participate in this attack or remain at the compound for support was politely shuffled out to a waiting van, as Mark had arranged a safe house for them for a few days before he would take on the task of figuring out where to resettle them, or simply releasing them.

Now that John clearly saw the size of his pack, he, Andy, Mark, and Kevin all participated in interviewing every one of them to determine the level of their firearm proficiency, their individual skills, and particular attention paid to anyone with military, LE, or hunting experience. John had a plan, he had his men and women, and he had to figure out where all of the pieces of this puzzle fit together. This would be a multifaceted operation, one in which there would be ample opportunity to help both here at the compound, on the outskirts of the camp providing support, and in the team who breached the camp and participated most directly in the attack.

For that, John needed men he could count on to act decisively, and he would need to spend most of the next day learning the team, coordinating their movements, and learning to work as a pack rather than a bunch of individuals. It was daunting work.

Kevin, the former F-Class shooter from California, headed up the sniper detail. He found among the volunteers eight with substantial hunting experience. While not up to his level of shooting, these were men and women who intrinsically understood how to lead targets and account for holdover at ranges under three hundred yards, and knew enough anatomy to place their shots where they would put their targets down. Kevin would need to look through their growing armory and secure as many bolt-action rifles with magnified rifle scopes as possible, including John's and Andy's if necessary. He might also need to press these people into service on the reloading bench to build up as much ammo as possible in the time they had available. And spend time adjusting the rifle scopes to work with individual lengths of pull, and cut down stocks if needed. The challenge was daunting.

Mark would run the TOC at the compound, oversee the drone operators, and manage communications once they were online. Mark had argued against Kevin going with the sniper teams, but Kevin insisted he was the best long-range shot in the entire cell, and Mark reluctantly agreed. Mark instead fell back on the other drone operators and commo guys Kevin had been training over the past weeks. A couple of the volunteers who showed skill flying the drones, a father and teenage son pair who flew model airplanes together, were welcomed into the TOC and quickly put to work learning the controls and getting familiar. Mark was also happy to add another IT worker to the TOC.

Several of the remaining volunteers who lacked the firearms-handling experience to join the assault, or the computer or radio experience to man the TOC, were put to work in a massive support operation by Vicky and Rachel. Housing, clothing, and feeding this small army was going to be a chore in and of itself, to say nothing of managing the homestead.

John, Andy, and Randall surveyed their six volunteers: two former police officers, three military veterans, and one security guard. None had what John would count as substantial experience with direct-action assaults, including John. He wished he could have lucked into an infantry vet for this team and would have happily handed the team off to the more experienced man. Andy was quick to point out that during the past month they had done nothing but accrue experience far in excess of what they previously held.

"Andy, the problem is we have always had the advantage. The numbers were never that lopsided, two on four at the worst. We always had the element of surprise. We struck from the shadows and could have disappeared just as fast. This time, we are kicking this dragon in the balls and sticking around for the fireworks. This could get really bad," John explained.

Andy looked his friend squarely in the eye. "John, if you think we can pull this off, I'm in one hundred percent. If I have to drag your ass home, we will pull this off and get back here. Don't talk like you're quitting before we've even started."

John nodded, his mind still troubled. "Okay, then let's get these men armed and get started right now. It isn't too late; we can get some practice in while it's dark, do some weapons handling in the daylight, and fix any issues we find tonight. Hopefully by tomorrow we'll be ready."

John and Andy met Kevin in the shop as he was sorting through the various weapons they had collected, looking for suitable rifles for his sniper team. He also grabbed a few standard M4s they had lifted from dead agents, intent on using these for suppressive fire.

"I'd kill for a belt-fed machine gun to send along with you guys. That would really help us out if things get hairy," John said flatly.

Kevin nodded enthusiastically. "Tell me about it, but a handful of full-auto M4s ought to fill in. I already grabbed anything with a scope on it, and I'm bringing along my FAL and my F-Class rifle. I guess this is what you had in mind, hitting their depot and dragging guns home every time you got the chance."

"That was the idea. An army needs the tools of its trade. Which reminds me, see that big hard case right there? Make sure you take it with you, and remind me to show you how that works. It may come in handy," John replied.

"Will do. What's your plan? My guys are going to be in here all night loading match ammo. Figure I'll let 'em sleep through most of the day so their eyes are rested."

"We're getting our group out in the field behind the property right now. Going to work on coordinated movements, nonverbal communications, learning to sweep rooms, and that sort of thing—how to work together without flagging each other. There's a lot to learn and very little time to learn it. At some point, it probably wouldn't hurt to show everyone here how to use a C-A-T tourniquet and a pressure bandage, just in case," John said, both to exchange information and organize his thoughts verbally.

"Yeah, we can put Vicky on that. She worked as an RN for years before George was born," Kevin related.

John silently kicked himself for never wondering how she had come by her obvious skill tending wounds. "Good enough for me. I hope we aren't bringing wounded home, but this could turn into a real flap really quick."

The conversation wound down and the men set about their own individual tasks. John and Andy had secured enough Glock 17s and M4s for each of their six men.

"You know, you ought to leave that hipster pistol here and take a Glock," Andy chided.

"Listen, dickhead, you ease up on my CZ," John poked back.

"All I'm saying is we need to all carry the same ammo and mags. Hell, you're the military guy, you know this," Andy continued.

John absolutely hated the idea of ditching his CZ for a Glock. He had detested the guns since his first introduction to them and found the idea of carrying one personally aggravating. But he didn't disagree with his friend. He did insist on keeping his personal AR instead of one of the full-auto M4s. Andy likewise kept his. The lack of automatic fire would be more than made up for by their familiarity with their own firearms they had personally built.

John asked Mark to task one of his people with securing clothing and sturdy footwear for everyone. The first stop was the shop, where the various spoils of Andy and John's raids were being housed. Most of the members of their rapidly growing cell found matching sizes within the piles of boots, trousers, and shirts intended for the same agents who hunted them now. Those that didn't left their sizes with Vicky to go secure in the local community in the morning since she was one of the few left at the site the agency didn't have on a "capture or kill" list at this point. Mark would later insist on sending an armed escort with her as a precaution that John happily welcomed. John was relieved to see Mark finally seemed to have his head fully in the game, planning ahead for unforeseen events.

John and Andy drilled their six-man group for several hours that evening almost until daybreak. Simple things like light discipline, only illuminating a potential target for a second to identify and shoot, not flagging teammates with the muzzle of their weapons, transitioning from rifle to pistol and back, tactical reloads—all these things had to be drilled and practiced.

"I think they're getting it, John. You can tell these guys are the right ones. They didn't take a ton of training to fall back into their old habits," Andy encouraged.

"Agreed, just need to work on hand signals and coordinated movements after they get some sleep. We can do that in the light where we can see each other better, but I wanted to get started in the dark and stress them out to see how they reacted. The eight of us have a real chance to pull this off," John said in agreement. "There is one thing though, Andy. If I go down, you have to keep these guys moving. Do not stop for me and get yourselves killed. Just Charlie Mike and finish this."

Andy looked to his friend with an obvious look of shock. "I'm not leaving you behind, John. Rachel would literally kill me with her bare hands if I come home without you."

"If I go down, and you guys try to pull security around a dead body and get shot to pieces, the agency will come after this cell and tear it apart. All the work we did, every life we took, everything will be for nothing.

We have to end this tonight, or we might as well all die in that place," John said with finality. "Promise me."

Andy couldn't form the words and merely nodded. He questioned to himself if he could do it, if he could leave his friend behind wounded or dead. He did not question whether or not John could, and held no malice towards John for that revelation. John was not the same man he was a month ago, or years ago when they met. He wasn't the same carefree, jovial man he had once known. John was a soldier again, and he would not let anything cloud his mind from the mission ahead. Andy realized, not for the first time, he had to find that same mindset sometime in the next twelve hours.

The weary assault force walked off the field behind Mark's home around 0300 that morning. John went to his room where his family was. Andy had relocated out to the barracks with the other single men, giving his room freely to one of the husband and wife pairs who had joined them recently. Many of the assault force simply collapsed into their bunks and were fast asleep in moments. John insisted on showering and addressing some hot spots that were developing on his feet from the long day-and-night operation and training he had endured before crawling into bed with his wife.

His sleep was fitful, dreaming of the violence he had brought to people throughout the past month and of the violence that lay ahead of him. The agent whose throat he had cut, and the look of shock and fright on his face as he could not draw his next breath. The sniper attacks. The body bouncing along behind Andy's Jeep on the way to the compound's front gate. The agent he had executed in Mark's shop. He saw every face, every man, and their angry looks stared at him accusingly for taking their lives from them, for taking them from their families and friends.

He awoke with a start, quickly sliding his watch onto his wrist and checking the time: 0700, a late start for him most mornings but a justified one after the day they had previously. Still, he had a lot of work to do.

He rubbed his eyes with the palms of his hands to encourage them all the way open, then noticed his wife absent from his bed. In her place was his daughter, Kay. She was softly snoring, her hair draped over her face like a blond curtain. She had always made a habit of crawling into bed with one of her parents whenever one of them, usually John, had left for work in the morning. He gently leaned across the bed to kiss her forehead and pull the sheets up around her shoulders, then felt a single tear slide out of the corner of his eye as he prayed he would see her grow up. He willed it away, reminding him the only way to that end was through this camp tonight. There could be no life without freedom, no peace before war; he could not raise this child in a country that wanted to imprison or execute her father. He had to see this through.

After pulling on his jeans, threading his Cobra belt through the loops, and pulling on a shirt, he holstered up and left the room quietly. He found no others awake at this hour, only his wife taking a shift at the TOC, monitoring radio traffic. "All quiet, honey?"

She jerked, not realizing someone else was awake. John could move his 240-pound frame so quietly across a room when he intended to, it was easy to be snuck up on, especially when usually his heavy steps marched across the floor, announcing his approach. "Good morning, love. Everything's quiet. Sounds like the agency isn't sending out a single patrol this morning. I'm not sure if that's lack of manpower or they're just scared, but nothing is coming our way. Vicky left with her escort just a few minutes ago, heading into town for some provisions and clothing. She said to radio her if you need anything before she gets back. And Kevin and his snipers were up till 0600 loading ammo and working on rifles. He said to expect them to be down for a few hours longer than usual to get them rested."

John nodded. He and Vicky had had a rough start to this unlikely relationship he had developed with Mark's cell, but he had to give credit where it was due, she was all in. "I think we're fine. We have plenty of equipment and ammo from raiding supply shelves and taking what we can off dead agents.

182

I'm going to get a mug of coffee and head into the shop to get everyone's gear together. I'm sure some of these guys will have their own thoughts on arranging gear, but I need to at least get their shit together and get mags loaded before they wake up. We have a lot of work to get done before this afternoon." John kissed his wife on the lips, lingered just for a moment, treasuring that kiss like his very breath, then made his coffee and went about his task.

John headed into the shop to secure plate carriers, magazine pouches, individual first aid kits, hydration bladders, and small assault packs for his team. He and Andy already had all this equipment, having brought it with them out of their preps, but his team had come to them with nothing more than the prison jumpsuits they wore and needed a full complement of everything. The irony that he was arming and equipping them with the stolen equipment of the very agency that hunted them, some of it from the dead agents who had worked so hard to imprison them, was not lost on John. *Beggars can't be choosers*, he thought.

By the time Andy found him in the shop, he was at the workbench, working the Uplula benchloader, with several cans of 5.56 in front of him, empty magazines on his left and a growing stack of full magazines on his right. He had also made a point of loading eight mags with only twenty-eight rounds for easier loading on a closed bolt before the men went hot, denoted by a strip of electrical tape around the magazine body.

"You got an army you're trying to supply?" Andy said, half joking.

"Actually, yeah. I figure with the setups for all of our plate carriers, I need four mags each for the eight of us, I have a speed pouch on my battle belt for one more, and I have assault packs for all of us I intend to stuff with some extras along with smoke grenades and those CS grenades we found. Just trying to plan ahead. If this turns into a row, we don't need to run out of ammo trying to shoot our way out. And with the M4s these guys are using, if they flip to full auto, they can burn through some ammo quick," John reasoned.

"Need a hand?" Andy offered. He could see the sweat through his friend's T-shirt and see him shifting his bulk back and forth on the wooden stool. He wondered how long John had been working that morning, and worried he would burn himself out if he kept pushing.

"Thanks Andy, I'm good. I could use another refill on the coffee, and after that I need you to go get the rest of our team up. See if someone from HHC is getting breakfast started, and get those men eating. Lots of protein, easy on the carbs, and make sure they check their feet for blisters and their bodies for chafing. We can't afford to have a man down for silly shit before tonight," John answered.

"HHC?" Andy questioned.

"Sorry, old habits. HHC is the acronym for headquarters company. I'm falling back on my Army vocabulary," John said, ramming another thirty rounds into a magazine.

Andy nodded and went off to accomplish his task. John looked to the pile of magazines on his right. Figuring eight men, four magazines for a basic loadout each, plus five more in each assault pack, he was about two-thirds of the way to being finished for his assault team. Once he had that done, he would spend another hour loading magazines for Kevin's sniper support team. They would have to task someone to finish loading so John could get to work with his team, but it would give them a head start. Many hands make light work was the phrase John had grown up with and the work ethic he had been raised with.

Doing the Right Thing

John Arceneaux was the oldest of two boys. He had been largely raised by his stay-at-home mother, while his father worked hard to provide a living for his family. Money was tight, but they never went without. He had learned often and early the value of pinching pennies, budgeting, and not being wasteful with anything. Chores around the house were modest when he was young, growing with him. What was once feeding the family dog and taking out the trash grew into John doing small home repairs with his father and helping work on the family cars. John's mother and father worked relentlessly hard to teach their children the value of hard work and patience. John's father found quickly that his oldest son grasped this first lesson much more readily than the latter.

"John," he said one day, "there are three ways to get ahead in life. You can be born rich, and we weren't. You can be born lucky, and I don't think we have much of that either. Or you can work hard, really hard. If you outwork the next guy every day, even when you don't think you have anything left to give, you'll get ahead one day. But you have to learn some patience along the way. You have to learn to work twice as hard and wait twice as long for the moment when you can get ahead. If you learn to do both of those things, you'll be just fine in anything you do."

John took his father's words to heart, even if patience was a hard virtue to learn for him. When he grew bored with high school, his grades slipped. This was more due to John's boredom with primary school than any lack of intelligence, but his father drove the point home that he had to finish his commitments. It was another lesson for him, to persevere even when he was ready to quit and move on to something else.

Along the way, probably after a failed attempt at mowing the lawn properly and having to mow the entire lawn a second time, he learned that the fastest way to accomplish a task was to do it right the first time.

John's father also taught his son the two lessons that led to his greatest confrontations throughout his life: to always do what he thought was right no matter the consequences, and to make his own decisions. "You have to make your own decisions, not follow what everyone else is doing. I'm not going to be around forever to watch out for you. You have to learn to take care of yourself and make your own decisions because ONLY you will suffer the consequences for them, good or bad. And you have to be really careful not to do the wrong thing just because everyone else is doing it. If you do what you think is right, then you'll accept the consequences just fine."

It was with great frustration that he was reminded of these words when his son wanted to enlist in the Louisiana National Guard when he was only seventeen. They had fought and argued, neither willing to give ground. John's father wanted to protect his son from the reality of one day going to war, remembering the way he had seen friends come home from Vietnam decades prior. John wanted to serve his country, to protect others, to do his part to secure the country that had given him the freedoms he treasured. "Dad, you always told me I had to make my own decisions, to do what I thought was right. This is right. Not everyone can join the military, but I can. Someone has to go because not everyone can."

John's father eyed him with a look of pure frustration. "But why is that someone you?"

John just looked up at his father and replied, "Because I can, and others can't." It was a simple, but not flippant answer. John saw himself as having a duty to protect others, no different than defending smaller and weaker kids from being bullied in school years prior. He had to go, because he was able and others were not. Someone has to go drive away the wolves so the sheep can live in peace. It would be some years before he could find the words to describe to his father what he felt, but that was his way of seeing it.

His father signed the paperwork, and John shipped off to basic training between his junior and senior years of high school.

At seventeen years old, he was five feet seven inches tall, weighed 175 pounds, and was every bit the idealistic young kid most seventeen-year-olds are. The day he graduated basic training, his parents saw a young man two inches taller and nearly fifteen pounds lighter, with a hardened look in his eye. Their son, whom they had worked so hard to raise, had become a soldier.

Years later, after his deployment to Iraq and Hurricane Katrina, John had left the National Guard and settled into the quiet life of a husband and father. John's father had no illusions about who his son was after all these years. He was a doting if not stern father, a loving husband, a hard worker and good provider for his family. He was also every bit the idealist he had been years prior, occasionally prone to diatribes about the government overstepping their authority on a host of issues from free speech to illegal search and seizure. John's most vitriolic speeches were reserved for the state's curtailment of gun rights.

"Dad, I don't know what it's going to take for people to wake up and get it through their thick skulls. I mean, in 1778 we only had one gun law. That law says 'everyone can have any damned gun they please, and the government can't screw with them about it.' Then we get laws making 'short-barreled' shotguns and rifles illegal 'cause no military uses them, even though they did. Then we get laws making full-auto guns more heavily regulated, even though the previous law heavily implied the government couldn't regulate firearms used by the military, which full-auto guns damned sure are. Then states and cities start passing handgun laws, and we have to waste years fighting them before the Supreme Court strikes them down, but SCOTUS won't state plainly what the Second Amendment has always meant and clear out all these existing infringements. And no one gets upset or protests. It's like people don't mind handcuffs as long as you don't put them on too tight."

John's dad was not as vocal about the issue as his son, but he too was troubled by what he saw as a progressive but constant move towards restricting people's rights and freedoms. It troubled him, but his personality was drastically different from his son's. "I think if the day comes they outlaw it all, I'm going to have to hide my guns. No way I'm handing them over while the government and criminals all keep theirs."

John looked to his dad and shook his head. "Did it ever occur to you the day they try to take your guns isn't the day to hide them. That's the day to load them."

"What are you saying, John?" his father asked.

"I'm saying, Dad, if the government, or anyone, ever comes to my door to take what's mine, they are going to have to fight to take them. No different than anyone else kicking down my door to take my family or my property. I don't care who it is, they have no right to take my freedom or my property, and I won't allow it. It just isn't right." John said this levelly, without blinking. He just met his father's eyes and said, plainly, he would shoot anyone who tried to disarm him.

"Can't fight the whole government, son. No one can."

"I can't. You can't. A hundred of us can't. A thousand can't. But sooner or later, the numbers will add up, and yes, you can absolutely fight the government. Remember the Alamo? Those men held their ground knowing they couldn't win, but their sacrifice motivated the rest of what would be Texas to fight the Mexicans for their state."

"So you're saying you'll be a martyr."

"No, I'm saying I will do what I think is right, damn the consequences. If enough people do what I do, then we'll win. If there aren't enough people left in the country who have the balls to do the right thing, then it's better I not live to see it," John said. The anger in his voice wasn't directed at his father, it was directed at the millions he knew would accept that yoke of tyranny rather than fight. For themselves, for their country, for their rights. Just like 1775, those with the will to do the right thing would be the minority while the rest of the country would stand in the middle like sheep.

John knew there would be far more sheep among his countrymen than sheepdogs. But no matter what, he would do the right thing.

John's attention snapped back to reality as he reached into the ammo can in front of him and felt sheet metal. He glanced at his watch and realized now was a good time to leave the rest of the loading to the next person, go get breakfast in his belly, and get his team together with all their equipment.

He knew he was looking at adding forty to fifty pounds of gear to each of his team in the way of body armor, magazines, rifles, belts, sidearms, and their small packs. They needed to get all their gear sized to them individually so it wouldn't move around on their bodies unnecessarily, and they could get used to the additional weight and bulk. Things they had practiced the previous evening, like weapon transitions, were made more difficult by the addition of body armor. Running, and more importantly changing direction quickly or stopping, would be very different with the additional weight on their upper bodies. John expected the three veterans on his team probably had worn armor before; he heavily doubted his two LEOs and the security guard had. He thought it best to bring everyone up to speed together, and quickly.

He found his team sitting at the table with Andy, vigorously replacing the calories they had lost the previous evening. All were dressed in the Dickies tactical pants Andy and John had fished out of their pile of tactical gear pilfered from the agency storehouses, and an odd assortment of T-shirts apparently from various sources. Each also looked very refreshed by the long sleep they had that morning. Some opted for shaving, while others let their beards grow in. They looked like what they were, not professional soldiers, but like a militia. Each also wore their sidearm on their belt, causing John to wonder if that was their own unanimous decision or at Andy's insistence.

"Get some grub in, guys. We have some work ahead of us. I've got everyone's gear put together and magazines loaded, but we need to get everything sized to you and do some drilling with the extra weight so you aren't surprised by it later. Andy, where's Rachel?" John asked his friend.

"She's out back with your daughter, eating on the porch," Andy replied between bites.

John grabbed his plate and headed out to sit with his family, reminded again that the time he had with them was precious and possibly very short. He found them at the table on the back porch with Mark, Vicky, and George. He sat and thought they looked absolutely ordinary sitting here together eating breakfast, belying the reason these people were all joined together right at that moment. "How did it go this morning, Vicky?" John asked.

Vicky worked to swallow a spoonful of eggs before she spoke. "Fine, John. We didn't run into any trouble, and I got a couple of days' clothes for everyone. Fortunately, Mark has always been a closet prepper, so we had plenty of hygiene supplies and toiletries to cover everyone else. If we take in anyone else, we'll have to figure out living accommodations. Our house and the barracks are almost filled to capacity."

John nodded. "Mark and I will need to have a conversation about everything after this evening is done. I'm thinking the thing to do is to split the cell in half after this is over. Not sure what everyone else's feelings are, but the bigger we are, the bigger the target. Splitting our manpower but staying coordinated gives us some insulation and eases the load on your guys. I know this has to be stretching your resources to feed and house all these people."

Mark nodded. "It's a stretch, but this is what we signed on for, John. I'm glad you got these people freed. We'll figure out the details after tonight, but putting that camp out of commission once and for all is going to take a lot of pressure off of us. We won't have to hide quite so much anymore. What are you guys up to today?"

"As soon as they finish breakfast, I'm getting them into all their gear, and we're doing a dress rehearsal of sorts. Few men react well to having fifty extra pounds of gear strapped to them, and they need to figure out how that weight and bulk will change things. We're also working on our nonverbal communication today, hand signals and learning to work as a team. Once we get inside the compound, I anticipate splitting us up. An eight-man team has a lot of potential for flagging and friendly fire. We need to be able to anticipate each other's movements, to know where the guy on your right is going to go before he goes there," John related to everyone.

"Sounds like that'll take a lot longer than a morning to teach," Mark remarked.

"Usually, yes, but it is the hand we've been dealt. We can't put this raid off any longer, so ready or not, we're going in tonight," John replied. He sat between his wife and daughter, eating in silence as his mind wound through the task ahead of him. As he had admitted before, his specialty in the military was hardly the sort of assault and direct action they had in mind for this raid, but between the eight of them, that was the task ahead, and John intended to rise to the occasion. He was just finishing his meal when Andy led the procession of armored, rifle-toting men out the back door towards the field. John went to stand and Andy waved him off.

"I've got them for a minute. Eat with your family. Mike over here"—Andy indicated to one of their assault team who was also a military veteran—"suggested some buddy rushes, whatever the hell those are."

John mentally filed away the face and name of the team member who appeared to have recalled some of his long-ago military training and had the confidence to rise to the occasion when others did not. If the occasion came to split his team, he would tap this man to lead the other half and keep Andy with him. He finished breakfast with his family while watching the men practice advancing on a target, one covering the other, and noted that he was right to insist on drills this morning.

They were initially clumsy with the added weight influencing their balance, figuring out how to shoulder the rifle around their plate carriers and find their magazines for reloads. Practice brought proficiency, and inside of a half hour, the men looked much smoother.

After John left the table, he armored up and joined his team. They worked on hand signals, drilling them to watch the team leader for direction and learning to coordinate their movements without speaking. John well knew the noise of the assault, the constant gunfire and yelling of less disciplined people, would make verbal communication much clumsier and slower, not to mention giving away their own position. By insisting on near silence, they could exercise another small advantage.

After an hour, the men retreated to the barracks, dropped their armor on their bunks, and reviewed the drone camera footage of the camp. John identified the location to breach the wall, pointed out the guard towers, and warned his men of the locations of the main office and the agent barracks and of the prison barracks. He severely doubted, having just shipped out their prisoners, that the camp would have any more, but it was something they had to verify. John also asked Andy to remind him to pack a second small assault pack with a few spare Glock 17s, magazines, smoke grenades, and IFAKs just in case they found prisoners who needed to be armed.

The plan was simple, if not audacious. Kevin's sniper team—now awake and in the shop, working feverishly to prep their own gear and load more .308 Winchester ammunition for their sniper rifles—would take out any exterior lights while leaving the interior ones lit both to illuminate their targets and to blind them to activity outside the wall in the shadows. Under their cover, Randall would back their van-turned-enormous-breaching-charge up to the southeast corner of the detention camp. They would detonate the van to destroy the wall and cause as much confusion and havoc as possible; then John's eight-man assault team would enter the compound.

John had made it abundantly clear to everyone they were not going to take prisoners; they were going to destroy the camp and every agent within. While this news caused some worried looks as the men wrestled with their consciences, it drew no argument. Everyone was well aware of the hell these agents had brought to these men, their families, and their neighbors, and the weight that placed on one side of the scale had to be balanced with their lives. It was a simple, if not brutal truth.

After their training and briefing, John regarded his watch to see it was 1500, 3:00 p.m. in civilian terms. He released the men to spend time relaxing or with their spouses if present, for two hours, to meet up at the TOC at 1700 sharp "ready for war," as John put it to them. John went first to check in with Mark and see how he and the TOC were doing with their preparations, then to Kevin to check and see if they needed help.

"We're good, just about to finish up," Kevin replied. "Every sniper has two hundred rounds for their rifles, and my support guys have twenty mags each for their M4s. I don't figure we'll need that much, but if we need to use suppressive fire to hose down the camp, we'll burn through quite a bit. And we're stationary, so we can camp a little heavier than your guys." Kevin's assessment of the situation was spot on, and John found nothing else to recommend.

"I'm getting my guys together in the TOC at 1700—sorry, 5 p.m.—all dressed for the party. I figure we need to leave here at 1730 on the button. By the time we reach the camp, it'll be after dark. We can all roll together. Your guys will have time to circle around in the tree lines before we have to get started, so you don't have to leave early or rush. I have a handful of penlights we can use to signal to each other around the camp when everyone is in position. You still have that radio rig in your van we can use to jam their comms?" John asked.

"I do, but that also jams ours. I worry if you guys don't have radios to communicate back and forth with each other and us, you'll run into trouble," Kevin cautioned.

"We'll be using hand signals for most of it, but I concede your point. Say jam their comms from the moment of the first sniper shot, plus about three minutes after we enter the camp. We'll have them on the back foot, and shutting down their comms will hurt them a lot worse than us. After that, they'll be in the fight, comms or not, and you can kill your jammer so we have comms back. Sound like a plan?" John reasoned.

"It does," Kevin answered. "You think we can pull this off?"

John looked at Kevin, reaching for his words. Here was a young man, several years his junior, who John was just realizing had undergone a drastic change since the open hostilities had started. Once an idealistic, liberal hipster millennial, precisely the sort of person John would have openly derided, Kevin was now a very different man. He had spent the last twenty-four hours committing multiple felonies and plotting to murder a few dozen agents of the United States federal government because their actions disagreed with his ideals and with the US Constitution. He had been an idealist, then a zealot, and now he was an honest-to-God insurgent. The journey he had walked to where he stood today was a very different and much longer journey than John's. John had always been emotionally prepared and equipped to defend his family and himself from anyone, violently, ruthlessly. John only needed to be provoked. Kevin was the polar opposite. He had turned from a sheep into a sheepdog.

"Yeah, I think we can. I just don't want to have to bury anyone when this op is over, so please keep your head down, Kevin," John said genuinely.

Kevin just nodded his head, thinking to himself, *I don't want to bury anyone either, not myself, not you.* Kevin and John had begun this odd relationship on very rocky ground. John's brand of violent and blatant aggression was unsettling to Kevin, a rational man not given to using force against his fellow man, but the more time he spent watching John's campaign, the more radio chatter he listened to, the more drone footage he watched, he saw the simple truth John had shown him.

There are three sorts of people in this world: sheep, sheepdogs, and wolves. Sheep are preyed upon by wolves; sheepdogs protect the sheep. Kevin had come to realize that this man, though his ways were brutal, was not a wolf, not an animal, not a heartless beast. He was a sheepdog, driving away the wolves using the only language they understood. In that revelation, Kevin gave himself to becoming a sheepdog like John, not because he yearned for the blood and violence that would follow, but to protect the sheep who could not and would not protect themselves. He would do what he felt was right.

"While I'm thinking about it, pull that hard case over and let me show you how to assemble and load this monster. Andy and I fished a Barrett M107 out of the agency's supply depot that might come in handy," John explained.

A Long Row to Hoe

John sat next to the van with Randall, Andy, and his assault team, having a cigar. They were a mile away from the camp, giving Kevin and his sniper team a half-hour head start to get into position before they approached closer with the van they would use to breach the wall. John figured they were easily far enough away to be hidden from view, and with all of their gear in the van or Andy's Jeep, they were not likely to alarm anyone if they were seen. John had pulled out enough cigars for the team, several of whom happily accepted the luxury. Some of the assembled men made small talk or discussed tactics. John let his mind wander to his wife and daughter, whom he had left at the compound hours earlier...

He had spent his last hour with the two of them, as he struggled mightily with his emotions. He hated to leave them, and the fear he would never see them again gnawed on him. His wife and daughter simply held him in silence. Kay had cried when he said he had to leave tonight. John hadn't completely related to her he might not be coming home, but Kay was an insightful enough child at her age to understand the severity of her daddy's situation. Rachel likewise fought the tears mightily, not wanting to push doubt or questions into her husband's mind. She wrestled with herself hard, knowing that John's own mind was already conflicted, not wanting to leave his family but knowing the task ahead of him had to be seen through.

"We'll be okay, John. Just come home to us," she had whispered in his ear before kissing his cheek.

John could only nod his head. He was so choked up his voice would be little more than a hoarse whisper. When his watch beeped, he gave them one final squeeze and a kiss and left them in their room.

As he shut the door, he stole one more glance at his wife and daughter, their red-ringed eyes and worried faces burning their way into his mind. He swore, to God and anything else that existed, he would come home. No matter what, he would come back to his family.

He met his team at the TOC and started getting his gear together. He laced up his Salomon hiking boots, tightly and with heel locks to make sure they stayed put on his feet. He cinched his Cobra belt tightly around him, then wrapped his web belt around his waist. Once buckled, he dropped his CZ into his duty holster and made sure the retention hood was locked down, then donned his armor. Unlike the repurposed agency armor his men wore, his was OD green and showed heavy use from years of ownership. Across the front he wore a three-cell magazine pouch; on his back was a full IFAK where he could still reach it if he had to use it for self-aid. His battle belt held spare magazines for his CZ, a taco pouch for another AR magazine, and a tourniquet immediately behind his sidearm. John's gear had been put together years prior to repel a home attack or a mob of looters, as he had seen after Hurricane Katrina. Now he was wearing it to go fight his own government. His mood was heavy. Not angry, but deadly serious.

"Thought you were ditching the hipster pistol," Andy poked, trying to lighten his friend's mood.

"If I need a Glock, there'll be plenty lying around on the ground five minutes after we start. Besides, if we end up having to burn through all our rifle ammo and we're down to handguns, we're in deep shit anyway," John said. "What's the matter, afraid I'll outshoot you with my hipster pistol?" he added, poking back.

Andy just grinned. He was falling back into old habits from working as a first responder, using humor to ease the mood when danger or death was afoot.

"Alright, everyone, listen up. We're on the road at 1730 sharp. Everyone has maps of the compound. None of them have been marked with our planned positions or routes in case anyone is captured, so pay attention to the briefing and don't make any notes. Keep it in your heads.

Likewise, whatever else you do, don't allow your radios to be captured. Agency catches one, they can penetrate our secure comms, so smash them or swallow them if you're about to get caught.

"When we get close, the assault team and breaching van will pull off the road and give the snipers a half-hour head start getting in position. Kevin, you're on your own to get your people where they need to be. You know where we'll approach from, so you signal us with a penlight, short tap, when you're ready. If you don't see a response, tap again every ten minutes till you get one. Once you get a confirmation we're ready, knock out their exterior lights and hit any targets of opportunity. If your guys can't make head shots at their range with their equipment, aim for the top of the plate carrier. Even a hit on top of the carrier will spray spall into their faces and take them out of the fight," John lectured.

"Once we back the van up to the corner of the compound and blow the wall, Randall, you stay in the wood line and keep that lane clear. If we find any prisoners, they are coming back through that hole and you are their rally point. If you have critically wounded, throw them in the Jeep and haul ass back here to the compound. We have enough seats in the two vans for my eight plus Kevin's guys, but it'll be tight. And if shit goes south, you are our rally point. If you see agents trying to barricade or secure that hole, put them down hard. Kevin, same for your guys around that corner, keep them from slamming the door shut on us.

"Now, assault team, once we get in, our first order of business is to hook hard right, stay close to the wall so we only have to pull 180-degree security, and move to the prisoner barracks. If we find anyone inside, I'll have some party favors to give them if they are in the fight. If not, we escort them out of the camp. From there, each of you are on search and destroy orders, every agent goes to see Jesus tonight. I don't care if he's the janitor with eight kids, all of them. We are not just here to destroy this camp, we are here to send a message, and it has to be bloody to get the point across. Anyone not ready to follow through, drop your gear and stay here with Mark's team for reassignment.

Everyone who comes with me, get your shit together 'cause we have a long row to hoe tonight."

A long row to hoe, that was the old country saying he had used, and it was amazingly accurate. What lay ahead of these men was going to be a night of violence, blood, and death. If everything went better than John dared to hope, he would bring his entire team home in one piece. They would have struck a devastating blow to the agency in this area and an embarrassing one to the agency as a whole. Other cells, even other citizens acting on their own, would see what happened here and realize they had the power to fight back against this tyranny. John, Mark, Andy, Kevin, Rachel, Vicky—they all would have begun something bigger than themselves. Their fledgling insurgency would be the start of something much more. This would be louder than the first shots at Lexington and Concord. This would be the day the People, not just a random lone wolf or two, put their collective foot down and said NO.

And if tonight did not go as planned, they would die. Some would escape, only to be hunted down later. The agency would shrug off their assault and, further enraged by their attack, would call in all the assets they needed to finish the job they had started. Any man not killed in action would be tried as a terrorist and summarily executed, if history had taught them anything. John would never see his wife's smile or hear his daughter's laugh again. His jaw tightened and his brow furrowed as he pushed these thoughts from his mind. He said he would come home, and he would, no matter what it cost him.

He glanced at his watch, impatience filling him. Five minutes remaining. He took another long draw on his cigar, feeling the smoke fill his mouth and swirl around his tongue before letting it tumble out of his mouth. He mentally reviewed his men's equipment, went over the map he was picturing in his head, everyone's positions, the routes to their objectives, the guard towers, tried to figure out where they would have decent cover to reload or repack their magazine pouches from their packs—all these things his mind worked over.

Andy caught his eye with a nod. "Stop, you'll just drive yourself nuts thinking about whatever you're thinking about," he warned.

"Just trying to think things through, Andy, and make sure I haven't overlooked anything. A mistake at this point could kill everyone," John replied.

John checked his watch again. Three minutes left.

Patience, John. John heard his father's voice in his head. *Got to learn some patience.*

I suck at patience, Pops. I'm better at working hard, he thought back.

Patience is hard work. Why do you think it's so hard to learn, the voice said back. John smiled. He wondered what his father would think of his oldest son at a moment like this. Would he understand why John had killed so many? Would he rationalize it like John was at war again? Or would he see his son as a crazy person, shooting government agents for no reason. Maybe when this was over, he could ask him himself. He hadn't spoken to his parents since the day the agents came to his home, both to protect his family and to keep the agency off his parents' doorstep. He had a fair idea his father had done exactly what he always said he would, and hidden his firearms to prevent their seizure. He hoped the agency had not gotten as far as his mother and father's home by now, knowing they would likely have been carted off to this very detention camp if not shipped to Angola. When this was over, he would have to go find them.

His watch beeped. "Alright, guys, get armored up, and keep your chambers empty and safeties on till we dismount closer to the compound. Randall, I'll ride with you in the van, everyone else in the Jeep. When we get close, headlights off. Once you guys are in position, wait for Kevin's signal and answer it so they can get this party started," John instructed. With everyone loaded up, the two vehicles made their way down the road towards the detention camp.

"You ready?" Randall asked.

"No. You?" John replied.

Randall just smiled. "At least you're honest about it. Son, you'll do just fine. Your heart's in the right place, and you keep your head when things get hectic. Just work on bringing your boys home and let the pieces fall where they may."

John leaned his head back against the headrest, closed his eyes, and took a deep breath. He let it out through gritted teeth as his eyes opened, working to get himself focused. He had to do this job right, or everything would be for nothing. Tonight, he had to summon that part of him he had put away years prior. He had to become the soldier once again, the man willing to kill other men without remorse. He and his men had a long row to hoe tonight.

Cry Havoc

Chief Shorts lay in his bed that evening. He hadn't slept since the previous evening, wrestling with the revelation that two more agency personnel had been murdered, the prisoners he had worked so diligently to capture apparently released, and the insurgency obviously growing. His own personnel at the camp numbered less than thirty, himself included. He had insisted, almost to the point of a fistfight, that the guard towers be manned tonight for their own safety. He had also lobbied hard that his agency immediately send him any and all aid available before they were forced to suspend operations in the area and evacuate. He knew the career suicide he would be committing to follow through on that threat, but at this point his options were steadily dwindling to that or risk an all-out mutiny among his men.

He heard his radio, with its volume turned low, begin to whine loudly. He glanced at it, reached for it, and changed the channel to their designated backup, only to find the same whining noise. Every channel he tried, he was met with the same result. He got up, laced his shoes, and left the comfort of his room in the TOC, heading for their communications room. He found the night watch wrestling with the same problem.

"What's the issue, Agent?" Shorts demanded.

"I don't know, sir, some sort of interference. It isn't our equipment. We're getting bombarded with some sort of signal that's screwing with our radios," the agent answered, clearly puzzled by the source of the problem.

Shorts turned on his heel, heading for the barracks. The hair on his neck was standing on end. He was nearly to the barracks when he heard a muffled pop and one of the exterior searchlights shattered. His head involuntarily snapped towards the light as he stopped in his tracks.

At that moment, another pop, another searchlight. Then another. Now all of the searchlights on the southern end of the compound were out. Then the boom of a high-power rifle sounded, followed by shouting.

"We're taking fire!" one of his agents in the guard tower shouted. "One down. Can't see where they're shooting from!"

Shorts nearly lost control of his bladder. They had been the victims of sniper attacks and harassment every other night for weeks, but this felt different. He shouted to the men to take cover, and rushed towards the barracks. He found several bleary-eyed agents rushing to get dressed, roused from their slumber by the sound of the rifle and shouting.

"We're under attack! They're taking out our searchlights, and our agents are taking fire from the wood line. I need every agent up, armed, and reinforcing the wall right now!" Shorts barked. His voice was strained by the near panic he felt. Two more gunshots sounded, then more, and more. He stopped counting after more than two dozen rifle reports shattered the quiet of the camp.

He ran across the camp back towards the TOC when he heard the bellowing of a V-8 engine approaching the southeast corner of the wall...

John was waving Randall back while Andy pulled security. All the agents were in a scramble looking for cover while Kevin's snipers rained down on them from the wood line. John was focused on getting Randall into position, up against the corner and oriented in line with the southern wall. His goal was to make as big a hole as possible. He also had the forethought to hook a tow cable from the van to Andy's Jeep so the men there could pull the remnants of the detonated van out of the way of the hole in order to facilitate their egress and keep the lane clear. When the van thudded solidly against the wall, Randall threw it in park, and the three men raced back towards the rest of the team. The nine of them took cover as John motioned for the remote detonator.

"Well, here goes nothing. Cry 'Havoc,' and let slip the dogs of war," John remarked to no one in particular. He mashed the button, ensuring his entire body and everyone else was shielded from the blast, and his ears were assaulted by a thunderous noise that threatened eardrums for hundreds of yards. When he returned his attention to the van, he saw little more than a chassis and part of a cab. The reinforcements they had added had done their job, and most of the blast was directed straight back into the wall, blowing an enormous hole along the southern edge.

"Randall, get that Jeep moving and clear that van. Give us some cover. Anyone comes out of there who isn't us, put them down. Watch for red lights," John instructed. He had given each of his men a pair of small red chemlights to use as markers for themselves, and had several in his extra pack for POWs. This would act as a primitive but effective IFF, identify friend or foe, system, ensuring that Randall and Kevin's snipers would not accidentally shoot at any of them in the chaos.

John jumped out from behind cover and charged towards the compound. Andy and the other six men trailed close behind, rifles all at low ready except for the two at the end, who were both angled up, watching the top of the wall and the guard towers. With Randall watching their back, they didn't need rear security, but John had stressed that the men in the rear's primary responsibility was to watch up high for threats the men in front would be less able to see.

Kevin stole a glance through his sniper rifle's scope at the assault team rushing from the wood line towards the compound, with his finger resting solidly against the side of the trigger guard to preclude friendly fire. The sniper to his left fired another shot.

"Got another one. I think they're hunkering down. I don't see anyone in those towers anymore," he remarked.

Kevin nodded his head. "Keep your eyes open, Donnie," he said to the one to his immediate left who had shown the greatest immediate skill at longer shots. "Keep hitting the towers and the top of the walls if you see anyone. Everyone else, shift down to inside the camp. Looks like our guys blew a thirty-foot hole in the wall.

You see any guys you can identify as agents, put them down. And watch carefully for our guys. They have red chemlights on the front and back of their armor. We don't want to nail our own guys."

Kevin zoomed in his own rifle scope, looking for targets at ground level. He also thought about the large hard case on the ground next to him. John had sent it with him, taken from one of the supply depots, on the offhand chance Kevin needed it. Within was a Barrett M107. Incorrectly called a "sniper rifle" by many, it was in reality an anti-material rifle meant to make short work of lightly armored vehicles and even low-flying aircraft. Kevin had been warned the muzzle flash and report would be awesome if he had to use it, but if he needed to punch a hole in something his .308 Winchester would not, it would come in handy. He dedicated his full attention to his rifle scope and worked to cover the assault team.

John was the first through the wall, finding nothing but smoldering rubble and the remnants of an apparent guard shack. He quickly sidestepped to the right, with his back facing the wall, and scanned for targets while the rest of his team poured through, keeping close to the wall and passing behind him. Andy roughly clapped him on the shoulder, signaling everyone was in, and John swept to the right following the wall. Their first target was the prisoner barracks, which was on this side of the agent barracks. If they could reach it and clear any prisoners out, they would then be free to engage anyone inside the walls without worrying about friendlies.

John's mind was a flurry of activity as his eyes scanned in a constant pattern, looking for movement in the dimly lit camp. Kevin was apparently good to his word, as his snipers had made quick work of the agents in the guard towers, and no harassment came from above. His eyes registered movement up ahead, and his rifle came up to his eye as he triggered his light. Seeing two agents, both being blinded by the 600-lumen weapon light, he fired two shots each, dropping them in their tracks.

He of all people knew body armor was not impossible to defeat, and the armor-piercing ammunition they had loaded up most of their mags with was more than capable of punching through the armor the agents wore. The same was unfortunately true in reverse though; their armor would not guarantee them that the agents' returning fire would not slice through their armor.

The eight men continued forward, the barracks coming into sight as John peeled off to the left towards the front door. As they had rehearsed, Andy stuck close to him to be the second man into the room right behind John, while the two men in the rear spread out to guard the rest of the team while they made entry. It was a formation they had rehearsed numerous times and required no additional coordination or verbalizations. John planted his bootheel solidly against the door right by the knob, and it gave as he rushed in, his light switched to constant on to blind and disorient anyone inside as he swept to the left. Andy followed, sweeping to the right. They found no agents, only four terrified people wearing prison orange. John and Andy switched off their lights.

"Listen, we're here to get y'all out of here." John spoke loudly and forcefully.

The assembled people eyed him warily, unsure who this bearded man wearing body armor was. The oldest man in attendance approached John. "My name is Eddie. This is my wife and two friends of ours. Who the hell are you?"

"John Arceneaux. I'm here with the Minutemen. Do you want to get out of here or not?" John was abrupt, not having time for formal introductions or small talk. He needed to get these people on their feet and the hell out of the camp before the agents could assemble and get their bearings.

"Hell yeah, we want to get out of here," the reply came.

"Out-fucking-standing. Here." John unshouldered his extra pack, tossing it at the feet of the four adults. Eddie opened the pack to find six Glock 17s, loaded, and spare magazines. He also found several lengths of cord with chemlights tied to them. "Each of you grab a gun and a spare magazine; leave the rest there. Put one of those chemlights around each of your necks and snap them.

Those will identify you to our men outside so you don't get shot to shit on your way out."

"What about you guys?" Eddie questioned.

"We have work to do. You need to get your people to safety. When you get outside the wall, go straight forward and look for a flashing light; that's our guy waiting for you. Run, don't walk, straight to him, and get your asses behind cover," John ordered. "Andy, everyone else ready?"

"Yeah, John, I've got two guys pulling security in the doorway. They popped a couple of agents running around half dressed. I don't think they've gotten their shit together yet, but we need to move," Andy replied.

John grunted. "Alright, everyone, follow me. My team will walk you out. If you see anyone who doesn't have a red chemlight on them, consider yourselves free to defend yourselves. Get the hell out of here and stay with Randall until this is over." With that, John turned on his heel, marshalling his team together. "Get ready, guys. Get these people moving right behind me. Keep your eyes peeled. Mike, once we get these people out, you take your three and sweep to the west to clear out any agents you find. I'll take Andy and our other two and sweep east. We meet at the TOC. Clear?"

Mike nodded vigorously, checking his watch. "Turn your radios on, guys. Kevin ought to be done jamming by now."

Everyone switched their radios on just in time to hear Kevin's voice.

"Guys, let me know how things are going in there."

John replied, "I've got four pax heading out, orange jumpsuits marked as friendlies. We're walking them out now."

The team charged out of the barracks, running quickly to the hole in the wall. John was ten yards away from the wall when he heard the distinct sound of an AR rapidly shooting from outside the wire.

"Contact southwest guard tower. Someone is up there taking shots at us. Can't get a bead on them, trying to suppress," the radio reported.

John rushed to get the prisoners clear of the wall. "Mike, get your guys and go smoke that shithead out. Circle around and burn anyone you find. Don't take any chances," he barked.

Mike motioned his men together with a wave of the arm, and they were gone.

John grabbed his microphone strapped to his body armor. "Pax coming out. Hold fire." He then looked quickly to Andy. "C'mon, let's not stand around with our pants down, waiting for someone to notice."

John's team backtracked along the path they had just travelled, heading towards the agent barracks. John had no illusions about the next phase of the plan, there could be a dozen agents in that barracks, and by now even the most inept of them had to be ready for a fight. John motioned Andy over and dug in his pack, looking for his trump card, a couple of CS tear gas grenades. When John had found these in the agency equipment depot, intended for riot control, he immediately seized them. Andy didn't see the immediate utility in them, but John had explained at the time: people who can't see or breathe can't fight.

John approached the barracks, followed closely by Andy and his other two men, cautiously looking for evidence of an attack. As they rounded the corner, they came face-to-face with an agent clutching a Glock 17 in his hands and apparently without his rifle. He motioned to point at John, but John, already at the ready with his rifle, was faster. John fired three rounds, the first two striking the agent's plate carrier, the third bisecting his collarbones.

"Andy, grenades!" John shouted.

Andy passed one grenade to John as he pulled the pin on his own and hurled it through the unguarded door. John's followed soon after.

"You two," John ordered his team, "post here and shoot any of these fuckers who try to run out, and stay clear of the doorway. Andy, with me!"

The two of them ran towards the back door of the shotgun-style barracks. John watched for agents while Andy shot the lock and doorjamb before kicking the door in. When the door gave, both men stood shoulder to shoulder and liberally hosed down the entire barracks with their rifles.

With the mist from the CS, their lights lit up and blinded anyone inside if the gas had not done its job already. They aimed for the shadows created by their lights, and for the windows. John had recognized that in order to clear the room, he would have to enter, but doing so without a mask would be tough. Blowing out the windows would clear the gas enough to only be irritating, not debilitating.

John left Andy at the doorway, with the rest of his team securing the other door, and entered the barracks after slapping a full magazine into his rifle. The gas was clearing, but enough lingered to scratch at his throat and tear up his eyes. He thought back to basic training when he had first been exposed to CS, and remembered well how badly it could disorient people. Unfortunately, the agency had never taken the apparent time to expose their agents to it in order to train them and build up any sort of tolerance, as was common in the military and most police forces. John walked along, finding several dead or dying agents and finishing the ones not already thoroughly perforated. He was most of the way to the other side of the barracks when he felt an impact in his back and a searing pain in his shoulder. Then he heard the noise. He had been shot.

In the wood line outside, Kevin heard the radio: "John's down. I repeat, John's down!"

Kevin snatched the radio off the ground to his right. "Is he okay? What's going on?"

Andy's voice came back. "He was clearing out the barracks; someone took a shot at him and hit him in the back. We're checking him now."

Kevin's stomach turned. His worst fear was for this attack to result in casualties on their end, and his thoughts shifted to Rachel and Kay. How would he go back to the compound without their husband and father and tell them what happened? How could he? He was thoroughly caught in his own anguish when he heard the rumbling of an approaching vehicle.

"Everyone, give me eyes. Why do I hear a vehicle approaching?" Kevin plead into the radio.

"Agency Humvee approaching, turret-mounted weapon. It's coming down the road towards us!" Randall's voice warned.

Kevin looked to his right with terror as he realized too late, not all of the agency personnel had been back to camp yet. He looked at the black Humvee, with its armor plating and a belt-fed machine gun in the turret, approaching the detention camp.

"Oh Jesus," he said to himself. "Assault, you have an up-armored Humvee, belt-fed machine gun, approaching the camp!"

No Plan Survives First Contact

Andy ran into the room after John, without regard for the stinging of his eyes or the protesting of his lungs. He hurled himself through the barracks, barely diverting his attention from his fallen friend to put two more rounds into every agent who had fallen. He would not be victim to another agent playing possum. He was out to make sure they all were on their way to their maker. He reached John, transferred his rifle to his left hand, and roughly yanked on the grab handle on the back of John's armor, pumping his legs hard and pulling urgently to drag his friend facedown through the room towards the front door, where the rest of their team was pulling security. He hazarded a glance down to see blood soaking into John's armor close to his left shoulder.

When he reached the doorway, he yelled to the other men, "Get your asses in here. One of you watch each door and keep behind cover. Kevin just said there's an agency Humvee approaching with a belt fed!"

The men took up positions watching for hostiles while Andy reached for the clips on each side of John's armor.

"We don't have time for this shit, go!" John shouted, trying to shove his friend away.

"I'm not going home without you, motherfucker!" Andy replied, shoving John roughly down to the floor and yanking the back of his armor up over his head. He saw the wound, just above the armor plate on John's left side, and ripped his T-shirt to expose a surprisingly minor wound. "You lucky son of a bitch, the armor caught the round. You got cut by the spall!"

"If it isn't that bad, then we'll deal with it later. Did I hear you say belt fed?!" John shouted while sitting up and securing his armor back to his body.

"That's what Kevin said. Humvee, machine gun in the turret," Andy replied. He worked to marshal his emotions back to the task at hand. Later, much later, he would admit he had been driven nearly to tears in equal parts by the fear of his friend dying in front of him and the realization that the injury was minor.

"Dammit!" John shouted, exasperated. He reached for his mic on his armor. "Everyone on channel, put eyes on that Humvee and report. We need to neutralize them right the hell now!" Then John heard the rhythmic thumping that could only be an M240B medium machine gun. John well knew the balance of firepower had just shifted heavily in the agency's favor, as the medium machine gun could pour out a volume of fire none of their assault rifles could match, and the Humvee's armor would shrug off anything they could throw at it. They only had one chance...

Kevin was hunkered down in the wood line behind a fallen log, hoping it was enough cover to protect him from the maelstrom of flying lead the Humvee was pouring into the wood line. It was readily obvious their gunner could not easily see his targets but had a good enough idea where they were to hose down the area.

"John, we're taking fire out here. One of my snipers is down. No one can get a shot on this guy while he's trying to cut down the whole damned forest," Kevin shouted into the mic over the roar of the machine gun. His men would occasionally spray a thirty-round magazine towards the Humvee in vain as the armor of the truck and turret did their jobs. They had come to this fight with the advantage in numbers and surprise, but the momentum of the battle was quickly shifting as the agency Humvee brought overwhelming firepower and protection to their side.

Back inside the camp, John raced out of the barracks with the rest of his team in tow. "Team two, meet me at the south wall, buster!" John shouted, unconsciously using the term *buster*, military jargon for bust your ass, or hurry. The tone of his voice communicated loud and clear the urgency. The eight men quickly converged at the south wall, conscious of possible attacks from their rear but laser focused on the Humvee trying to tear apart the rest of their forces.

212

"Kevin, you still have that hard case I left with you?" John shouted into the mic.

"Yeah," came Kevin's response. "But I can't reach it with this going on."

"Got it. Pop smoke to give you some cover; throw the smoke grenades out in front of your position. When you hear us start firing, get that damned Barrett up yesterday. It'll punch through their armor. Hit the turret with a full mag then aim for the engine and driver. Randall, check in," John ordered.

Precious seconds ticked by before he heard Randall's voice. "We're behind cover. Don't think the Humvee sees us."

John looked to his men. "Alright, guys, you two," he started, picking two men at random, "pull security on our asses and make sure no one tries to sneak up on us. Everyone else, when I say the word, start laying it in on that Humvee. Aim for the turret. Let's see if we can get that smartass to put his head down."

The assault team took cover behind the wall on either side of the breached section, while the security guys put their backs against their teammates, watching for a possible ambush from within the camp. Then John flipped his AR from safe to semi, raised his rifle towards the turret, and began taking as well-aimed shots as he was able. He knew the turret setup from his Army days; it was armored and shielded fairly well from a ground-level assault in all directions. He could just make out the top of a helmet above the armor and had little hope he could actually take out the gunner. His intention was simply to get his attention away from the south sniper team until Kevin could get the M107, a semiautomatic .50-caliber anti-material rifle, set up to take the Humvee out. With its thick armor and bulletproof windows, none of their rifles stood a chance of hitting the men inside. Their only hope was with the big .50.

The rest of his assault team joined in, most following John's lead, using semiautomatic fire to conserve their ammo. Unlike the teams outside the camp, who were stationary and had brought extra ammo, John's team had to stay mobile and could not afford to be wasteful.

213

Every shot was meant to hit the turret gunner, or at least get his attention. It did not take many shots before they saw the turret quickly swivel in their direction.

"Get back!" John shouted just before a torrent of .30-caliber lead filled the air, spraying back and forth to both sides of the opening in the wall. "Kevin, get that rifle up RIGHT THE FUCK NOW!" John shouted into his mic, barely hearing his own words over the noise of the machine gun and the impacts on the wall.

Kevin yanked the handle on the hard case, pulling it to him behind the log. He scrabbled for the latches, then flung the case open, diverting his attention to make sure the Humvee was not angling back towards them for another attack. The tracers loaded along with the ball ammo in the gun's belts gave the impression of a stream of light in the dark pouring towards his teammates, who had taken cover behind the wall to escape the withering fire directed at them. Kevin looked down into the case to see the enormous rifle in two halves, as it would be for transport. The Barrett was a nearly five-foot-long rifle when assembled and was typically packed into its case in two halves, which had to be assembled prior to use. Kevin cursed himself for not having paid better attention when John explained how to put this damned thing together.

"Kevin, what's the holdup? Those guys are screwed if we don't get that rifle going," Donnie shouted.

"Gimme a second. Some assembly required," Kevin hollered as he jogged his memory and started fumbling to put the rifle together.

At the wall, John's team was waiting for brief moments when the machine gun stopped between bursts, to crane their rifles around the corner and spray a burst of fire towards the Humvee, both to hold their attention away from the wood line and to encourage them not to approach. John held little hope that would last long, as their armor gave them an advantage, and eventually they would run out of patience. If that Humvee reached the wall, they would have nowhere to hide, and Kevin would have no shot at the Humvee to take it out.

"Contact rear!" one of his team shouted. The counterattack from the remaining agents that John had feared had arrived.

"John, we're fucked if we stay here!" Andy shouted.

"And they're fucked if we don't," John replied loudly.

John took the lead, holding his position but turning around to engage the three agents who were firing at them from around the corner of a building. He knew they were sitting ducks, but if they did not hold the line, the Humvee would either come forward and burn them out, or return its attention to Kevin's group, taking the M107 out of the fight. "Andy, take our two guys, go around the back side of that building, and burn those guys down! GO!"

John's forceful tone left no room to argue, and Andy reluctantly left his friend's side, taking off running along the east wall towards the other side of the building their assailants were using for cover. John alternated between taking shots at the corner of the building to cover his team, and taking shots at the Humvee to keep them from advancing. "Kevin, any day now!" John bellowed into his microphone.

Andy pumped his legs hard, running for the building with his two teammates working hard to keep up with him. He could feel his legs protesting, and the soreness in his back from the extra weight of his armor, but gritted his teeth and charged onward. He had to stop these guys before John or someone else ended up dead, and he could not afford to slow his pace even for a single step.

He reached the first corner, cautiously angled around to clear the corner, then ran to the next one. As he turned the next corner, he saw the three agents, all huddled against the wall, taking shots at John and the rest of the assault team. They had neglected to post a rear guard. Andy raised his rifle, placing the red dot of his optic on the nearest man, and fired two shots. Then two more. And again, until all three men were down. "John, your ass is clear!" he shouted into his microphone. Then Andy heard the thundering report that only a .50 BMG could make.

Kevin had finally gotten the rifle assembled, remembering he had to hold the bolt retracted in order to close the two halves of the rifle together. He inserted the takedown pin, cycled the rifle, and dry fired it, then yanked two loaded magazines out of the hard case. They were comically large, as was the ammunition. Kevin had never fired a .50 cal before, since they had been so heavily regulated in California and so expensive few people where he lived owned them. It took him a few extra seconds to realize the magazines were a "rock and lock" design rather than inserting straight in like an AR. With the magazine firmly inserted, he pulled back on the bolt handle, compressing the surprisingly stiff recoil spring, and let the rifle cycle to load its first round into the chamber. He left the bipod folded, opting to rest the rifle on the log he was using for cover.

When he flipped up the scope covers and found the turret in his sights, he squeezed the trigger for the first time and briefly wondered if the rifle had malfunctioned and blown up in his hands. The noise, the pressure, the blast, the recoil—everything about firing this weapon was incredible. The .50-caliber armor-piercing incendiary ammunition fired by the M107 was more than four times heavier than Kevin's 168-grain match bullets he fired from his .308 Winchester, and despite the immense size and weight of the projectile, it had even more muzzle velocity. The first round struck the turret, punching a neat hole in it before the incendiary charge detonated. Kevin paused ever so briefly when he realized the immense recoil of the rifle had driven the optic back into his face, causing the scope to cut his eyebrow. The impact and blood stunned him for a brief moment, just long enough for the turret to start its traverse back towards him, recognizing the greater danger now lay behind the Humvee.

"Oh no you don't!" Kevin shouted, and quickly pulled the trigger again, sending a shot flying just over the top of the Humvee. The rest of his ten-round magazine all connected with the turret, slicing through the armor and killing the gunner as the turret stopped its traverse.

Kevin worked feverishly to find and hit the magazine release, flinging the shoebox-sized magazine out of his way and reaching for the full one as the Humvee throttled up and began to move. Kevin would later wonder what drove him to the emotion he felt, but he was determined not to let the Humvee that had shot one of his snipers and tried to kill them all leave with anyone alive. He rammed the last magazine into the well, yanked the charging handle, and raised the rifle, bringing the optic in front of his eye as he heard John's voice in his mind. "Aim for the engine block, then the driver."

Kevin fired once, then twice at the engine block, hearing the satisfying noise of the engine grinding itself to a halt. With the Humvee stationary and the driver's door facing him broadside, he put his reticle on the door and pulled the trigger eight times, marching his shots back towards the rear of the truck. Anything bigger than a rat in the truck would be hard-pressed to have survived the assault.

John watched Kevin from the wall as he emptied his M107 into the driver's door of the armored Humvee, satisfied that the API ammo had done its job killing both driver and passenger if there was one. "Good job, Kevin! Everyone check in, casualties or wounded?" John called into his microphone.

"Couple of scratches here, nothing serious," came Randall's voice.

"I've got one casualty south. He's gone." That was Kevin.

The other sniper teams reported no injuries or casualties. John turned around to see Andy jogging forward with his team. "We're good. Fuck, I need to run more." Andy puffed.

John pounded his fist on his friend's shoulder, as close to a hug as he could manage given the present situation. He had anguished over sending his friend off without him towards danger, but in the moment his military mind and instincts had taken over. He saw his close friend as a soldier and ordered him into battle. He would reflect on that decision later and question whether or not he could have lived with his friend's death if that had come to pass. Right now, he had one more order of business.

"Andy, hold this. Everyone else, circle around and make sure you leave no one behind breathing," John remarked, unslinging his rifle and handing it to his friend.

"Fuck are you going?" Andy shouted, exasperated.

"I'm going to see that little asshole Shorts, and I'm going to end this," John said, a dark smile spreading on his face. He drew his CZ from his holster and marched off towards the camp's TOC.

Shorts was in his office, rifling through his desk drawer, looking for his agency-issued sidearm, and sweating profusely. The radio chatter had died down substantially, then stopped altogether. Whoever these people were, they seemed to have killed all of his agents and even managed to disable the Humvee that had arrived late from its nighttime patrol. Shorts was still fumbling through drawers and shuffling paperwork when he heard the door to the TOC slam against the wall.

He heard the sharp thudding of bootheels striking the polished floor, stopping occasionally, then resuming their travel. He was still looking for his Glock when a man wearing jeans and body armor turned the corner. Shorts looked up, from the hiking boots, the dirty jeans, the green-colored plate carrier, up past the handgun levelled at him, to the bearded face and angry eyes of John Arceneaux. The revelation dawned on him just as the gun fired, striking him in the shoulder. Shorts was rocked back away from his desk into his chair by the 9 mm slug that shattered his shoulder, dropping his arm limply down to his side.

"Do you know who I am?" John spat. He made no attempt to conceal his anger and indignation. John was seeing the faces of the men and women whose lives had been torn apart, the children traumatized by watching their parents beaten and killed. He saw the terror in his daughter's eyes. He saw the look in his wife's eyes when he killed those first four agents. He saw his friend lying on the ground, shot by one of these agents.

Shorts nodded his head, too frightened to speak. He recognized the face of the man, the one who had turned up missing after his first failed raid and lost team. The face of the man who had killed the second team, minus Agent Johns. The face he suspected was responsible for the sniper attacks and all the ill that had befallen his agents for weeks. The pictures he had pulled from John's DMV record and social media showed a sometimes serious, but happy family man playing with his daughter or hugging his wife. The man who stood in front of him today was none of those things. Shorts saw the anger, the contempt, and the pure murderous intent in his eyes, like Death itself come to collect a soul on his list.

"Good, then we can skip the introductions, you little bastard. Pick up the phone and call your boss."

In Washington, DC, rather late for official business, a phone rang in the Secretary's home office. He grumbled loudly, looking at the caller ID and wondering what that little idiot wanted to talk about at this hour. "Shorts, this had better be damned important for you to call me this late," the man shouted.

"Shut up and listen," a gruff voice that did not belong to Gary Shorts barked, silencing the Secretary.

"Sir," Gary Shorts's voice started, "I am sitting here with a man by the name of John Arceneaux. He is holding me at gunpoint and wants me to give you a situation report on the New Orleans area operation. Are you ready to take that report?"

The Secretary was shocked and fumbled for his words. "Go ahead."

Shorts's voice sighed into the phone. "Sir, all agency personnel but myself are dead. I have been assured that if that is not a fact at this exact moment, it will be within a few minutes as Mr. Arceneaux's team continues to check the facility. Our prisoners have been freed, our camp is in ruins, and all of our men are dead. All but me."

The Secretary's mind reeled at the news. How had an entire detention camp, two hundred men strong, been destroyed?

Shorts had made mention of several casualties and more people quitting, but this was beyond comprehension. "Do you have anything else to report, Shorts?" the Secretary questioned.

"No, sir." Shorts sobbed. Then the gunshot sounded, followed by several more as John emptied most of his magazine into the former chief LEO of the New Orleans detention camp. He replaced the empty magazine with a fresh one, falling back to his old habits, and replaced the CZ in his holster before picking up the bloody receiver.

"Now," the voice of John Arceneaux snarled into the phone, "let me be frank with you, sir. This man and his agents and your agency are responsible for gross violations of the civil rights of US citizens, not the least of which was breaking into my own home with the intent of harming my family and me. I am putting you on notice, personally, that if these hostilities continue, the cost in human suffering will be both immense and on your head. Louisiana is, as of right now, a US Constitution zone. We will have our free speech, and we will have our gun rights and every other right you jackbooted hoodlums have seen fit to try to take from us. And we will fight to keep them. You and your men stay out of my AO, sir, or come here at your own peril."

The line went dead. The Secretary stared, with his mouth hanging open, at the phone. He struggled to force his mind to make sense of the events that had just been brought to light. An outright insurrection had just been sparked in Louisiana and had openly challenged the authority of his agency and indeed the entire US government. He slapped the receiver and dialed the president's Secret Service detail, hoping to reach someone at this late hour to inform his boss about what he had just learned.

Curtain Call

The flurry of activity that followed the next morning sent shock waves through the United States political apparatus and its various agencies. News of the destruction of the detention camp, the murder of more than thirty agents, and the beginning of outright hostilities between US citizens and their own government were alarming to say the least. Not since 1861 had the country been in the precarious situation it found itself, in which it was now faced with having to use its own military and national police forces to subdue not a single man, not a handful, but potentially thousands of people as the insurgency grew. Unlike the American Civil War, which was largely fought along geographic lines, the reality of the Minutemen was that the decentralized nature of their cells meant this conflict could potentially be fought nationwide, with hostilities boiling over across the nation. It was a situation the president and his advisors argued over mightily, deciding how to respond.

At the same time, the Minutemen revived their old party trick and prepared a full-scale international news release. Unlike the first one, which had detailed the heavy-handed approach US government agents were using to secure those firearms not given freely, this time the release was of drone footage from the attack. With Kevin's and John's teams assaulting the camp, Mark and his small army of drone operators had put everything in the sky they could manage, all either live streaming the video to a receiver in Kevin's van or recorded to be downloaded later. Mark was also glad they had managed to intercept the phone call John had made to the agency's higher headquarters, the Secretary of the Department of Justice no less. It was self-incriminating to John, but was also an incredible rallying cry for the rest of the Minutemen cells.

They saw, finally, the way to win their fight. The detention camps, all of them nationwide, had to be targeted and destroyed. Once that was accomplished, the agency's ability to conduct operations would be drastically marginalized, and further operations meant to free captured gun owners could commence. John had been right, the insurgency was indeed giving rise to an all-out rebellion.

BBC news: BBC news reporting from on location at the United States Capitol in Washington, DC. Reports are still coming in indicating prior reports regarding isolated hostilities directed towards US government agents and officials may have been severely understated. News has reached us through unofficial sources, only partially corroborated by the White House press secretary, that a US government facility in the vicinity of New Orleans, Louisiana, was attacked last night, suffering severe damage and dozens of casualties. The terrorist group Minutemen has openly claimed responsibility for the attack and has indicated their intent to continue and escalate hostilities towards the US government and its agents unless their demands are met: for the right of citizens to keep and bear arms to be restored, for the censorship of free speech to be suspended, and for the political prisoners of the US government to be immediately released. The White House has not confirmed all of the details and will not confirm or deny that the censorship of the internet is even taking place, though we have been receiving our information from an unnamed and independent source. We will continue to report as details come in, and we await an address from the White House for further information.

The combined assault and sniper team returned to the Minuteman compound in the wee hours of the morning, to treat their wounds and bury their dead. Kevin considered them lucky to have only lost one man, a member of his sniper detail who died barely ten feet away from him when the Humvee's machine gun cut him down. The elation at reuniting the team with their friends and loved ones was clouded by breaking the news to the new widow, a task John would not allow anyone else to attend to.

222

After scarcely a few moments to hug his own wife and daughter, he walked to the woman with a somber look on his face. Both of their tears started before he even spoke.

"Ma'am, what is your name?" John felt like an ass for not even knowing, though he had scarcely known any of these people long enough to get acquainted.

"Mary," she huffed out between sobs.

"Mary," John started, "your husband was a brave man, as brave as any soldier I ever knew. He gave his life trying to change something bigger than him, bigger than all of us, and I'm proud to have known him if only for a short time. I am so sorry we couldn't bring him back to you." John struggled hard to keep his voice, even as the tears flowed freely down his cheeks and onto his bloody shirt. He thought back to the moments in time he had to say goodbye to soldiers he had served with, to send them off to the next life. He remembered the widows and the children who would grow up without their father or mother, the families who would miss their sons and daughters and brothers and sisters. He did not know the words then, and he did not know the words now, to express his deep remorse that this man had lost his life and this woman had lost her husband. He could only stand there and hold her shoulders while she grieved.

They held an impromptu but reverent burial for the man, whom Kevin identified as Thomas Jameson. Each man and woman present, though they had known him little, felt the loss. He had given his life trying to change the world, and John personally hoped his sacrifice would be remembered one day in the pages of history like great men had been before. John, Mark, Kevin, and Andy all worked to bury the body while many of the others filed inside the house to rest and comfort Mary.

"I still can't believe we won," Kevin remarked.

"We haven't, not yet," John said simply. "But at least we won the battle."

John worked the shovel while his mind wandered. He was relieved to be alive, glad to be back in the arms of his wife and daughter, yet he felt incredible guilt for the man they were interring in the earth right at that moment. Had he been right to demand they attack that camp?

Should he have just given up in the first place and spared all of these people? What about the families of the men he killed? Hundreds of other women and children besides Mary would not see their husbands come home after what he had done; what of their sorrow? How many families had he shattered? How much suffering could a human being cause and not be forever damned for it?

"Don't do that, John." It was Andy's voice. "You didn't kill this man. He believed in what we are doing, and he walked the walk right along with us. His death isn't on your hands, it's on theirs. It has to be that way."

"Maybe, but what about all the men's deaths that are on my head? All the blood? How many more people am I going to kill, how many more families will I destroy? Is this worth it?" John's words came out like a tortured sigh.

Mark looked up to John. "Do you remember what you told me, John? You said the faster we ended this, the fewer people would have to die. How many people died before you fought back? How many families were destroyed? How many children taken? How many more would have lost everything this past month if you hadn't done what you did? Don't fall on your sword because you lost one man trying to save thousands."

John closed his eyes when he felt the stinging sensation of tears. He knew Mark was right, every war risked casualties, and the one man they were laying to rest had given his life to save others. John felt foolish for dishonoring his memory by losing sight of that. "I know you're right. Just give me a second, guys. I thought my days laying fellow soldiers to rest was long past, and it's not something I've ever gotten used to."

With the task finished, John turned to find his wife, Rachel, sitting on the back porch, waiting for him, while Kay and George played in the yard. He sat beside her, wiping his wet eyes. She laid her arm around his shoulders, stopping when he winced. She had forgotten the wound to his shoulder.

"You were damned lucky, John," Rachel said evenly.

John only nodded. The bullet that had struck his armor and glanced off, the flesh wound, could have been much worse. Closer to the plate carrier, he wouldn't have had a scratch. An inch higher and left, he might have punctured a lung and died. These were the kinds of things your mind wanders over after the fight is over, which he couldn't burden his mind with at the time. "I was. But I had to do this, honey. Now we have a little bit of breathing room."

"Breathing room for what?" Rachel asked.

"To rest. To reload. To get ready. The battle is over, the war isn't. We haven't won, we've only just started…"

The Coming Storm

That evening, nearly the entire population of the United States of America sat near their televisions, their smartphones, their tablets, waiting for an emergency address from the White House. Rumors abounded about the terrorist organization that had attacked a government facility in Louisiana, and the people were scared. Reporters had all told various stories, some from unofficial sources, that this attack was provoked by a government agency exceeding its authority, but the reaction from much of the population was motivated by their fear. Sheep react equally to sheepdogs and to wolves, making little distinction. The room hushed when it was seen that the president, not his press secretary, was approaching the podium.

Live from the White House: My fellow Americans, I am saddened to confirm that earlier reports that a United States government facility was attacked late last night are accurate. Early reports indicate severe casualties, including our local station chief, who was a veteran civil servant of more than twenty years. My condolences go out to the families and friends of our dead.

As your commander in chief, it is my responsibility to ensure these aggressive acts are brought to heel, and the guilty punished. To that end, I am sending a resolution to Congress, which I urge they pass with all available haste, to suspend Posse Comitatus and enable us to deploy the full weight of the United States military on home soil so that we may find and capture these antagonists. The murder of these agents is only further evidence that we must maintain control over our nation, and those who would destroy the peace we have worked so hard to secure must not be allowed to succeed.

We will stand together and demand in a unified voice that this aggression against our country cease, and back that demand up with the force of the world's greatest military.

John and Mark sat at a terminal in the TOC watching the address when John stood and turned to leave. He stopped to raid Mark's beer fridge and grab a cigar on his way out. Mark stood to join him, following suit. He found John sitting on the back porch, in his usual spot, roasting the cigar while drawing before offering his cutter and torch to Mark. He clenched the cigar in his teeth and used one of his meaty palms to wrench the cap off his beer before taking a healthy swig.

"What are you thinking, John?" Mark asked.

"Suspend Posse Comitatus. That son of a bitch is going to use this to finally get the police state they always wanted. Never let a tragedy go to waste. It's like what they did in New Orleans after Hurricane Katrina all over again. Back then, they were stealing property and taking guns 'for everyone's own good.' Now they're actually going to put the Army and Marines out in the street to keep everyone safe. I swear, Mark, 1933 must've been a long ass time ago, because everyone forgot what happened the last time a country pulled this little stunt," John said. His history nerd credentials were showing again, as he referenced Hitler's coming to power, the consolidation of the federal police forces and military, and the total control over the citizenry of Germany. Only this time, John feared it would not be anti-Semitism that drove the witch hunt, but the fear and hatred of freedom itself and freedom-loving people.

Mark nodded his worried face. "What do we do, John? This isn't just a couple of hundred agency guys, this is the whole damned military. That's what, a million active duty and another million reserve?"

"Pretty close," John said. "But there's two things you're overlooking. Firstly, I don't think they'll send all two million straight here to smoke us out. They can't, they still have national security concerns to deal with all over the globe. That, and this might blow up in their faces."

"How?!" Mark demanded.

"Because," John said patiently, "the men and women they would send aren't going to bomb people in a faraway land, they're going to be sent to bomb and shoot US citizens. And that's a very different emotional pill to swallow. Ask me how I know. The White House is used to snapping its fingers and getting what they want, but this is a situation the US public hasn't been faced with in several generations. A lot of people are going to put a lot of pressure on Congress to keep the Army out of their damned neighborhoods, and if they value their seats, they will listen. If the White House only sends the National Guard, that works out even more to our favor, because Guard assets are local and under state control primarily. They'll be even less sympathetic to government guys getting smoked for grabbing guns. In any case, we just keep playing our game and let them play theirs. We aren't done yet."

The next morning, John and Andy had loaded up in Andy's Jeep with Donnie. Donnie had been Kevin's right-hand man on the sniper detail and had felt Thomas's death more than many of the Minutemen because he had been so close to the man when he lost his life. When Thomas had been hit high in the chest that evening, he looked to Donnie right next to him, knowing his life was over. He reached out and grabbed Donnie's sleeve as he stayed behind cover and looked into the man's eyes and said, "Whatever happens, tell my wife I love her, and find my son." He died moments later with his eyes open, and the sight had burned its way into Donnie's memories. Donnie insisted John and Andy help him keep that promise.

Kevin's prodigious computer skills enabled him to hack the DCFS computer system and find the records of one Thomas Jameson Jr. and the address of the foster home the state had placed him in after he had been taken from his parents weeks prior. The three men left early that morning, with Andy's Jeep loaded down with enough firepower to get out of any trouble they might come across, and an extra day's clothing, food, and water in case they had to camp out of the Jeep before returning.

228

The three men accepted that they were all fugitives from justice, and if caught, they might have to shoot their way out of trouble, but reuniting Mary with her son after Thomas Sr. had lost his life was the least they felt they could do.

Two hours later, they arrived at the foster home. "Andy, let me go by myself. Maybe I can talk this out without things turning into a row. I'd rather not have to shoot these people if I can help it," John said.

Andy nodded. "Okay, John, but if I see some shit start, I'm coming."

"Fair enough, brother." John smiled genuinely. After all they had gone through, he did feel as though these men and women he had thrown in with were more than just strangers. They were a growing family, and he was going to work hard to get these children back to their families, through diplomacy if possible, and through violence if necessary. He opened the Jeep door, careful to make sure his handgun was tucked into his jeans and not visible, and approached the front door, walking up the path from the driveway. When he reached it, he found a man roughly in his late fifties staring warily at him through a screen door.

"Can I help you, sir?" he asked.

"Sir, I sure hope so. I understand there's a young man who's come to live with you recently, goes by the name Thomas Jameson Jr.," John started.

"Tommy. What do you want with him?" the man said brusquely. He was used to deadbeat parents trying to circumvent the system and come see their children after DCFS had removed them. Something about the look of this man didn't strike him as a doper. He looked like an Army veteran, something he would recognize after his own service. He had the straight posture, the laser-focused eyes, the confident and direct speech. He also had the air of a man used to hurting people if he was forced to.

"Sir, I have come to take the boy back to his mother," John said simply. No point beating around this bush.

"His mother is in jail," the man replied.

"She was, and her husband. I broke them out, and Thomas is dead. I've come to take the boy back to his mother and to explain what happened to his father," John said evenly.

The man's eyes softened. He knew the boy would be crushed to hear about his father's death. It had become obvious over the past two weeks how close they were. "How did he die?"

"He died holding the hand of that man in the back seat of that Jeep behind me. He died with me, fighting against the same people who put him and his wife and thousands in jail just because they didn't think their government had a right to take their guns. He died a hero, and his son deserves to know the truth and to be consoled by his mother," John answered.

Realization dawned on the man's face. "You. You're that man on the TV. The Minuteman."

John nodded his head. "I am. Whatever you have heard about me, or us, understand that I'm not here to harm Tommy or you. I'm just trying to put things back right. Sometimes I have to use a rifle to do that, but I was hoping not to today."

The man looked at John's face and saw his emotions painted across it. "Come on in and help me get the boy's things together. He's a good kid. I'd have been happy to have him live with us permanently, but he should be with his mother. Just promise me you'll protect them, son. You're playing a dangerous game here."

John looked into the old man's eyes, then up past his shoulder, into the house to the mantel above the fireplace. A picture of a younger man in uniform, wearing DCUs like John had worn in Iraq. First Marine Division. Medals and unit citations. He was looking at a Marine, one who had kicked the same sand in the same part of the world he had. A man who had seen the horrible cost of a totalitarian regime heaped upon the people under its control. A man who had witnessed the horrible cost of an insurgency upon the native land.

"Do you think we were right to do what we have done, sir?" John asked him.

The man paused and looked at him. "I think you knew the answer to that before you asked, and you should trust yourself that you have made the right decision. Trust yourself, and follow through with it. Let come what may, but always do the right thing."

About the author

Phil Rabalais is a born Texan raised in Southeast Louisiana. He enlisted in the Louisiana Army National Guard, deployed to Iraq in 2004, and again for his state's Hurricane Katrina relief mission. After his enlistment, Phil graduated from Southeastern Louisiana University in Hammond, Louisiana, with a BA in business management. He is a staunch free speech and Second Amendment advocate, a self-admitted prepper, and the host of the *Matter of Facts* podcast. The podcast is based in no small part on his belief in self-reliance, small government, and the right of people to defend themselves. He lives in Mandeville, Louisiana, with his wife of ten years and their daughter.

Synopsis: One man's terrorist is another man's freedom fighter.

The inalienable right of citizens of the United States of America to keep and bear arms has been rescinded by the changing tides in US politics, but not all is peaceful. The Minutemen take up the task of resistance, and place themselves on a collision course with the very country they call home. What will the consequences be for the men and women on both sides of the conflict, and for their country? What happens when peaceful people are pushed to violence by intolerable circumstances? Where does one draw the line between fighting for one's freedom, and open insurrection?

Made in the USA
Monee, IL
01 March 2021